The Alpine Fortress

ROWENA KINREAD

Published by Goldcrest Books
www.goldcrestbooks.com
publish@goldcrestbooks.com

ISBN: 978-1-9192133-1-6

I dedicate this book to my granddaughter Pia.

Never lose the sparkle in your eyes nor your heart-melting smile.

A national redoubt, or national fortress, is a strategically chosen area where the remaining military forces of a nation can retreat if the main battle is lost or if defeat seems inevitable. Typically, this location has natural defensive advantages, such as mountainous terrain or a peninsula, and serves as a last stronghold to maintain national independence and continue resistance during a conflict.

The Alpine Fortress was a World War II redoubt planned by Heinrich Himmler in late 1943. It was intended to provide a retreat for Germany's government and military forces in an area stretching from southern Bavaria, through western Austria, and into northern Italy.

Although Hitler never fully supported the plan, and it was never seriously implemented, it became a useful propaganda tool. In the war's final months, the Allies were misled into diverting significant resources southward to capture this supposed stronghold, which ultimately proved to be fiction.

Contents

Glossary
(in alphabetical order)

The names of all the towns, cities and villages, rivers, valleys and mountains, tourist attractions, restaurants and hotels are real and exist as and where described.

Aérospatiale AS 332: a helicopter that civilians call a 'Super Puma' and in military circles is sometimes nicknamed the 'Cougar'.

Altaussee mine: a salt mine that was used to hide art treasures of inestimable value that the Nazis had stolen from castles, museums, churches, and private families (mainly Jewish) during World War II. The treasures were recovered in 1945 and, as far as possible, returned to their rightful owners.

Archenkanzel: a famous viewpoint with beautiful views of Lake Koenig and the pilgrimage church St. Bartholomä.

ATC: abbreviation for air-traffic control.

The Barmsteine: two rock towers, the pinnacles 841 and 851 metres above sea level, in the northernmost part of the Hasel Mountains in the Bavarian Alps. They rise above the Austrian town of Hallein and lie on the border between Salzburger Land in Austria and Berchtesgadener Land in Germany.

St. Bartholomä, Berchtesgaden: a famous church of pilgrimage.

Le Bourget, Paris: the busiest private jet airport in Europe.

BND: abbreviation for **Bundesnachrichtendienst**, which is the Federal Intelligence Service for Germany and directly subordinate to the Chancellor's Office. It is equivalent to the British M16. The BND headquarters is in central Berlin and is the world's largest intelligence headquarters.

Federal Police: Germany differentiates between Territorial or Regional Police, responsible for safety in districts, and their Federal Police, responsible for the safety of borders, airports, motorways, rail stations, and many others. Inside these two separate bodies are many smaller departments, for example, the **Kripo**, responsible for crime.

French DGSE: The Directorate-General for External Security is France's Foreign Intelligence Agency, equivalent to the British MI6 and the American CIA.

Eagle's Nest (German: das Kehlsteinhaus): a building erected atop the summit of the Kehlstein, a rocky outcrop that rises above Obersalzberg near the southeast German town of Berchtesgaden. It was used exclusively by members of the Nazi Party for government and social meetings. It was visited on fourteen documented instances by Adolf Hitler. Today, it is open seasonally as a restaurant, beer garden, and tourist site. It is owned by a charitable trust.

Not to be confused with: **The Berghof:** Adolf Hitler's holiday home in the Obersalzberg of the Bavarian Alps near Berchtesgaden, Bavaria, Germany. He spent more time here than anywhere else during his time as the Führer of Nazi Germany. It was also one of the most widely known of his headquarters, which were located throughout Europe. Today the building no longer exists.

Kripo: German equivalent to British CID.

Kührointhaus: training centre of the German Federal Police.

Ice Chapel: the lowest-lying permanent snowfield in the Alps. Its lower end is only 930 metres high in the upper

Eisbach valley. The Ice Chapel is fed by mighty avalanches that slide down from the east face of the Watzmann in spring and accumulate in the angle of the rock face.

Lake Koenig: a natural lake in the southeast Berchtesgadener Land district of the German state of Bavaria, near the Austrian border. Most of the lake is within the Berchtesgaden National Park.

Linz: a town in Austria where Adolf Hitler was born and where he planned to open a museum for the fine arts after World War II.

Ramsau church: a picturesque church near Berchtesgaden.

Ratlines: systems of escape routes for German Nazis and other fascists fleeing Europe from 1945 onwards in the aftermath of World War II. These escape routes mainly led toward havens in the Americas, particularly in Argentina.

Rinnkendlsteig: a scenic and panoramic mountain trail from St. Bartholomä on Lake Koenigssee to Kühroint, offering impressive views into the depths below.

Rossfeld circuit: Germany's highest panoramic road. The Rossfeld Panoramic Road in Berchtesgaden, open year-round, winds through impressive mountain landscapes and diverse flora and fauna. As a starting point for unforgettable hikes, it passes by numerous inns and famous film locations.

Salzkammergut: spans the federal states of Upper Austria, Salzburg, and Styria (Steiermark). The Styrian part is also called Ausseerland.

Schatz: German endearment. Lit.: treasure.

Steinernes Meer: (literally 'Rocky Sea') a high stony plateau in the Northern Limestone Alps. As one of the nine sub-ranges of the Berchtesgaden Alps, the Steinernes Meer belongs partly to Bavaria and partly to Salzburg.

Straubing: a place with a high-security prison near Munich.

Toter Mann: a mountain near Ramsau.

Traunstein: a town in the south-eastern part of Bavaria, Germany, and is the administrative centre of a much larger district of the same name. The town serves as a local government, and has retail, health services, transport, and educational centre for the wider district.

Mount Watzmann: (2,713 m): the third highest mountain in Germany, and the highest located entirely on German territory. On its eastern side, Lake Koenigssee lies at its base, with the highest rock face in the Eastern Alpine Range, the famed Watzmann East Face. On the western side, the mountain looks over the unusual landscapes of the Wimbach Valley. Mount Watzmann's three peaks are called Hocheck, Mittelspitze and Südspitze. Its eastern face is a sheer climb of close to 2,000 metres and can only be scaled by experts. However, good hikers can reach the summit via another trail that leads past a large overnight hut called Watzmannhaus.

Wimbach Bridge: a bridge over the river Wimbach.

ZIS-5: a 4x2 Soviet truck produced by Moscow's ZIS factory from 1932 to 1948 (first one made at the end of 1930).

zum Wohl!: Cheers!

Main Fictional Characters in order of appearance/families.

Konstantyn Petrenko: a Ukrainian; prisoner of war in World War II. Ivanna's and Toby's grandfather, 1921-2005.

Ivanna Petrenko: Konstantyn's granddaughter 1993- .

Toby: Ivanna's cousin.

Mel: his wife.

Olivia: Ivanna's and Toby's cousin.

Hannes: Olivia's husband.

Alina Schuster: Ivanna's friend.

Kommissar Matteo Stocker: mountain guide for the federal police in Berchtesgaden.

Freya: his wife

Dennis: Matteo's friend and colleague.

Sven Wassmer: Course participant.

Mark Rogg: Course participant.

Christina (Tina): Course participant.

Nicole: Course participant.

Benni (Borya Koljic): Course participant.

Danny (Farouk El Hassan): Course participant.

Superintendent Harald Ebner: head of the Kührointhaus.

Rudolf Hoffmann: head of the district police in Berchtesgaden.

David Kraus: from the voluntary mountain rescue service.

Erik Benz: federal policeman for the motorway unit in Baden-Württemberg.

Robert: Matteo's friend and colleague.

Esteban Vargas also known as el lagarto/ the lizard, and in this book mainly referred to as the Argentinian, boss of the presently most powerful drug cartel in Argentina, the Los Ortegas clan.

Gerhard Weckmann also known as the 'Fridge' and changed his name to Felipe Vargas: high-ranking Nazi officer in World War II, escaped to Argentinia; the Argentinian's father.

Mr Andreas Buchenmeyer: Vice-President of the Bundesnachrichtendienst.

Kommissar Otto Beck: from the Kripo.

Sebastian Meier: IT expert

Jürgen Gross: name of police officer in Bonlanden

Thomas known as **Topper:** BND agent.

Stefan: BND agent.

Patrick: BND agent.

Julian: BND agent.

Detlef Riek: known as Didi, an antiques dealer.

Conrad Neuberg: well-known potholer from Berlin

Ludwig Fuchs: known as Foxy, leader of GSG 9 unit.

Emil: member of GSG 9.

Finn: member of GSG 9.

Henry Steger: mountain guide who works for the National Alpine club in Berchtesgaden.

Friedrich Horn: an eighty-three-year-old man who has lived all his life in Berchtesgaden.

Mehmed Dragovic: Bosnian commander of the Argentinian's private army.

Historical Characters in alphabetical order.

Cardinal Antonio Caggiano: a cardinal of the Roman Catholic Church in Argentina. He played a part in helping Nazi sympathisers and war criminals escape prosecution in Europe by easing their passage to South America.

Franz Xaver Gruber: Austrian composer of the carol 'Silent Night, Holy Night'.

Heinrich Himmler: a leading member of the German Nazi Party, and one of the most powerful men in Nazi Germany. He is primarily known for being a principal architect of the Holocaust.

Adolf Hitler: Austrian-born German politician who was the dictator of Nazi Germany from 1933 until his suicide in 1945. He rose to power as the leader of the Nazi Party, becoming the chancellor in 1933 and then taking the title of *Führer und Reichskanzler* in 1934. was central to the perpetration of the Holocaust: the genocide of about six million Jews and millions of other victims.

Mauricio Macri: former Argentinian president

Benito Mussolini: an Italian dictator who founded and led the National Fascist Party (PNF). He was Prime Minister of Italy from the March on Rome in 1922, until his deposition in 1943.

Juan Perón: an Argentine lieutenant general, politician and statesman who served as the 29th President of Argentina from 1946 to his overthrow in 1955, and again as the 40th President from October 1973 to his death in July 1974.

Still living:

Angela Merkel: a German retired politician who served as chancellor of Germany from 2005 to 2021 and was the first woman to hold that office.

Dr Dieter Romann: President of the German federal police.

Johann Westhauser: A German cave researcher. His complex rescue from the Riesending cave in 2014 received international media attention.

The Alpine Fortress

Inspired by a true story

Rowena Kinread

There is no fire like passion, there is no shark like hatred,
there is no snare like folly, there is no torrent like greed.

Buddhist Quote

Chapter One

IVANNA. JUNE 2022

Ivanna was sorting out her grandparents' loft and riffled through a pile of dusty old books. A map fell onto the floor. She picked it up, examined it and read the backside of the map, an account of her grandfather's time in World War Two. She showed it to her cousins.

"A map of the whereabouts of stolen Nazi treasure?" she wondered.

At first, they laughed, thinking that had any treasure been there in the first place, then it would long since have been discovered and removed. But Toby, who had been born and still lived near Salzburg in Austria, was lost in thought.

"There might be something there. A lot of treasure from those days still hasn't been recovered, and if the entrance to the mine was closed, like Granddad wrote, surrounding vegetation has had over seventy years to grow and make it unrecognisable."

The cousins listened to Toby intently. He was usually quiet, but when he spoke, he always had something relevant to add to the conversation. He was also a potholer. It wasn't his job – he worked during the day as an architectural draftsman – but he was an experienced potholer and a valued member of the regional voluntary rescue team for cavers. He had been part of the team that rescued Johann Westhauser in 2014. So, if anyone could weigh up the probability of the map's authenticity, it was Toby.

"You must have heard about the Altaussee treasure?" He saw his cousins' puzzled faces and continued. "In 1945 an American infantry unit was tasked with opening the entrance to the Altaussee salt mine and recovered fine art and jewellery hidden there. Among the thousands of paintings found were famous works from Rubens, Rembrandt, Titian, Bruegel, Tintoretto, Vermeer, Raphael, and Goya. There were crates full of gold bars made from melted-down dental gold from the concentration camps and dispossessed belongings from Jews, amongst them the Rothschild family collection. The Americans established the Central Collecting Point for recovered stolen property in Munich. These were returned to their owners, many of whom had emigrated to the States. This was just one salt mine, there are many.

"The salt mines have a constant temperature of eight degrees Celsius and seventy-five per cent air humidity. That's ideal for storing paintings. The Nazis stripped museums, galleries, and private art collections all over Europe. Of these, the best works were reserved for Hitler, who planned to open a museum in Linz. In autumn 1943, Hitler ordered that the most valuable works of art be stored in the numerous salt mines in Salzkammergut, a region on the northern edge of the Alps, to protect them from the enemies' bombs.

"When Germany began to be bombed by the Allied Forces, panic broke out, and in the last months of the war the intelligence of what was stored where and in which of the salt mines was lost. Treasure worth billions of dollars has not resurfaced even today.

"The abundance of riches was designated not just for Hitler's planned museum in Linz, but also for the 'post-war' era. Generals and brutal war criminals were organising their escape to Argentina or elsewhere. However, the loot was hidden under chaotic circumstances as the Allied Forces were already bombing Germany and Austria daily. So, it's a possibility that Grandfather's suspicion was correct."

"What should we do with the map?" Ivanna asked her cousins. "Do you think you could find the entrance, Toby?"

"That kind of thing is better left to the experts. Even if we did find it, and even if treasure were still there, what could we do about it? It would be heavy and belongs to… hmmm, I'm not sure, the German authorities, I suppose. They are keen to do the right thing now and would probably attempt to find the rightful owners, whether museums or private citizens. There may be a reward, but I wouldn't feel comfortable profiting from other people's misfortune."

"Me neither." Ivanna agreed, and the other cousins nodded. Ivanna looked at her cousins. She was the only one living in Germany. "I've no idea where to send it, though. It would probably get lost in the mass of mail somewhere. I would like some kind of receipt for the map and would be interested to find out in a year or two whether anything came from it."

Again, her cousins agreed. "You could simply take it in person to your local police station," Toby suggested. "They won't be responsible themselves. but they will know where to send it."

"Okay, I'll do that and let you all know what they say."

Ivanna folded the map up and put it in her jeans pocket.

Chapter Two

SUNDAY MORNING, 25 SEPTEMBER 2022

Ivanna left her flat in Bonlanden and hurried to the bus stop. Her blonde hair was tied back in a high ponytail, that swished back and forth as she strode briskly. She risked a glance over her left shoulder and let out a sigh of relief; nobody was following her. Had she finally shaken off her shadows or was she no longer a person of interest? She hoped the latter.

Ever since she had shown the police the map she had found while sorting through her deceased grandfather's stuff, she had been stalked. She couldn't understand it. The police had brushed her off when she had presented them with a sketch her grandfather had drawn of where Nazi stolen treasure was allegedly hidden.

"You will need more evidence than that," the officer had said. "Just recently a sixteen-year-old girl found a gold bar whilst swimming in Lake Koenig. The place where she found it was searched, but it was just the one gold bar and had nothing to do with Hitler's gold cache. Still, the newspaper report locked hundreds of gold-diggers to the lake and the police had their hands full dealing with them. Imagine the amount of money and other resources needed to follow up all the tip-offs given to us every year? The map looks very vague anyway, There's not a single town named."

"No. He was a prisoner of war, marched hundreds of miles through hostile territory, and was forced to work in a salt mine. He had no way of knowing exactly where he was, but he had to help unload the wooden crates himself. He drew a church and a river with an island in its midst. It was his view from the entrance of the cave. My cousin thinks it could be found."

"Well, if your cousin finds it, take some photographs. If you come back with photographic proof of the treasure, then the proper authorities would probably pursue your lead."

So why had the police been following her? Or was it someone else? Had someone overheard her conversation with the officer at the station? She tried to think back but couldn't remember seeing anyone else. She had spoken to the officer in a type of glass booth to the left of the entrance. At the back of the station there were two doors, one leading to an office and the other one perhaps to a restroom. A man had entered the station while she was speaking to the officer on duty. He was middle-aged and had the beginnings of a beer belly. He had given the officer a small wave, brushed past her and entered the office closing the door behind him. Could he have heard the conversation through the wall? But hadn't the conversation finished by then? She wasn't sure. It made no sense to her.

After she had noticed being stalked, she had gone back to the police station and made a complaint. The officer, the same man as before, had said that it was not the police following her, but at her insistence, he had unwillingly filed her complaint against 'two unknown men.'

Two days later, while she was on night duty at Stuttgart Airport, where she worked as a federal policewoman, her flat had been broken into. Her furniture had been upturned, drawers emptied onto the floor, food containers emptied. The mess was horrific but nothing was missing.

She had gone to the police station again, and as she entered, she saw the same officer as on the previous two occasions. She told him that she was a federal policewoman and showed him her identity card. He took her more seriously then and wrote everything down. He told her that as nobody had been injured and nothing was missing, it wouldn't be prioritised. However, he had gone round personally to look at her flat. "There's no serious damage done," he'd told her. "Your door lock is easy to pick. You should consider getting a better lock." Then he had left. She had been utterly pissed off. *The police were useless!*

Not worrying now, she got on the bus, took a back seat and relaxed until they reached the main bus station in Stuttgart. Soon she would be in Berchtesgaden, she thought, and nobody would look for her there.

Arriving at the station, she got off the bus and walked across the wide square to where the federal police minibus was waiting.

"Alina Schuster," she told the driver, who ticked her off his list. She took a rear seat and deposited her luggage on the place next to her, to discourage anyone from sitting there. Safe, she sighed. She looked out of the window and froze. The two men who'd been following her for days stood at a hot-dog stall. Dressed in shorts and T-shirts, revealing way too much black body hair. They looked like apes. They were both short and stocky, and their skin was olive-coloured, like Southern Europeans. Their biceps bulged so much that their arms hung away from their sides. They saw her looking, waved and took a large bite of their sausages.

What a cheek! Her heart began thumping wildly. Looking quickly away, she pulled her hood up and sank down in her seat. But they'd already seen her! Her pulse raced… what should she do? How did they know she was getting this bus?

Before she could decide on a course of action, the driver turned on the engine and pulled out of the station. The decision had been made for her. She was heading to the Bavarian Alps. Not until they reached the motorway and picked up speed did she sit up and look out of the rear window. There was no sign of her followers, but she didn't relax. Would they be in Berchtesgaden waiting for her?

She tried to calm herself. She was a federal police officer going on a training course. They weren't police, they couldn't just join in. But her efforts to reassure herself failed. She wasn't who she was pretending to be either. She decided to flee at the first possible moment after her arrival. She opened her rucksack and retrieved her phone. She dialled her cousin's number in Salzburg and left a phone message: "Change of plans. I'm coming sooner. See you tonight."

Chapter Three

SUNDAY AFTERNOON, 25 SEPTEMBER 2022

Matteo Stocker, mountain guide for the Federal Police, steered the Unimog sharp left across the Wimbach Bridge. Gravel crunched beneath the tires as he pulled up at the hiker's car park in a cloud of dust. The heat shimmered off the ground, the scent of dry pine and scorched earth thick in the air. It hadn't rained for weeks. The fire department was on red alert in the national park nature reserve.

He jumped out and scanned the area. Two officers waited near the information boards, shifting their weight impatiently. Matteo strode over, boots kicking up dust.

"Matteo Stocker," he introduced himself, eyes sharp. "You can get parking permits over there. You must leave your cars here for the week. The road to the hostel is private.

As the officers turned to sort their vehicles, the first of the police minibuses roared into the lot. Doors flung open, and officers poured out, adjusting backpacks and stretching cramped legs. Within minutes, the final buses pulled in, and a semicircle of twenty-five officers—eight women, seventeen men—formed in front of Matteo, their luggage stacked at their feet.

Matteo checked his watch. Four p.m. on the dot. For once, no stragglers. He lifted his clipboard, voice steady as he called names, marking off each officer with a flick of his pen. These men and women had come from all over Germany, drawn into the Bavarian Alps for a gruelling week of team-building and endurance training.

"That's great," he told them. "Everyone's here. I'm Matteo, your coach for the week. Take your luggage to the blue Unimog over there" – he pointed to the dusty vehicle in which he'd arrived – "then hike up the road to your left" – he indicated again – "until you arrive at the Kührointhaus, your hostel for the week. Take water bottles with you. It isn't far, just eight kilometres, but there's a difference of eight hundred metres in altitude."

A few officers groaned, and one man, with the beginnings of a spare tyre, complained, "I thought the course didn't start until tomorrow!"

Matteo smiled, showing his slightly crooked white teeth.

"No better way to shake off the travel fatigue." He let the statement hang, then added, "Stick to the road. No shortcuts. The terrain's tricky, and you're not equipped for it."

A few exchanged glances. He knew that look. He'd see them again soon—earlier than expected.

"Right, off you go. I'll take your luggage and meet you at the hostel in about three hours. Don't delay, a hot meal will be awaiting you."

Matteo left them, a few still grumbling half-heartedly, and drove up the steep gravel road to the Kührointhaus. It was closed to general traffic, but the police had a special permit. Not expecting any oncoming traffic, he put his foot down and swung round the hairpins enjoying himself.

Braking in front of the hostel, the air was thinner, cooler. The scent of wood smoke and fresh mountain air replaced the dry dust of the valley. Matteo left the vehicle, as usual, unlocked, keys dangling in the ignition. Who would steal it up here?

He greeted Dennis, the cook, with a thump on his back and sat down with him for a coffee, a large slice of cheesecake, and the latest gossip.

The first officers entered the grey stone building in just over an hour. They had taken the shortcuts between the hairpins, despite Matteo's warning. He knew that solely by the time they had taken. There were two of them. Presumably sporty types, they looked fitter than himself. These candidates were there for the team-building course, not the fitness programme. Matteo took their names and underlined them on his list.

"Well done," he told them. "You're the first ones to arrive and now have the honour of unloading the Unimog. Here's a list with the room allocations. Take the luggage to the corresponding rooms."

The men looked aghast. One protested, "We're not here to wait on the others!"

The other looked at Matteo sourly. "Is this supposed to be some sort of *punishment* for taking the shortcuts? It's worse than nursery school here!"

Matteo underlined both names a second time: Sven and Mark.

"No," he rebuked Sven, "although it was reckless after my warning. The team is only as strong as its weakest link. You are here to learn to help the weaker ones. It could be lifesaving."

Sven grunted. He snatched the list from Matteo's hand and went wordlessly outside to start bringing in the luggage.

More officers trickled in. Two hours. Two and a half. Three. The last exhausted figures stumbled through the doorway, flushed and aching. Matteo assumed they must all be present. He took out his list, pen poised.

Twenty-four. He counted again.

Still twenty-four. One missing. He waited ten more minutes.

Matteo's jaw tightened. There were only twenty-four; a female officer was missing.

The sun was dipping lower, shadows stretching across the mountain. The temperature would start to drop soon.

His gut twisted. She should have been here by now. Something was wrong.

Chapter Four

7 P.M. SUNDAY EVENING, 25 SEPTEMBER

"Alina Schuster?"

Matteo repeated the name louder. The officers turned around and looked at each other but nobody came forward. Matteo looked at his watch. Seven p.m. She should be here by now.

"Did anyone notice Alina? Were you in groups together?"

A young woman cleared her throat to make herself noticed. Looking at the woman next to her, she said, "I think she might have been with us. She didn't introduce herself, but about a third of the way up she said she needed to pee. She told us not to wait. Said she'd catch up. But she didn't and I can't see her here."

"Pee? Did you see where she went?"

"She ran off into the forest. I thought she was going to crouch behind a tree."

"Okay, thank you…?"

"I'm Christina… Tina."

"Did anyone else see Alina, maybe coming out of the forest later on?"

A man put his hand in the air. "I'm Benni and this is Danny." He pointed to the man next to him. Matteo recognised them as two guys who had arrived in their own car. "We were walking behind Tina and saw Alina run into the woods. Not later though, sorry."

"How many colleagues were behind you?"

"Behind us? Nobody, we were the last."

Matteo raised his eyebrows. Usually those who arrived in cars were the quickest to start on the hike. "Well, it's not really possible to get lost on the way up here," Matteo said, shrugging. "Maybe she stumbled while going to take a pee and twisted her ankle or something. Do you think you can show me where she left the road?"

"I think so, yes."

"Good, come with me then."

Matteo went to a cupboard and removed some torches and gave one each to Benni, Danny, Tina, and her friend Nicole.

"You four come with me. We'll drive down the road and search for her before it gets dark. Everyone else stay here, sort your rooms out and settle in. Dennis!" he called to the cook. "Can you wait here till we get back? We shouldn't be gone long."

"No probs," a deep voice rumbled from the kitchen next door.

Matteo grabbed a coil of rope from another cupboard and hurried outdoors. Just before he got into the car, he had a thought and ran back inside. He looked at the list of room allocations, sprinted up the stairs two at a time and knocked, entering a room with three beds. It was empty. He found Alina's case on the floor – a holdall made from some sort of flowery material. He picked it up and went back downstairs, then locked it in the equipment closet.

Then he returned outdoors and got into the Unimog with the four officers, and drove slowly downhill.

"Keep your eyes peeled, she could be anywhere by now," he urged them.

They were roughly halfway down the road when Nicole called out. "Stop! This is where Alina left us."

Matteo stopped the car, and they all got out.

"Are you sure?" Tina asked her. "I thought it was further down."

"Me too," Benni agreed.

"I'm not really sure, everywhere looks the same," Nicole conceded.

Matteo peered into the forest and called the name clearly, "ALINA!"

The others joined in: "ALINA! ALINA!"

Nobody answered, and Benni said, "It was definitely further down."

Matteo flashed his torch into the trees. "You are sure she went *left* into the forest, not *right*?" he checked.

"Yes, yes," they all agreed.

Getting back into the car they continued until Danny called out, "Here! I think it was here!"

Matteo slowed the car and looked at the others. "Do you all agree?"

"Everything looks different from this direction," Tina said, excusing her uncertainty. "Wouldn't it be better to go the whole way back to the car park and then turn back up?"

"It's getting dark," Matteo said. "Let's call from here and if she doesn't answer we'll do as you suggest."

The five called again and again as loud as they could. When they stopped shouting, it was so quiet that Matteo could hear himself breathe. He took a few steps into the forest flashing his ultra-vision torch. Nothing! Nobody returned their calls, and the torchlight revealed no signs of Alina. Worried, Matteo drove further downhill until they reached the car park, reversed the car, and started retracing their tracks back up the mountain. As he did so, something irritated him. Had he noticed something peculiar at the car park? He tried to remember. A thought niggled his brain but evaded him. They stopped several times on their way back, got out of the Unimog and yelled. To no avail. Alina had vanished.

Chapter Five

10 P.M. SUNDAY NIGHT, 25 SEPTEMBER

Matteo drove back to the hostel. The remaining officers had eaten but were sitting or standing in small groups, awaiting the return of Matteo and their four co-participants with, hopefully, Alina.

"There's no sign of her," Matteo told the group. "You four get something to eat in the kitchen and I'll go to the office to ring Superintendent Ebner to let him know that Alina is missing. I'll see you all back here in fifteen minutes." He left the room buzzing with subdued chatter and popped his head round the kitchen door to Dennis. "Can you join me in the office after you've warmed up their food? And save something for me please, I'm starving!"

He rang his boss's number. "Matteo, is something up?" Harald Ebner had recognised the number on the display.

"You could say that. An officer has gone missing!"

"Huh? You haven't been anywhere yet! Do you mean someone didn't turn up? You don't need to ring me up on a Sunday evening for that!"

"No, sir. Everyone was at the car park, but when we

arrived at the hostel, one female officer, an Alina Schuster, was missing. A couple of her colleagues saw her dash off into the forest to pee. I've spent the last two hours going back down the road with four volunteers, searching for her, but there's no sign of her." Matteo had to repeat his story twice until Ebner finally grasped the situation.

"For goodness' sake! Why didn't she pee at the car park? There are toilets there!"

Matteo hoped his boss didn't expect an answer to that. He remained silent.

"All right, I'll ring the District Police first and let them know, then I'll come. Stay at the hostel until I arrive and if she turns up ring my mobile."

"Yes, sir."

Matteo rang Freya, his wife of four months, to let her know why he wasn't home yet and that presumably he would need another couple of hours. She laughed when she heard why. "That's a new one, lost one before you even started. Maybe you scared her!"

Dennis knocked on the door, saving him from answering. Matteo quickly said goodbye to Freya and turned his attention to Dennis.

"What did the boss say?" Dennis asked placing a dish of steaming goulash on the desk along with cutlery.

"Ah, table service! Thanks, I owe you one. He's going to inform the District Police and then come here. We're to stay here until he arrives," Matteo said between mouthfuls. "God, I was starving! What do you think about Alina? What were the officers saying? Did you pick up any interesting snippets?"

"A few wondered whether it was part of the course…"

"What!? For heaven's sake, don't tell me that conspiracy theories have reached Berchtesgaden!"

"Well, there were quite a few heated discussions on the scale from conspiracy theories to dumb blonde jokes. I think when you returned without her though, they began to realise it was serious."

"Let them wait till the police come and start taking statements!" Matteo groaned. "Oh, it's going to be a long night."

Matteo went with Dennis to the common room. "I've spoken to Superintendent Harald Ebner, head of the Kührointhaus," he told the awaiting officers. "He is notifying the District Police this very moment that Alina is missing. He will meet them here shortly and we are all to wait for them. No one is to retire to their rooms yet. The police will want to speak with all of you."

Nobody complained. Sven volunteered to start a search party. Several more officers stepped forward to also offer their services.

"For the moment, we must all wait," Matteo repeated. "We have a few minutes until they arrive, though, and could use the time by starting on a few preliminary chores. Normally, when you arrive, I would give you a short history of the Kührointhaus and discuss the plans for the week. I think I can skip that for the moment, but I'd still like to inform you of your duties. You will stay in the hostel by yourselves and..."

Someone wolf-whistled, someone always did. Matteo grinned, as was expected of him, and then signalled with his hands to calm the laughing police officers down. "You are all adults and responsible for your own actions. In the mornings you must be ready in front of the hostel at eight a.m. with the appropriate clothing and equipment."

Groans and murmurs of discontent circulated the room. "In case anybody thinks that they are here for a holiday, then I must disappoint you. This is a course to ingrain certain procedures which could be lifesaving. *So,* in the mornings you can help yourselves to breakfast, there are plenty of groceries to last the whole week. Afterwards, you will clean up after yourselves. Dennis here…" – he beckoned to Dennis to show himself and he came forward and took an exaggerated bow – "will prepare a hot meal for you every evening at seven. You must lay the tables yourselves and clean up afterwards. You need to appoint one person to be your leader. He or she will make sure that everywhere is tidy and that the doors and windows are locked at night-time. We also need someone in charge of fire prevention. Who shall it be?" Danny stepped forward to volunteer. "Good. I'll show you where the fire extinguishers are while your colleagues choose a leader."

Ten minutes later Matteo and Danny returned, and Tina said she'd been chosen as leader.

"Good, here are the keys." Matteo dug in his pocket and gave her two keys on a ring. "The second one is for the storage building. I'll show you that tomorrow."

*****

The sirens were ear-splitting as an assortment of emergency vehicles with flashing blue lights braked before the hostel. Matteo went outside to greet his boss. Harald Ebner was talking to Rudolf Hoffmann, head of the District Police, and David Kraus from the Voluntary Mountain Rescue Service, whom the latter had notified. An ambulance stood nearby.

"Ah, Matteo, here you are! I was just explaining the situation to Police Commissioners Hoffmann and David."

Matteo shook hands with Rudolf Hoffmann and slapped David, whom he knew personally, on the arm.

"I can only imagine that Alina took one of the shortcuts between the hairpins and stumbled," Matteo said. "But she didn't answer our calls."

"You didn't search there though?" David double-checked.

"No, I had four of the course participants with me, but we didn't have the right equipment."

"Good," Ebner confirmed. "It would've been against the regulations."

"If she'd answered our calls, I would have anyway. But she could be anywhere, and it was already getting dark."

"You don't think she could've veered off towards Schönau?" Hoffmann enquired.

"Well, not by mistake, unless she's blind!" Matteo was a bit confounded by the question. To go to Schönau, Alina would have had to pass nearby the hostel.

"No, she'll have fallen on one of the shortcuts." David was certain. "I'll get my men together and we'll set off immediately. She could be unconscious."

David went over to his men, divided them into three groups, and they drove off in cars to the start of each shortcut between the hairpins.

"Let's go inside to wait." Ebner made a sweeping movement with his arms to include the police from the various departments, medics, and the emergency doctor. "David will radio in with a message as soon as they find anything."

The District Police began to take statements from the course participants and Harald Ebner went around introducing himself. Matteo disappeared into the kitchen and looked for something to eat. He was always hungry and could eat as much as, and whatever, he wanted, without putting even a gram of weight on, much to the annoyance of Freya and his female colleagues. A few minutes later Dennis joined him, and they sat down with mugs of coffee and generous portions of plum cake.

"How long do you think David and his men will need?" Dennis asked.

"Depends on how soon they find anything. At the most an hour."

"It's just that my prosthesis is getting sore, and I wondered if I could go home?"

"Oh goodness, I'm sorry, I didn't think! Yes, of course, go home now and take it off."

"Okay, good night then, I'll see you tomorrow."

Dennis left. He had lost his left leg, just below the knee, several years ago in the course of his service in the GSG 9. He was protecting the German ambassador in Libya when his car was ambushed. He wore a prosthesis and didn't even limp. Nobody could tell that he was disabled but after a long day of standing, his stump became red and sore.

An hour passed and then a second. Harald Ebner came into the kitchen and sat down with Matteo. One after the other looked at the time on their mobile phones. Eventually, Rudolf Hoffmann joined them with a pile of paper statements. "My men have finished interviewing the officers," Hoffmann informed Matteo. "As far as I'm concerned you can let them all retire if you want."

Matteo stood up, glad of something to do. "I'll be right back."

He returned just as David opened the front door, and the men in the kitchen rushed out to meet him.

"Nothing." He shrugged his shoulders. "I can't understand it!"

"How far could you see with your lights?" Ebner asked.

"Far enough. No other vehicles here that could have picked her up?"

"No," Matteo replied. "We would've noticed. Wait!" he said. Something clicked in his brain. "When I drove back to the car park tonight, a black Golf was missing. It was there when I met the officers this afternoon and afterwards it was gone. I knew something was different!" he said, feeling triumphant that his memory had returned.

"But that doesn't mean *anything*." Ebner dismissed Matteo's revelation, and his feeling of euphoria sank. "It probably belonged to a hiker returning late."

"Oh, and Alina came on one of the minibuses anyway," Matteo remembered, feeling stupid.

"Well, there's no more we can do tonight," Hoffmann said. "Tomorrow morning the mountain rescue team can search the shortcuts in daylight and David can get a helicopter up in the air."

"I must ring her parents and let them know she's missing," Ebner said. "Then we might as well all get a few hours' rest before dawn."

Matteo took his leave.

✳✳✳✳✳

Ebner had already looked at Alina's file and seen that her next of kin were her parents and that she lived with them at their family home. He wondered briefly whether to wait until the next morning before phoning. However, if something serious had happened to Alina and he hadn't promptly informed the parents of her disappearance, there would be trouble. It was regulation to inform the next of kin immediately. It was well past midnight when he rang their number, steeling himself for a grilling. The telephone rang fifteen times before a deep, grumpy voice barked, "Yes!"

"Good evening, this is Superintendent Ebner from Berchtesgaden. I'm sorry to disturb you so late, but I'm afraid I must inform you that your daughter is missing."

"Is this some kind of sick joke or something!" Mr Schuster's voice bellowed down the phone so loud that Ebner held it slightly away from his ear.

"No! Of course not! I assure you that we do not ring the next of kin in the middle of the night as a joke!"

"Well, I can assure you that my daughter is peacefully asleep in her bedroom!" boomed Mr Schuster.

Chapter Six

1 A.M. MONDAY, 26 SEPTEMBER

"What! How is that possible? There's no way she could have got back to…" – he checked the file – "Stuttgart in that time. I mean, I suppose it could be possible with a car, but she came with one of our minibuses!" Ebner searched his brain wondering if it were possible by train via Munich.

"I don't know what you're talking about. Our daughter hasn't been anywhere; she's been at home all day."

"No, no, she was here! We've spent the last six hours searching for her! You must be mistaken. Can you check her room, please?"

"For goodness' sake, what on earth is going on? I saw her before she went to bed. Are you implying I'm lying?"

"No, no, of course not. Look, can I speak to her myself?"

"It's the middle of the night and she's been a bit off colour recently. Can't it wait until tomorrow?"

"It's all right Dad, give him to me." Ebner heard a female voice at the other end of the line.

"Well, if you're sure…"

"Hello, this is Alina speaking."

Ebner took a deep breath to stop himself from exploding. "I'm Superintendent Ebner, head of the Kührointhaus. We have spent the last six hours searching for you! How did you get home and why didn't you inform us immediately?"

"I wasn't in Berchtesgaden. My best friend and colleague, Ivanna, took my place on the course."

"Ivanna? Ivanna who? Why haven't I been informed about the changeover? Why didn't she say anything? She answered to your name! Wait! Does this mean that Ivanna is missing now?"

"Her full name is Ivanna Petrenko. Yes, I'm worried that she may be missing. You weren't informed, sir, because… because we didn't tell anybody. We hoped we wouldn't be found out…"

Ebner had been in the service for over twenty years and was not only well trained but also experienced. Nevertheless, something like this had never happened before. He clenched his teeth together, willing himself to stay calm. "This demands a lot more explanation from you. Go to your superior first thing tomorrow morning and make a full written statement. For the moment you are suspended from all active duty, but you must remain available for additional questioning at all times until further notice. Do you have a photograph of Ivanna that you can send to me by email?"

"Yes, sir."

"Well do that immediately. It will help to know who we are looking for. Where does she work?"

"At Stuttgart Airport, sir. Like myself."

"And the name of your direct supervisor?"

"Detective Inspector Jan Huber."

"I shall ring him immediately, so he'll know to expect you in the morning."

"No sir, *please*. I'll explain everything but could you wait to call him, just one day?"

"You're not in any position to ask favours! You do realise this is a serious offence, don't you? It's fraudulent behaviour. You could lose your job and your status as a civil servant."

"Yes, I know, I'm sorry. I hope that Ivanna is okay. It was my fault, not hers. The blame is entirely mine."

"We've been searching for her since seven. She seems to have disappeared from the face of the earth. There's no trace of her."

"Please, let me explain everything to you. I applied for the course six months ago and was really pleased when I got a place. Ivanna went last year and told me how much she had enjoyed it. Then ten days ago I realised I was pregnant. I was so shocked. I didn't know what to do..."

"Well, the rules are clear. Due to safety precautions, pregnant women cannot take part in the course. You just had to tell your supervisor. Someone else would have officially had the chance to take your place, and you could've reapplied after the child was born."

"But that's the problem! I don't know whether I want to keep the child or not. I must get used to the idea of being pregnant myself before telling anybody... especially the supervisor... he's the father!"

"Your supervisor? Are you a couple?"

"Not exactly. He's already married and has two children."

Silence. Ebner couldn't speak. Alina rushed on, babbling desperately. "Ivanna realised immediately that I was troubled. I confided in her, and it turned out she had her own problems. She was being followed by two stalkers. She'd issued a complaint at her local police station, and they'd taken a statement, but had not done anything. She was frightened. So, we decided to swap. She hoped that her stalkers would lose her and forget about her if she went to Berchtesgaden. She thought it was unlikely they would follow her there. We don't look alike but we're a similar height and build and we both have shoulder-length blonde hair. She knew that we didn't have to show our identity cards. It seemed to be a perfect solution. Do you think her stalkers followed her and kidnapped her?"

It was a lot of information to digest. Ebner contemplated it. "That does indeed throw the events in a new light. Detective Inspector Huber has abused his seniority and taken advantage of a female subordinate..."

"It wasn't like that, sir!" Alina protested.

"Hear me out. No matter what you thought, or he led you to believe, that is officially the case and is as such a criminal act. Who is your superintendent?"

"Mangold, sir."

"All right, I'll tell you what I'll do. I shall ring Superintendent Mangold first thing tomorrow morning. He will no doubt want to speak to you first and then Huber. Just tell him what you told me. I shall also ring the police station and ask for a copy of Ivanna's statement. Do you know which station she went to?"

"Bonlanden, sir."

"Good. This could be a lot more complicated than we thought. Did she describe the men to you or speculate why she was being followed?"

"I don't think so. My mind's a mess, I was so preoccupied with my own troubles. Oh, poor Ivanna! I should have asked more."

"Don't worry about that now, but if something comes back to you, get in touch. I'll give Mangold my contact details and ask him to pass them on to you. We may need to speak again. Now then, I'm not your father, but if you'll accept the advice of an older man, I strongly recommend you decide quickly whether you want this baby or not. If you want to pre-warn Huber, although he doesn't deserve it, get in touch with him first thing in the morning."

"Yes, sir, thank you."

"That's all I can do, I'm afraid. Whatever you decide, I wish you all the best. I must ring Ivanna's next of kin now."

Chapter Seven

4 P.M. SUNDAY, 25 SEPTEMBER

Ivanna perked up as the minibus drove through the picturesque town of Berchtesgaden. She'd been on the same course last year and knew that they were close to their destination now. The bus slowed down and navigated the narrow Wimbach Bridge carefully. Some of her fellow passengers "oohed" at the view of Ramsau church before the backdrop of the Alps and shot photographs. Her thoughts were elsewhere. Full of anxiety, her eyes wide open, she scanned the car park. Her heart sank as she recognised them almost immediately. Standing amongst the other police officers, chatting nonchalantly as if they belonged there, were the two apes.

How did they know she'd be coming? She realised she had stopped breathing and took a large gulp of air. What to do? Her colleagues had already left the bus. The driver noticed her and reminded her to take all her belongings with her. She dragged herself along the aisle, desperately trying to think of some way to escape. Her mind, already on overdrive, failed her. She had scarcely put one foot on the ground as the door of the minibus hissed shut and the driver pulled away.

She walked over to a tall girl with broad shoulders she'd noticed on the bus earlier, and her friend. "Hi, I'm Alina," she introduced herself.

"Hi, my name's Tina," the girl replied.

"And I'm Nicole. Are you looking forward to the course?"

"Oh yes! It'll make a nice change from the daily routine." Ivanna was spared making more conversation as their coach for the week introduced himself and gave instructions. Luckily it was a different guy than last year. That was one worry gone. She doubted anyone else would remember her. Matteo was tall, slim and fit with shortish, untidy brown hair and huge brown eyes. A ready smile made him enormously attractive but a glance at his left hand showed a wedding ring. Typical, she thought, all the interesting men are spoken for. Oh well, she had no time for romance on this trip. While he talked, Ivanna examined the other course participants closely. Her eyes returned repeatedly to a middle-aged, balding man with the beginnings of a spare tyre around his belly. He answered to the name of Erik Benz. She was sure she'd seen him somewhere before, but where? She racked her brain but it failed her. She pushed her thoughts aside as they were called upon to put their luggage in the Unimog. As Ivanna dumped her holdall in the back of the car, she thought, I must disappear immediately, on the way up to the hostel. She began to forge a plan. She would hang back with Tina and Nicole and wait until the apes were out of sight, then make some excuse and run off.

The course participants began to march uphill to the left as was expected of them. Luckily for her, Tina and Nicole didn't seem to be in a rush to set off, but unfortunately the apes were hanging back, too. They went to their car and pretended to look for something on the back seat, but she could see them watching her. She wondered whether she was being paranoid or if they were waiting for her to set off and wanted to follow her. She was scared and dug her hands into her pockets so no one could see them trembling.

Eventually just the five of them were left. Tina and Nicole set off at a leisurely pace and she had no alternative but to join them. The apes followed at a distance. Ivanna felt hysterical... what was she going to do? Should she confront them? No, they would just deny everything. Could she confide in Tina and Nicole? But what could she say to them when even the police hadn't believed her? She felt alone and her heart thumped. They passed the first hairpin and Ivanna realised that the apes were temporarily out of sight. An idea began to form in her mind. She counted the seconds until the apes reappeared around the corner... nearly twenty, would that be long enough?

As they approached the next hairpin curve, she picked up her pace and told her colleagues hurriedly, "I've got to pee. Don't wait, I'll catch you up!" Counting the seconds, she ran as fast as she could into the forest and searched for somewhere to hide. She saw a pile of leaves beneath an ash tree, threw herself to the ground and covered herself completely with them. Her heart was thumping so hard it felt like the ground was vibrating. She lay stock-still and waited.

Just a few seconds later she heard running footsteps. "Where is she? She can't have got far," she heard one man saying. She clasped her hands tightly together and prayed they wouldn't find her. She listened to their footsteps, slower now, searching. One man spoke again, and a creepy laugh followed. She was glad she hadn't understood whatever he'd said.

A spider started crawling along her upper arm. She wasn't scared of spiders, but it tickled. It crept along her shoulder and up her neck. Then it crossed her cheek, turned and sidestepped towards her nose. She felt an urge to sneeze and clamped a hand over her nose and mouth to try to suppress it. Please, let the apes move on, she pleaded silently. The spider's tracks itched and tingled. It was torture. She could feel the impulse to sneeze, and tried to stifle it, but she couldn't prevent a smothered sneeze. The silence that followed was as quiet as a rock concert was loud. The apes' footsteps were approaching her. She could sense them through the forest floor and her heart seemed to stop. Suddenly an arm plunged through her blanket of leaves and a hand grabbed her ponytail and pulled her up to a standing position.

She shrieked and struggled, kicked and lashed out with her arms and legs, determined to break free. "What do you want?" she screamed frantically. One of the men put a hand over her mouth to silence her. She bit him hard, and he swore, taking his hand away, and she spat at him in his face.

"Hurry up!" the man told his partner. "She's a bloody fury!" He held her hands so firmly in his grasp that Ivanna had no chance to break away. The second man filled a syringe with some unknown fluid and stuck it into her arm. After that, everything went black.

*****

Tina saw Benni and Danny follow the girl calling herself Alina into the forest. Earlier at the car park, the two men had stood out amongst the officers like two penguins in a forest. She had taken note of their names, wondering what had happened to the real policemen. These two were obviously imposters. She told Nicole to carry on walking and if necessary to cover for her. She dashed into the forest, scurrying from one tree to the next, attempting to avoid being noticed by the two men. She observed them finding Alina and giving her some sort of injection. Then Alina blacked out. Tina waited. She heard the men discussing something but couldn't decipher their words. Danny ran off, leaving Benni alone with Alina. Tina wondered whether she should try to rescue her, but short of shooting Benni and probably Danny too, there was nothing she could do. Her instructions were to 'observe only'. She obeyed. Just a few minutes later a black Golf stopped on the road. Danny got out, and together with Benni carried Alina to the car and shut her in the boot. Benni tapped on his watch and Danny drove off. Tina took a photo of the number plate and then hurried off. It was still nearly six kilometres to the hostel, so she started to sprint until she caught up with Nicole.

"Wow, have you run the whole way? You don't look the least bit flustered, You're not even breathing hard. How often do you train?" Nicole asked.

"Every day, at least ten kilometres, so that was nothing."

"I took my time," Nicole apologised.

"It's okay, I'll explain later. Don't say anything yet just follow my lead."

They went indoors and waited with the others. Just before seven, Benni entered the hostel with a red-faced Danny in tow. Danny was out of breath and had large patches of sweat under the armpits of his shirt.

Tina sidled up to Sven and spoke quietly. "I'm not sure what's going on. Benni and Danny aren't who they say they are. Alina tried to hide from them in the woods, but they found her, gave her an injection that made her unconscious and then put her in the boot of their car and Danny drove off. He can't have gone far though, as he's back here now. I photographed the number plate. Maybe Zehra can find out who it belongs to."

"Well done," Sven praised her. "So, we were right to split up. Matteo's going to notice she's missing in a minute. Say she was with you but nothing else for the moment until we understand what's going on."

Chapter Eight

7 A.M. MONDAY, 25 SEPTEMBER

The next morning Matteo arrived at the Kührointhaus at 7 a.m. He remembered that he had locked Alina's luggage in the equipment cupboard and went to get it. Although unlikely, he thought that maybe the contents would give them a clue to her whereabouts. The cupboard was locked as he'd left it, but when he opened the cupboard door, her holdall was missing. He was thunderstruck. Despite being positive he hadn't, he unlocked the other cupboard doors just in case he had mistaken the correct one, but her luggage was gone. Nobody had broken the lock, so that just left Tina who had the universal keys.

He ran upstairs and knocked urgently on her bedroom door several times. Nicole opened the door with a toothbrush in her mouth, mumbling, "Just a moment…" She rushed to the bathroom before the toothpaste dripped. Another girl with waist-length dark brown hair, chocolate-coloured eyes, impossibly long, bushy eyelashes and a long, straight, aristocratic-looking nose sat on a bed. The third bed, presumably Tina's, was neatly made and empty. He saw the keys lying carelessly on the top blanket and her luggage on the floor next to it.

The girl on the bed said. "Hi, I'm Zehra. Did you want something?"

Matteo forced himself to remain polite. It wasn't Zehra's fault, after all.

"Yes, I'm looking for Tina. The equipment cupboard has been opened and Alina's luggage removed. As she was the only one with the key, I wanted to ask her why she removed it, but now I can see that the keys I gave her are on the bed. Do you know where she is? I must speak with her."

Zehra looked at her feet and then looked up again. "I don't know where she is, but she was talking a lot to Sven last night."

Matteo was partially distracted by her eyelashes. Were they real? Whatever, she was a real stunner, he thought appreciatively. "Okay, thank you. If you see her, tell her I want to speak with her as soon as possible." Matteo pocketed the keys and went to Sven's room. He knocked on the door, and when nobody answered, he entered. The room was empty. Feeling annoyed and irritated, he went back downstairs. It was already seven thirty, and the participants were getting ready to start their course.

He went outside. Harald Ebner had just arrived with deep shadows under his eyes and his short hair was sticking up at the back like a parrot's tuft. His face was as long and thunderous as the Grim Reaper. David Kraus and Rudolf Hoffmann were also present with their units. Ebner informed them that Alina was in good health at home. Ivanna Petrenko had secretly taken her place and was the young woman missing. The news caused an uproar. Matteo remained still and quiet. Yes, basically it was possible, he thought, but what on earth for?

His friend and colleague, Robert, arrived and stood next to him. Ebner passed Ivanna's photograph around and filled them in with the details they needed to know, including the possibility of kidnap.

"That doesn't make sense," Matteo protested. "The kidnappers would have had to have followed her on the trek up here, but there was no one else at the car park, and anyway, I would have passed them on the way."

"What about that black Golf you noticed missing?" David reminded him. "Maybe someone was waiting in the car until you all set off and then ran after the group."

"But someone would've noticed!" Matteo insisted.

"Unless we have more bogus police officers on the course," Robert said casually. The group looked at him dumbfounded. He shrugged. "It wouldn't hurt to do an identity card check."

"We checked everyone's personal identity cards yesterday evening," Rudolf Hoffmann intervened. "They were in order. Everyone is who they are supposed to be." An audible sigh of relief encircled the men.

"The mountain rescue helicopter will be arriving any second and we'll search for Ivanna. We have infrared cameras on board and I'm reckoning on speedy results," David informed them. "I'll send four men to scour the shortcuts again all the same. Maybe in daylight they'll discover some clues."

"Should Robert and I continue with the course? Wouldn't it be better to call it off and send everyone home?" Matteo asked Ebner.

Ebner stroked his chin. "No, I expect we'll find Ivanna now in daylight. We'll send her home, but the remaining participants can complete the course as usual."

"Well, I should tell you that I locked Ivanna's luggage in

the equipment closet yesterday evening. This morning when I went to retrieve it, it was gone. The cupboard hadn't been broken into and the only person with a key, apart from myself, was Tina. When I tried to talk with her earlier, she wasn't in her room, but the keys lay carelessly on top of her bed. I'm afraid anyone could've 'borrowed' them."

Ebner groaned and Hoffmann pricked his ears up.

"Where is Tina? I'll speak with her. Stealing property and withholding evidence from the police is a crime." Hoffmann spoke with a deep, threatening voice. He couldn't conceal his annoyance.

Matteo agreed. "Yes, at the very least she didn't take her responsibility seriously." They both went indoors to find her.

They saw Tina immediately in the common room, checking her backpack. She had dark shadows under her eyes.

"Come outside with us for a moment, please," Hoffmann ordered. Tina looked puzzled at his harsh tone but did as she was told.

Once out of earshot from the other participants, Matteo asked sternly, "Where were you last night?"

"That's none of your business!" Tina retorted crossly and glared at the two men, her hands on her hips.

"It's none of my business as long as you look after your responsibilities, but the equipment cupboard has been opened and... Alina's" – Matteo made an instant decision to pretend they were still searching for Alina; he wanted to test Tina's reaction – "...luggage has been taken. You were the only person with the key!"

Tina gasped. "Oh! I locked the windows and the door and then I went upstairs and left the keys on my bed. Wait a minute... they must be there now. I'll go and get them!"

Matteo removed the keys from his pocket. "No need, I have them here. That means anybody could have gone into your room and taken the keys."

Tina blushed guiltily and looked downcast. "Yes, I suppose so. I'm sorry. I mean… I didn't think. I mean, who would want to steal Alina's luggage? Whatever for?"

Matteo frowned and studied Tina. She had said the name Alina convincingly. She was exceptionally tall, just under two metres, with broad shoulders and a pale, plain face. Her expression was bland. Matteo wasn't certain she had told the truth, but he couldn't prove otherwise. He looked at Hoffmann, who gave him a slight nod. Matteo put the keys back into his pocket. "I'll keep them for the moment. See you at eight."

*****

Robert was already waiting for him at the meeting point, as were most of the participants. He counted those present. Twenty-one instead of twenty-four.

"Three still to arrive," Robert whispered.

Matteo took his mobile out of his pocket to check the time. Damn the battery was empty. He sprinted quickly back to the hostel, went to the office and plugged his mobile into the charger. Then he ran back to Robert who told him it was 8 a.m. "Same procedure as every Monday," Matteo answered and grinned. "Who is it today? Let me guess… Erik and…"

"Wrong. Sven and the gorillas."

"Sven? Ah, he probably didn't get much sleep last night. Apparently, he's close to Tina. She looked tired, too."

"Tina? Really? Oh well, ten press-ups per minute as usual?"

"As always, yes. I don't feel lenient today."

They waited a further three minutes. Sven came rushing out of the door. "I'm sorry," he panted. "I was looking after Benni and Danny, they're not well. They were up all night with diarrhoea and sickness. I've given them Imodium and they're flat out now."

"A stomach upset?" Matteo asked.

"Yes. They said that, while travelling to Berchtesgaden yesterday, they had stopped at a fast-food fried-chicken outlet. Apparently, it tasted all right at the time, but last night, throwing up, the thought of deep-fried, battered chicken was nauseating. So, they suspect the chicken was off or the frying fat old or something."

Matteo looked at Sven. He looked as if he had been in a fight. His face was bruised and scratched, and one arm had a cut. But that hardly had anything to do with Benni and Danny, especially if they were ill. He looked at Robert and shrugged his shoulders. No press-ups this morning. Pity, Sven had a good excuse.

"All right," he conceded, and began to speak to the group. "We've all had a short night. This morning we'll take it gently with a brief hike to a scenic view called the Archenkanzel. It has a spectacular view over Lake König and a famous church of pilgrimage called St Bartholomä. We'll return here for lunch. This afternoon we'll meet here again at two for the aerial assault course at the high ropes park. At six this evening we'll finish for today. Robert and I will distribute your equipment, Nordic walking sticks and backpacks which you may keep after this week. Any questions?"

Nobody answered, so Matteo and Robert went towards an outhouse used for storage, asking Sven and Erik, who were standing next to them, to give them a hand. They went inside, and Matteo, the tallest, started removing backpacks from a top shelf. He asked Erik to distribute them. Erik was the oldest participant – he must be at least fifty, Matteo thought – and he already had an impressive beer belly. He wondered how he would manage the strenuous treks over the next two days. In the meantime, Robert and Sven counted out twenty-two pairs of Nordic walking sticks. When they had finished, they all went outside, and Matteo locked the door.

Robert asked Zehra to help him demonstrate how to adjust the length of the Nordic walking sticks to the correct height for personal use. Then he showed the group how to hold the sticks to get the maximum effect for fitness.

They set off along a steep, narrow pebble path. Every now and again an open metal drain was buried diagonally in the path to get rid of surplus water when it poured down. There were often sudden weather extremes in the Alps. Robert was in the lead, chatting animatedly with Zehra. Peals of laughter echoed back to Matteo, who was at the end of the line, making sure everyone was safe and didn't get left behind. He accompanied Erik, whose breathing was laboured. He was struggling with the uneven terrain and steep incline. They were lagging a long way behind the others. Matteo was a bit worried about him. How would he manage the rest of the week without holding the others up too much? Well, it wasn't far today. He decided to leave him be. Tomorrow on their long trek he would have to think of a different solution.

The tangy, resinous aroma of pinewood and mossy Alpine earth filled Matteo's nostrils. He breathed in deeply. It calmed him after the excitement of the last seventeen hours. Hopefully, David would find Ivanna not too badly injured, and life could return to normal. Following the path around a bend, the craggy, snow-topped pinnacles of

Mount Watzmann loomed up in front of him. The sight never failed to lift his heart. Loud cursing interrupted his thoughts. Erik had tripped over a metal drain and was sitting on the path, holding his foot. Matteo hunkered down, removed Erik's shoe and felt his ankle.

"Ow, that hurts!" Erik complained. Matteo saw no redness or swelling but maybe Erik had overstretched a ligament.

"Let me help you stand up. See if you can put pressure on your foot."

"A little, but it's painful."

"Okay, let me help you sit down on that bench over there." Matteo pointed to a wooden bench beside the path, just a few feet away. Erik hopped awkwardly on his good foot. Matteo reached in his pocket for his mobile to ring Robert to let him know what had happened, before suddenly remembering that he had left it recharging in the office. "Wait here, I'll just let Robert know that I'm returning to the Kührointhaus with you. I'll be back in a moment." Matteo set off jogging, caught up with Robert, spoke to him briefly and then returned to the bench. He'd only been absent for ten minutes at the most. Erik was gone.

Chapter Nine

8:30 A.M. MONDAY, 26 SEPTEMBER

Matteo gasped like a fish spluttering for water. He checked behind the bench, at the same time realising how ridiculous that was. There was nowhere to hide here in the middle of a meadow. He took long, determined strides back to the hostel. He was bubbling over with anger. He'd only been gone ten minutes, maximum. Who the hell did this Erik think he was? He could hear the helicopter taking off and waved to David as it swirled over him, flattening the grass and scattering clouds of dust. Matteo wondered briefly if the helicopter should start looking for Erik, too. No, he'll have returned to the hostel alone, the prat!

Matteo returned to the Kührointhaus, half expecting to find Erik on the way. He would give him a piece of his mind! But he was nowhere to be seen. His 'sprained' ankle had obviously been a ruse, if he could disappear so quickly. And he'd fallen for it! What was wrong with the group this week? Were they on *Candid Camera*? Matteo went inside, opening doors and scouring every room. Erik had vanished!

Entering the office last, he found his boss sitting at the desk with a mug of coffee. Matteo plumped down on a chair opposite him without waiting to be asked. He noticed his boss gawking at his untypical behaviour and hurried to explain.

"Erik's buggered off. He pretended to sprain his ankle. I left him alone just ten minutes, to inform Robert that I was returning here with him, but when I got back to where I'd left him, he wasn't there, and he's not here either."

Ebner opened his mouth and closed it again. He tried to speak but words failed him. On the third attempt he reached for the telephone and started dialling. "That's it!" he told Matteo. "I'm ringing for the buses. I'm sending everyone home. Call Robert and tell him to return immediately. Something's going on here but I've no idea what!"

Matteo unplugged his mobile from the charger, left the office and went to the common room, so that they could both telephone in peace. He sat down at a table and dialled Robert's number. He heard it ringing once, twice... he perceived a blast of cold air behind him and then whack! His head exploded, his vision turned black, he slumped forward onto the table and, having no balance, sideways then backwards again. He slithered to the floor unconscious.

*****

Ebner ordered the buses and wondered why Matteo was needing so long. As he stood up to go to look for him, the telephone started ringing. He went back to the desk and picked the receiver up. It was David from the mountain rescue team. They had sighted a body lying on a rocky ledge on the wall of a narrow gorge below the Archenkanzel. The terrain was so steep that it was impossible to land the helicopter. However, they had let his colleague down on a winch and he had confirmed that it was indeed a body. A dead woman. The colleague had said that the woman's face had been battered badly and he suspected foul play. If this were the case, the mountain rescue team would no longer be responsible. They had to inform the Kripo. They were now flying back to headquarters. He had given the Kripo the coordinates and they were already on their way to the corpse. Ebner asked him if it was Ivanna but David couldn't say. His colleague had said that it was a female, but the face was too damaged for identification. They would have to wait for an autopsy and probably DNA testing for a definite identification.

"Her face smashed?" Ebner repeated. "Could that have happened from the fall?"

"I don't know," David replied. "We'll just have to wait for the autopsy."

Ebner put the receiver down and headed towards the door again to see what Matteo was up to. The telephone rang again. This time it was Rudolf Hoffmann from the district police. David had informed him they had found a body and Hoffmann had then rung the Kripo. The Criminal Investigative Police were responsible as soon as a crime had been committed, and this didn't look like an accident. He just wanted to let Ebner know that the Kripo were on their way to the Kührointhaus. Ebner told Hoffmann he was sending the course participants home and that he had already ordered the buses.

"Good that I told you then," Hoffmann said. "Don't let anyone leave before the Kripo arrives. They'll want to take statements from everyone."

Scarcely had he put the receiver down when it rang again. It was David. He sounded unusually short of breath.

"There's a forest fire," he called urgently down the receiver. "It's below Mount Toter Mann and spreading rapidly. I've informed the fire brigade. You're not in any immediate danger. I just wanted to let you know."

"Give me strength!" Ebner groaned. "How many calamities can happen in twenty-four hours? I don't believe it!"

"I expect some inconsiderate tourists lit a campfire. It just takes one spark. It's much too dry for this time of year. The firefighters have been on red alert for two weeks now."

"Thanks for letting me know."

Ebner, now seriously worried about Matteo, who still hadn't returned, left the office quickly before the telephone rang again. He saw him straight away, flat on the floor with a pool of blood behind his head. He cried out and rushed over to him. He was breathing, thank goodness. Ebner dialled emergency services and they promised to come immediately. He touched Matteo's shoulders gently. He groaned and murmured, "Aah, my head…"

"The ambulance is on its way," Ebner reassured him. "What happened?"

"Don't know, hit…" Matteo managed to say. Ebner went to the kitchen to get some ice. He saw a Nordic walking stick lying on the floor between Matteo and the front door of the hostel. It looked like it could have been the weapon. The perp may have thrown it away, Ebner thought. He gave it a large berth, he didn't want to destroy any evidence. He entered the kitchen, ripped a plastic bag from a roll and filled it with ice cubes and water. Then he returned to Matteo and tenderly dabbed the bag on the back of his head, carefully avoiding the wound.

Matteo's mobile buzzed. It was on the table vibrating and going around in circles. Ebner picked it up and answered. "Yes?" It was Robert.

"Hi, Matteo. Did you try to ring me earlier? I've just noticed that I missed your call."

"It's Ebner here. Matteo has been assaulted. All hell is going on. Come back with the participants promptly. I'm sending everyone home; the buses are already ordered. David has found a body, though, so now the Kripo are involved. They will require statements from the officers before they can leave."

"Jeepers! How's Matteo, is he all right?"

"He's been hit on the head. The ambulance is on its way. Oh yes, and a forest fire has broken out, too, beneath the Toter Mann. It doesn't concern us, though. We aren't in danger, but the road from Ramsau to Berchtesgaden might be blocked."

"Christ, I don't believe it! I'm on my way. What on earth is going on this week?"

*****

The ambulance took the road via Schönau and reached the Kührointhaus in under eight minutes. Ebner let the paramedics in, and they found Matteo sitting up on the tiled floor, leaning back against a table leg and holding the bag of ice on his head.

They gave his wound a quick look and one medic took his blood pressure while the other set up a mobile ECG. A screech of tyres on the gravel drive announced the arrival of the doctor on duty. He rushed through the door, a little lop-sided from the weight of his medical case. "What have we got here?" he asked the medics quickly, relaxing a little as he saw Matteo sitting up and conscious.

"Patient has received a severe blow to the back of his head. Blood pressure 188 to 115, pulse 120; ECG without findings."

The doctor looked at the ECG himself and then the wound.

Matteo groaned. "My skull has shrunk!"

"Have you vomited?"

"No."

"Do you feel dizzy?"

"A bit. It's getting better now."

The doctor looked into Matteo's eyes with a pen-torch and told him to follow his finger with his eyes. He moved it back and forth. "Good," he said, satisfied. "I'll give you something for the pain, then we'll get you to hospital for an MRT, just to be on the safe side." He rang up the hospital in Traunstein to tell them to expect Matteo.

Robert returned with the course participants. There was a cacophony of noise, everyone asking questions all at once. Matteo's head thumped wildly.

Ebner shouted. "Quiet! Go to your rooms, all of you. Pack your things and stay there until you're called. Go on now, get out of the way so the medics can work. You'll be informed shortly." The officers filed reluctantly upstairs.

Peace restored, Matteo shot Ebner a look and whispered, "Thank you." He beckoned Robert over. "Can you let Freya know? Don't let her worry, though. I'll be fine."

"Of course. Is Erik at hospital in Traunstein, too?"

"Erik? Oh, you don't know. Erik has run off. He only pretended to sprain his ankle."

"What! But in that case, where are Sven, Mark and Tina?"

"What do you mean? Aren't they with you?"

"No, they insisted on helping you. I wanted to stop them, but they ran off before I had a chance to hold them back, and I couldn't leave the remaining officers alone."

Matteo put his face in his hands.

"We must get going now," the medic said.

"Yes. Robert, tell Ebner what you've just told me, and don't forget Freya!"

"Okay, I'll just check on Benni and Danny first, to make sure they're all right."

"Benni and Danny? Oh my God, I forgot all about them! I searched every single room earlier looking for Erik. They weren't in their room. They've disappeared too!"

Chapter Ten

10 A.M. MONDAY, 26 SEPTEMBER

Robert watched the ambulance drive down the road. Then he went back into the Kührointhaus to double-check on Benni and Danny. He sprinted up the stairs, two at a time, and checked their room. It was empty, as Matteo had already asserted. The beds were made and their luggage gone. He wasn't hopeful but he looked inside Sven and Mark's room, then Tina's room. None of them were there. Nicole and Zehra said they hadn't seen Tina since she left the hike. That made a total of seven officers missing. Robert returned downstairs deep in thought. He wanted to speak with Ebner but he was on the phone. He remembered Freya and gave her a ring to let her know that Matteo was on his way to Traunstein hospital. She said she'd drive there to give him a lift home. Robert turned his mobile off and waited for Ebner to finish his call.

*****

The ambulance needed an hour to drive to Traunstein. Matteo spent the time puzzling how Benni and Danny could have left the hostel undetected. There had been people outside the hostel all morning: the mountain rescue team, the district police, Ebner. Somebody must have seen something, or had they had help? Could Sven, Mark, and Tina have concealed them? But why?

As for Sven, Mark and Tina, where were they? He would surely have seen them if they had returned from the Archenkanzel to the hostel. No, they must have doubled back, hidden until Robert had passed them with the other participants, and then taken the Rinnkendlsteig descent along the north-eastern foothills of the Watzmann. They would need to be experienced high Alpine mountaineers for such a formidable route, but he wouldn't put it past them. They had been acting suspiciously. Ebner should ring their superior officer, he thought, hear what he had to say.

Suddenly he had a thought. What if they hadn't gone at all? What if all five of them were tucked away in the storage building outside? The keys could've been copied when stolen the night before. Wait – maybe Erik was with them too! Heavens knew what they were all up to, but it was certainly something criminal if they were going to such lengths.

"Stop the ambulance!" he called out. "Turn around, I must return to the Kührointhaus immediately. Hurry, put the siren on. It could be a matter of life and death."

Chapter Eleven

11:30 A.M. MONDAY, 26 SEPTEMBER

Robert picked up a Nordic walking stick lying on the floor, inwardly tutting at the disrespect some officers paid to expensive equipment. He was about to tidy it away in the storage cupboard when he noticed blood on his fingers. Horrified, he realised that it must have been the weapon used to knock Matteo out. He held it carefully at arm's length and entered the office.

Ebner had finished on the phone and was consulting with Rudolf Hoffmann. "I've brought a present for you," Robert said, holding the stick out to Hoffmann. "I think it may have been used to assault Matteo. There's blood on it."

"Oh yes, I saw it too," Ebner agreed. "I forgot about it, sorry, but I didn't touch it."

"That's all right," Hoffmann replied. "I'll get the forensics team on it. If we identify the perp, we'll need concrete evidence in court, and hopefully they'll find some DNA, or at least fingerprints. We can rule yours out later, Robert." He retrieved some latex gloves from his pocket, squeezed them on and took the stick outside to one of his men to take to the lab.

When he returned, Ebner suggested that they all move to the much larger seminar room before the Kripo arrived. "I just wish I knew what was going on," he said. Robert told him that Danny, Benni, Sven, Mark, and Tina were all missing too. Ebner put his hands over his face. "It's a nightmare!" he exclaimed and sat down with a groan.

When everybody had moved to the seminar room, Ebner went to a large whiteboard at the front of the room and began writing a timeline of events as reported to him.

Sunday 4 p.m.: Ivanna Petrenko arrives at the hikers' car park and says she is Alina Schuster.

Sunday between 4 p.m. and 7 p.m.: Ivanna Petrenko disappears.

Sunday 7.30 p.m. till 10 p.m.: Matteo, Tina, Nicole, Benni, and Danny search for her but to no avail. Matteo notices that a black Golf vehicle is no longer at the parking site. NOTE: Is this important? The remaining participants stay in the hostel.

"Do we know that definitely?" Hoffmann asked. "Couldn't one or more of them have left the hostel?"

"Well, everyone was present when Matteo returned, otherwise he would have said so," Ebner answered. "Wait a minute, I'll get Dennis. Maybe he noticed something."

Dennis had been called in early to prepare a light lunch for everyone. By the time the Kripo had questioned everyone, and the buses had arrived, it would be afternoon. Ebner went to the kitchen and asked Dennis to join them in the seminar room.

"I didn't notice anyone leave," he said. "But it could have been possible, I was paying attention to the cooking."

"I'll rub the last bit out as we're not sure and just stick to the facts," Ebner said.

Sunday 10 p.m.: Matteo informs Ebner of Alina's supposed disappearance.

Sunday 10.30 p.m.: Arrival of mountain rescue team, district police, and Ebner here at the Kührointhaus. The mountain rescue team searches the three possible shortcuts between the hairpins with no sign of the missing woman.

Nobody interrupted so Ebner continued writing.

Sunday midnight: Ebner informs Alina's parents that she is missing. However, she is healthy and well at home. She reveals that Ivanna had taken her place.

Sunday night: Someone steals Ivanna's luggage. Tina had the keys to the storage cupboard but claims innocence and says anyone could have taken the keys.

Monday morning: Matteo finds the keys on her bed. Danny and Benni get a bad stomach upset.

"We only have Sven's word for that," Robert thought out aloud. "What if they had already disappeared during the night?"

"I can't help but think that we're missing the larger picture," Ebner said. "At the moment nothing makes sense. I'll continue writing it all down though. Doing this makes it more transparent and the Kripo will be able to see the timeline of the events."

Monday 9 a.m.: On hike to Archenkanzel, Erik pretends to sprain his ankle and uses Matteo's short absence to disappear. Sven, Mark, and Tina vanish at the same time. David discovers a female body below the Archenkanzel and a fire breaks out below Mount Toter Mann.

9.45 a.m.: Matteo is assaulted here in the Kührointhaus by an unknown perp.

"Have I forgotten anything?" Ebner asked.

"I don't think so," Robert answered. "As to why Matteo was assaulted, I presume that the perp didn't want to be seen by him, but who knows? I've been asking myself why Ivanna's luggage was stolen. Maybe someone was searching for something. But what? Any ideas?"

"Perhaps we should ask Alina again. Ivanna must have told her something," Hoffmann suggested.

Ebner deliberated a moment and then dialled a number on his mobile. "I'm ringing Jan Huber, Ivanna and Alina's superior. Maybe he knows something."

Robert and Hoffmann could hear Ebner's phone ringing and a voice answering "Huber" at the other end. They remained quiet so Ebner could speak in peace, but they were also trying to listen. That proved difficult. Ebner asked questions and seemed to get several answers, but they couldn't hear the responses. A couple of times Ebner dug deeper. After a few minutes he thanked Huber and ended the call. He looked at his colleagues' inquisitive faces and reported.

"Huber told me that Ivanna had been on holiday in June. Her grandmother died and Ivanna went to the funeral in Ukraine. She stayed there for two weeks, together with her cousins, sorting out her grandparents' house and belongings. Apparently, she and her cousins had inherited the house and wanted to sell it. Huber couldn't recall Ivanna mentioning anything out of the ordinary. This was about three months ago."

"Hmm, I don't see how that helps us further," Hoffmann said. "Let's have a coffee while we wait for the Kripo to arrive."

Chapter Twelve

SUNDAY AFTERNOON AND NIGHT, 25 SEPTEMBER

Benni and Danny tied Ivanna's arms and legs together and Benni waited with her while Danny fetched their car. Together they carried the comatose girl to the Golf and locked her in the boot.

"She won't wake up for hours yet," Benni told Danny. "Hide the car and then hurry back to the hostel. We'll go back to her tonight." He hurried off up the hill, after the other course participants.

Danny reversed the Golf and drove back down the road, past the car park, over the bridge, and then turned right along the main road towards Berchtesgaden. He needed to find somewhere to hide the car, as nearby as possible, and then hurry back to the Kührointhaus himself.

The road followed the river Wimbach to his right and kilometres of dense forest to the left. Danny slowed down, not wanting to miss what he was looking for– one of the private roads for foresters which cropped up every few kilometres. There! He braked and turned abruptly into the forest, ignoring a NO ENTRY sign. He jostled along the stony mud track until he was out of sight of the main road. Then he turned left again and parked between some trees and scrub. He jumped out of the car, opened the boot, and finding Ivanna still unconscious, searched her quickly for the map. Nothing! Where could it be? He looked at his mobile and caught his breath. Twenty past five already. He needed to rush back to the hostel before he was missed. Making sure the boot was locked, he pocketed the keys and made a beeline to the hostel. He returned to the road, waded through the river and took a straight route up the hill, dangerous or not.

He spent several days a week at the gym but soon realised that he'd trained the wrong muscles for hill-climbing. His hamstrings screeched in protest. Sweat ran down his forehead, along his chest and down his armpits. Several times he misjudged his footing and slid back several metres down the steep slope between the trees, which scratched his arms. He persisted, trying not to panic because of the time, and reached the hostel out of breath, red-faced, and sweating profusely, just in time, at seven.

*****

Returning from their search for Alina, Tina and Nicole joined Sven, Mark and Zehra at a small, round wooden table in the corner of the common room. They talked quietly, their heads together. Sven sat so he could watch the rest of the room and its occupants. Their conversation was private. He didn't want anyone to come close enough to overhear them.

"Benni and Danny are definitely not who they say they are," Tina said. "Which means that something has probably happened to the two officers whose places they've taken."

Sven looked at Zehra, their IT expert.

"Benni is a Bulgarian named Borya Koljic. He has taken the place of Bernhard Mauch, who is a federal policeman, registered to take part in this course with his colleague Daniel Berger. They are both from Bamberg and were travelling together by car. There was a car accident late this morning along the German Alpenstrasse near Schneizlreuth. The preliminary police report says that two bodies were recovered. They haven't been identified yet, as the car, after coming off the road and plunging down the Weißbach Gorge, exploded and burned out. The road is narrow, steep, and windy. It is a famous, spectacular panoramic route but also a popular detour south, avoiding the motorway whenever there are traffic jams, which is often. I fear that the two bodies are Daniel Berger and Bernhard Mauch. There were no witnesses to the accident and the district police assume that it was caused by reasons unknown, possibly the driver being momentarily distracted," Zehra answered. "That the car broke through the crash barriers does worry them slightly though. They should've stopped a car going at normal speed."

"And who is 'our' Danny?" Sven asked.

"I was coming to that. His real name is Farouk El Hassan, an Egyptian. Farouk and Borya are both known to work for the Argentinian, which supports the theory that something big is going on."

"And what about the older man with a belly?"

"He is really who he's supposed to be, Erik Benz, and registered correctly on this course. He is a federal policeman who works for the border control along the motorways in the region of Stuttgart. He lives in Plattenhardt, quite close to Alina near Stuttgart Airport, so there could be a connection."

"I don't trust Erik Benz," Tina added. "He hasn't done

anything suspicious, but I don't know, it's just a gut feeling. He doesn't really fit in with the rest of the group."

"Okay," Sven said. "What we do know is that Benni and Danny have kidnapped Alina, or the girl calling herself Alina." His colleagues opened their mouths in surprise. "Well," Sven confirmed, "Alina has been thoroughly checked now, and the BND[1] can't find anything about her that could be in the least bit interesting to the Argentinian. Danny drove his car away with an unknown girl in the boot. We know that he can't have gone far, because he simply didn't have enough time before returning here at seven. But that still leaves way too many hiding places for us to find the girl before he and Benni return to her. As you all witnessed, Matteo locked the girl's luggage away, and now Tina is the only one with the keys to the cupboard. What I'm hoping for is that Danny or Benni will try to steal the keys and then the luggage. I think they're looking for something and haven't found it yet."

"So, we catch them in the act of stealing the keys?" Nicole asked.

"No, to the contrary. We make the theft easy for them and then follow them back to their car, disable them, and rescue the girl, whoever she is. Hopefully we shall get some answers from her. Right now, we don't know what is so important that the Argentinian has risked everything by leaving his safe exile," Sven answered.

"But how do you know that Benni and Danny haven't already found what they're looking for?" Mark asked.

"Their mission was to find the object. If they had it, they would have disappeared."

"Ah, I see. And when they find it in the luggage, they'll

───────────

1. BND: Bundesnachrichtendienst, which is equivalent to British MI5 or American CIA.

go to their car, get rid of the girl, and escape. But what if whatever they're looking for isn't in the luggage?"

"I still think they'll return to their car and try to extract the information from the girl. As I said, they didn't have much time until now."

"What are we going to do?" Tina asked.

"I would like you three girls to return to your room, leave the keys in plain sight and your door ajar. Then pretend to read or have a drink together and chat, whatever you like, but with the light on so that someone outside your door can hear and see you. I'm going to go back with Mark to our room and will insert a spyglass into the keyhole so that we can observe the corridor. I'm certain that either Benni or Danny will make some excuse to enter your room and steal the keys," Sven said.

"If you see them, pretend not to notice. On no account try to stop them. They are dangerous and will be armed. But don't worry, I'll be watching from our room, and as soon as it's clear, Mark and I will follow them to their car. Tina, stay in your outdoor gear. I'd like you to come with us. We don't know what sort of state the girl is in, and it might be better to have a female present. Nicole and Zehra stay here and cover for us if necessary. We don't have much time. In a few hours the officers will be getting up for breakfast."

"Of course I'll come with you," Tina replied. "How do you plan to disable Benni and Danny if they're armed and we're not?"

"Mr Buchenmeyer doesn't want us to kill them, he wants them for questioning. We must overlist them somehow and then tie them up. I don't have any handcuffs with me but plenty of cable ties. When you come to my room later, I'll give you some.

*****

Ivanna's mouth was dry, it felt like sandpaper, and she was terribly thirsty. Her head was splitting. Slowly her consciousness emerged through the dense fog of a drugged sleep. She pried her tongue from the roof of her mouth and licked her teeth and gums. She opened her eyes. It was dark… and quiet.

She realised she wasn't at home in bed and suddenly everything came back to her. One of the apes had injected her with something! She could feel where the needle had entered her skin. Panic arose in her breast. She took deep breaths and counted slowly to ten. Where was she? She raised her hands, and they knocked something hard. Her stomach lurched. She moved her feet but didn't get far. She bit her lips to stop herself coming apart. She was terror-stricken. The narrow space scared her. Was she in a coffin, buried alive? Oh God, please no! She kicked out with her legs and thumped the roof with her fists. But she wasn't in a neat rectangular container like a coffin, the sides were irregular and the roof convex. It felt like metal.

A car… she was in a car boot! Shaking, she fumbled for the inside lock. She could feel the cold metal. She twiddled the lock with her fingers, again and again until her fingertips were sore, but to no avail. She couldn't open it. She groped with her legs towards the back seat. She soon realised there was no escape there either. She swore. At some point the apes would return, and what would they do with her then? What did they want from her? If they wanted the map, then it was secure under the insole of her left boot, but then why hadn't they stolen it before, in Bonlanden? Ah, she had been working, she remembered, and wearing the same boots as today. She shouted for help. Once, twice, and then again and again until her voice gave way to a croak.

Nobody answered. She listened and heard faint birdsong.

Was the car in a forest? Hidden? *Nobody* would find her. She bit her lip to stop tears running down her cheeks, but they slid down her face anyway. She licked the salty liquid away with her tongue and concentrated on trying to work out what she could say to the apes to keep them from killing her, because she was positive that's what they would do, just as soon as they had the map.

Chapter Thirteen

SUNDAY NIGHT, 25–26 SEPTEMBER

Matteo told the officers they could retire to their rooms now that they'd given their statements. The three girls went to their room as well. Tina left the keys on her bedspread and the door slightly ajar so that anybody passing could see them. Then each opened a bottle of beer and chatted quietly, waiting.

Sven inserted a spyglass in his door lock so he could watch who was going back and forth along the corridor. There were so many men queuing for the bathrooms that it was busier than the Alexanderplatz in Berlin. Then he saw Danny knocking gently on the girls' door, and gave Mark a high five.

*****

The girls heard a soft knock on their door and Tina called out, "Come in!"

Danny entered. "Hi," he greeted them. "There's a long queue for the bathrooms. Are you waiting, too?"

"No, we have our own, all the women do. The organisers

obviously want to avoid complaints. We were just having a beer. Would you like one?" Tina asked.

"Sure, why not?" Danny plumped down on Tina's empty bed, next to the keys. He took a bottle of beer from Nicole. "Thanks, *zum Wohl!*" They clinked bottles and chatted for twenty minutes, till Danny stood up and said, "Well, I'll go and try my luck for the bathroom again, or I won't get any sleep at all tonight."

As Danny had sat down on her bed, Tina was certain he would steal the keys and had watched his hands, but she didn't see him taking them. When he left, the keys were gone.

"Did you see him pocket them?" she asked Nicole and Zehra. They shook their heads. Tina peered around their bedroom door and, seeing the corridor empty, bid them farewell and dashed to Sven and Mark's room.

The door opened before she could knock and closed again quickly. "Bingo!" she said. "Danny took the keys just like you suspected."

"Did he see you looking?" Sven asked.

"No, I was watching, but I didn't see him take them. When he left, the keys were gone. He's obviously a professional."

Tina, Sven, and Mark took turns looking through the spyglass. It lasted an agonising two hours until they finally detected Benni and Danny sneaking along the corridor, their luggage in hand. "We'll give them a couple of minutes," Sven instructed, looking at his watch.

Silently, they descended the dark staircase, their steps calculated and deliberate. Halfway down, they froze as they witnessed Benni stealthily relocking the storage cupboard. Clutching Alina's holdall along with their own luggage, he and Danny slipped out through the front door.

Sven slid to the window and watched as Danny upended Alina's bag onto the gravel. They sifted through her possessions with meticulous care, exchanging whispers as they inspected every detail of her luggage and the bag itself. Not finding what they were looking for, they repacked everything into the holdall before striding towards the outhouse.

Unlocking the door, they disappeared inside. Minutes later, they emerged without Alina's bag. They set off down the road at a brisk pace towards the Wimbach Bridge.

The night deepened and tension hung thick in the air. Sven looked at his watch again and nodded to the other two. "Right, let's go. We need to rescue Alina before they hurt her. Watch your feet. We don't want a twig cracking that alerts them to us." Sven, Mark, and Tina trailed behind Danny and Benni with careful precision, their footsteps silent in the woods, which were alive with animal movements and the occasional cry.

Benni and Danny were talking to each other. They spoke of a map they hadn't found and relief that they hadn't killed the girl yet. They needed that map, and they were willing to extract the information by any means necessary. Time was ticking; they knew they had to return to the car before their captive stirred.

Snippets of their conversation drifted back through the chilly air to Sven and his colleagues. "At least we know what they're looking for now," Sven whispered. "A map. If only we knew where their car is, we could try to get there before them and free the girl."

"Did you hear them mention Alina?" Tina asked. "I could only hear the name 'Ivanna', but it was several times. And 'El Lagarto'. Do you know who that is? Is he the Argentinian?"

"You heard that, you're sure? 'El Lagarto', or 'the Lizard', is the name the Argentinian is known by in certain circles. His real name is Esteban Vargas, son of Gerhard Weckmann, an infamous, high-ranking Nazi commander. Initially Weckmann supervised the allocation of mobile gas chambers and was responsible for the death of thousands of Jews in World War Two. In 1944, Hitler personally put him in charge of the transport and storage of the stolen art and other valuables, to protect them from the Allies' bombs. Ah, now I'm beginning to understand. Esteban is one of the most serious art collectors in the world. He must think that the girl has a map, or something similar, to the whereabouts of Nazi treasure. His father died quite a while ago, but maybe he told his son about the massed fortune and roughly where the secret caches were. Esteban obviously takes this map seriously. As for 'Ivanna', if they called the girl Ivanna, it would support our theory that Alina has nothing to do with this."

"But how could they know the girl has a map?"

"I don't know."

The moon rose, casting long shadows across the road. A heron screeched, causing Danny to jump and look around behind himself, but the officers were cloaked in deep shade. Sven, Mark, and Tina followed Benni and Danny stealthily the whole way to the Wimbach Bridge, now illuminated in the moonshine and offering no cover.

Sven turned to Mark and Tina. "Wait here," he said. "We mustn't get too close. I'll slip through the forest to see if they turn left or right after the bridge. Then we can continue to follow them, keeping to the edge of the woods."

Benni and Danny turned right over the bridge and then right again, towards Berchtesgaden. Following them was much easier than Sven expected; they seemed completely unaware that anyone was pursuing them. They didn't turn around once. Benni glanced at the sky and said something to Danny. They broke into a run.

*****

But it wasn't only Benni and Danny who were being followed. Fifty metres behind them, a silent figure clad in black covertly pursued Sven, Mark and Tina.

Chapter Fourteen

MONDAY, BEFORE DAWN, 26 SEPTEMBER

As Sven, Mark, and Tina passed the first forester's road on their left, Sven stopped and, slapping his forehead, told the others, "Of course, these roads run every couple of kilometres into the forest. They're for the forest workers and not open to the general public. I bet Danny drove his car down one of these tracks. If we turn left now, along the trail and then right again, in a kilometre or so we should find their car. Let's sprint and try to get there before them."

They set off at a brisk pace along the rutted lane. They weaved between the trees and through the scrub, jumping over thorny bushes, as if in a hurdle race. They reached the next forest trail, but not seeing the Golf, muscles pumping, chased on further. Even before they arrived at the next crossroad, they recognised the black Golf directly in front of them. Sven crouched down quickly and signalled to his colleagues to lie flat on the ground. Then they listened. In the distance, but unmistakeably audible, they heard footsteps coming along the track.

"Damn!" Sven exclaimed. "We're too late to rescue

Ivanna unnoticed. We're going to have to deal with them."
They put their heads together and discussed a plan. It
would be more difficult without guns, Benni and Danny
would certainly be armed. With a nod from Sven, Mark
and Tina fanned out, each taking up a position, ready to
strike at a moment's notice.

Almost immediately, Benni and Danny emerged from
the darkness. Sven's hand tightened around the makeshift
weapon he had found – a sturdy branch lying on the forest
floor. As soon as Benni passed him, heading for the car
boot, he pounced on him from behind and pushed him to
the ground, raising his stick and whacking him across his
face. Danny turned to help Benni, presuming that Sven was
alone. He withdrew his gun and aimed to shoot just as Mark
jumped on his back and Tina smacked the outstretched gun
with another branch, sending it spinning out of Danny's
reach. She dashed to pick it up, leaving Mark to wrestle
with him on the floor. Bloody fists were being hammered
back and forth. She had to wait to get a clear shot, then
aiming for Danny's underarm, she hit it accurately. It was
only a scratch, but Danny screamed out in pain. Mark took
advantage of the moment, turned him onto his stomach
and wrenched his arms back between his shoulders. Tina
tied his hands up and bound his feet together securely with
the cable ties. Leaving him biting the dust, she searched his
pockets, and finding the keys to the Golf, rushed to free
Ivanna from her prison.

In the meantime, Sven and Benni had been attacking
each other mercilessly. Mark took the gun from Tina and
hurried over to help Sven. Benni had a knife in his hand and
had taken up a stance, ready to plunge it into Sven's chest.
"Stop!" Mark ordered, pointing the gun at Benni. Benni
turned to look where the voice was coming from, and Sven,

using the distraction, leapt at Benni, knocking him to the ground. Mark ran over and together they trussed him up.

"Are you all right?" Mark asked Sven, who was getting up from the forest floor and flexing his right hand. He was breathing hard and looked terrible, with blood dripping from his nose, a cut on his upper arm and shiny red bruises on his face.

"Yes, nothing broken, just a few bruises."

Together they went over to Tina.

*****

After shouting for help until her throat was sore, Ivanna had dropped off into an uneasy sleep. The sound of shouting and fighting outside of her prison woke her up and immediately everything came back to her. She listened intently and realised that several people must be there, not just Benni and Danny. She banged on the roof of the car boot and shouted for help. Nobody answered, but she heard bangs and thuds and swearing. Dear God, please don't let the apes win this fight, she prayed.

Eventually she heard a key in the lock and tensed her muscles, ready to defend herself if necessary. The boot opened and a voice said, "Don't worry, Ivanna, we're here to help you."

Ivanna recognised the voice of the girl called Tina, with whom she had begun the hike from the car park at the Wimbach Bridge to the Kührointhaus. When was that? she asked herself. Crikey, it was only yesterday afternoon. It felt like a week ago, so much had happened since then. Tears of relief ran down her cheeks. "T-Tina?" she stuttered. "Thank you, oh thank you so much. How do you know my name? What have you done with the apes?"

"The apes? Oh, you mean Benni and Danny." Tina

laughed. "Don't worry about them." She stretched her hand out to help Ivanna from the car boot. Ivanna took it gratefully and lifted one leg over the edge of the trunk, then her vision spun. She felt dizzy and nauseous. "Hey, steady on!" Tina supported her. "Sit down a moment on the bumper." She reached into her backpack and gave Ivanna a bottle of water. "You'll feel better after a drink. Slowly now!"

Ivanna tried not to swallow the water too quickly, but she was so thirsty that the bottle emptied rapidly. Without warning, her stomach lurched. She rushed over to some nearby bushes and spewed next to them. Her stomach heaved and she was sick again. Beads of sweat formed on her forehead and her complexion turned chalky white.

Tina walked over and gave her a tissue to wipe her mouth. Supporting her elbow, she led her back to the car bumper and told her to sit. She passed her another bottle of water. "Just one sip at a time," she ordered. "Your body will be dealing with the after-effects of the drug they gave you."

Ivanna drank a sip. "What did they give me?" she asked.

"I don't know, but I'll look in a minute. It might be in their luggage."

"Luggage?"

"Yes, they were preparing to leave after they had got whatever they wanted from you."

"I don't understand."

"Well, don't worry for the moment. Just try to rest a minute until Sven and Mark finish tying up your two apes."

Ivanna turned around and saw the two apes bound and gagged on the ground. Two officers, presumably Sven and Mark who were on the course with them, were searching their luggage. Her head ached. She tried to work out how it came about that Tina and the two guys had come to her rescue, but the more she thought, the less she understood. She began to feel dizzy again.

Sven and Mark walked over to the vehicle and eyed Ivanna.

"How are you feeling?" Sven asked.

"Nauseous, dizzy, and very confused. Who are you and what's going on?"

They stood together in the glow of the waning moon, staring at each other and wondering how much they could trust each other.

Sven made an abrupt decision. "I'm going to ring Mr. Buchenmeyer. I'll be back in a couple of minutes." He walked off, out of hearing.

Ivanna folded her arms. Her heart thumped. She was terrified but knew she had to make a decision. She wanted to go to her cousin in Salzburg, but could she trust her rescuers? Maybe they were just as crooked as the apes, although they did seem a lot nicer. But appearances can deceive, can't they? She pondered and wondered what she should do, hesitating back and forth.

Sven returned and spoke to Ivanna. "Mr Buchenmeyer is vice-president of the Bundesnachrichtendienst. You may have heard of him?"

"Yes, I know his name, but how do I know you're telling the truth? That you really spoke to him and not to somebody else?" Ivanna asked, near to tears again.

"You're right to mistrust us. However, Mr Buchenmeyer has decided that we may trust you." He reached into his pocket and withdrew his BND identity card, telling Tina and Mark to do the same. Ivanna scrutinised the passes. The trouble was that she didn't have a clue what genuine BND ID cards looked like. She gave herself an inward kick and made the decision to trust the trio. As she saw it, she didn't have much choice.

"All right," she resolved. "There's a lot I don't understand, but I think the apes were after this." She bent down, removed her left boot, pulled out the insole and withdrew a folded piece of once white paper. "I found this map while sorting out my grandparents' belongings. My grandfather was a prisoner of war during World War Two and worked in a salt mine in the Salzkammergut region, in Austria. The map supposedly displays where the Nazis hid some of the treasure they stole. I showed it to a police officer at the police station in Bonlanden where I live, hoping he would know the correct address where to send it. He wasn't interested and brushed me off, saying I would need more proof than just an old map. Preferably photographic proof that the treasure really existed. I went home, and since then have been followed by those two," she pointed, "and my flat was broken into! So, I swapped places with my friend to take part in this course, hoping to escape them. When I saw them waiting at the car park, I tried to run away. I have two cousins who live in Salzburg and that's where I want to go, now!" she declared defiantly.

A branch cracked, birdsong erupted in the forest and Ivanna's eyes widened in terror. "Someone's here!" she cried. "The birds are warning each other!"

Sven looked between the fir branches to the sky. The first streaks of grey and apricot had appeared. "No, it's the dawn chorus. We're running out of time. Can you ring your cousin and ask him to pick you up here? You'll be safe with him until we can meet again. There's a lot we need to discuss." He gave her the map back. "This belongs to you, but maybe you'll let me make a copy later?"

"Yes, but I can't ring my cousin, the apes took my mobile."

"Come with me."

Sven walked over to the apes' luggage and told Ivanna to look for her phone. He picked up a small metal container and pocketed it. Ivanna held up her phone in triumph, and ringing her cousin's number, spoke rapidly to him.

"He's on his way to the Wimbach Bridge now," she informed the trio. "He knows where it is, and it'll be quicker than searching for this place. He'll be there in fifteen minutes."

"Super! Tina, go there with Ivanna. Wait until her cousin picks her up and then see that you get back to the Kührointhaus as soon as possible. Mark, I need your help for a couple of minutes, then you must also get back. If I don't make it on time, make some excuse for me."

The girls set off, Ivanna now confident that Sven, Mark, and Tina were trustworthy. After all, she still had the map and had regained her mobile.

*****

Once alone, Sven turned to Mark. "Mr Buchenmeyer said I was to give Benni and Danny a dose of their own medicine, literally. Afterwards, if you help me carry them to the boot, I'm to drive the Golf a bit further on down the road and leave it hidden. Four agents are already in a helicopter on their way here. I'm to give them the coordinates as soon as I've parked. Two will accompany Benni and Danny to the high-security prison in Straubing, where they'll be questioned. The other two will destroy any evidence or signs of a fight here. We're to return to the Kührointhaus and keep up our guise for the time being."

"We'd better get cracking then," Mark said, looking at the greying sky. "The early birds will already be eating breakfast."

Sven opened the metal box from Danny's luggage and removed a syringe and a phial of clear liquid. He carefully filled the syringe with the liquid and told Mark to hold Benni, who was tossing his head back and forth. As soon as the needle penetrated Benni's neck, he passed out. Danny's resistance was minimal; he knew he didn't stand a chance.

With Mark's help, Sven hoisted the two dead weights into the car boot and drove off in the Golf. Mark hurried back to the hostel.

*****

A dark figure watched as the car drove away. Then he extracted his mobile from his pocket and rang a number before he, too, set off back to the Kührointhaus.

Chapter Fifteen

12 P.M. MONDAY, 26 SEPTEMBER

Matteo begged the driver again, "Stop, Rüdi, please. It really *is* important!"

Rüdi was amused. He had been to kindergarten, junior and high school with Matteo. Nowadays they still often ran into each other. Berchtesgaden was only a small town and they both went climbing and were in the paragliding club together. They were good friends and trusted each other. Rüdi knew that Matteo tended to be dramatic. On the other hand, it was usually with good reason. He pulled in at the next layby, looking forward to some fun to break up an otherwise boring routine day.

"We're not a taxi, you know! The doctor rang up the hospital in advance. They're waiting for us." Rüdi smiled to take the edge from his words.

"Can you ring the doctor and tell him that the patient is refusing an MRT? He can't force me. It really is important that I return to Berchtesgaden as soon as possible."

Rüdi shrugged his shoulders and dialled a number. Matteo could only hear his answers. "Yes, sir." ... "Right." ...

"Yes." … "Will do." When he'd finished speaking, he told Matteo that the doctor had said that although he strongly recommended him to have an MRT, he could not compel him to. However, should the symptoms get any worse, he was to return to the hospital immediately.

The paramedic in the back of the ambulance with Matteo asked his colleague, "What now?"

"We're to return to base," Rüdi answered.

"And that's where?" Matteo enquired.

"You're in luck. Berchtesgaden."

"Great. Can I come with you then? It'll be quickest. You can let me out at the roundabout and I'll walk to the Kührointhaus from there."

"Yes, all right then."

The ambulance made good time to Berchtesgaden. Rüdi looked at his watch. "Oh, what the heck! We might as well drive you the last eight kilometres as well."

He crossed over the Wimbach Bridge and began to drive up the winding road to the hostel. About halfway up, Matteo's eyes sprang from their sockets. "What the hell!" he exclaimed. Walking up the hill in front of them were Sven, Mark, Tina and a further young woman.

"STOP! Stop immediately!" He barked at Rüdi.

Rüdi slammed his foot down on the brakes and the ambulance squealed to a halt just in front of the group. Matteo pulled the back door open and jumped out. He faced the group, feet apart and hands on his hips. "Where have you been?" he yelled at them. "And what are you up to? We've been looking for you everywhere and all sorts of strange things have been happening. Who are you even? And don't tell me Sven, Mark and Tina!"

"Sven, Mark, and Tina are our real names, actually, and this is Ivanna," Sven answered, putting his hand on the young woman's arm. "But you're right, we don't belong to the police force. We are employed by the BND. Not Ivanna, of course, just Mark, Tina and me. I'm afraid that when we left Robert at the Archenkanzel, saying we would help you, it was just a ruse. In fact, we took the quickest way to Mark's car at the hiking car park, hiding from anyone we saw on the way. Then we drove to Salzburg to pick up Ivanna at her cousin's house. We're on our way to the Kührointhaus now to explain everything."

"And to whom do I owe this assault?" Matteo asked, pointing to the wound on his head.

"That wasn't us," Sven replied. "You need it seen to."

"I've no time for that now. Why should I believe you? Do you have identity cards?"

"Yes." Sven showed him his warrant card and Tina and Mark followed suit.

"All right," Matteo conceded after examining the cards. "Get into the back of the ambulance. All of you, it'll be quicker." Matteo spoke quickly to Rüdi, and they set off on the last four kilometres to the hostel.

*****

In the meantime, David had arrived at the Kührointhaus. He was curious about the events taking place. He found Robert, Ebner, Hoffmann and Dennis in the kitchen drinking coffee. "Hi," he greeted them. "Have you heard anything from the Kripo about the body yet?"

"No, nothing." Ebner answered.

"It's still probably too early," David replied. "It'll take time till they retrieve the body and get it to pathology."

At that moment Ebner's mobile phone rang. It was Kommissar Otto Beck, from the Kripo. He told Ebner that he and his sergeant had been delayed, because after the firefighters got the forest fire under control, they had found the cause of it. Namely a dark-coloured Golf. Someone had set it alight, and the bonfire had spread to the surrounding shrubs and trees, all parched and dry from the drought. The car was completely burned out and contained two charred bodies. They were at the scene of the crime now to get an overview of the circumstances. Ebner should expect them in about half an hour.

*****

The ambulance rolled up in front of the door of the hostel. Sven, Mark, Tina and Ivanna tumbled out of the back followed by Matteo. He said thank you and goodbye to Rüdi and the paramedic, then followed the three agents and Ivanna indoors. As they entered the kitchen, Robert's jaw dropped. "Matteo!" he squawked. "I thought you were on your way to Traunstein!"

Ebner's coffee cup dropped from his hand, spilling scalding coffee over his trousers. It clattered to the floor and shattered. Dennis jumped up and gave Ebner a dishcloth. Hoffmann pushed his chair aside and dashed to the door in three strides. He slammed it shut and stood in front of it, preventing anyone from leaving the room. David stood up and offered Matteo his chair. "Sit down," he said, "you look terrible." Matteo accepted his offer, and Dennis placed a mug of coffee in front of him.

For a second nobody spoke, and then everyone started speaking at once. Sven held his hands up for silence. He passed his warrant card to Ebner. Mark and Tina did the same. Ebner looked at the cards and raised his eyebrows. "You're BND agents? So, what are you doing here? On a team-training course for federal police officers?"

"I'm sorry for deceiving you, Mr. Ebner. I can explain

everything, but before I start, my superior, Mr. Andreas Buchenmeyer, requests that you speak to him."

"Andreas Buchenmeyer? The vice-president of the BND?"

"Yes, and in direct contact with Dr. Bernhard Mahl, the president... that is correct."

Ebner sat up straighter in his chair. "Please wait for me in the seminar room," he told those before him. He waited until they had left the kitchen and then dialled the number. He had never spoken to Mr. Buchenmeyer before. Neither had he had anything to do with the BND. He felt honoured.

Chapter Sixteen

1 P.M. MONDAY, 26 SEPTEMBER

He was surprised when Mr. Buchenmeyer answered the telephone personally.

"Ah, Herr Ebner, I've been expecting your call. First, I must apologise for all the trouble we've been putting you through. My agent, Sven Wassmer, will clarify the factual situation to you as well as he can. At the moment, we are not sure of all the details ourselves. I would like you to support him in any way he asks, to the best of your ability. I also wanted to ensure you of the integrity of this operation and hope that the intelligence services and the law enforcement agencies can work together here to ensure a smooth exchange of information without losing time."

"Yes, sir, certainly."

"Splendid. One more thing, Agent Wassmer will be in touch with me daily, but if anything prevents him from doing so, then please call me instantly. Also, please feel free to ring me at any time, day or night, if you have any questions or are uncertain about something or even if you just have a bad feeling."

"Yes, sir, of course."

Ebner put the receiver down and went to the seminar room. Nicole and Zehra had joined the group. Ebner raised his eyebrows and Sven explained, "They belong to us."

"Aha. I was beginning to wonder if any of this week's group were Federal Policemen at all."

"Most, sir. I think sixteen," Sven replied seriously.

"Sixteen, not seventeen?"

"Well, we're not sure about Erik Benz yet. He doesn't belong to us, but strangely enough, I don't think he has anything to do with Benni or Danny either. Zehra is trying to find out more."

"I see. Well, as curious as I am about what you have to tell us, Agent Wassmer, the Kripo will be arriving any moment, and as we shall all be working together, I suggest we wait the extra few minutes. Any objections?"

"No, that will be best, but please call me Sven. We're all on first-name terms here."

"Fair enough, then call me Harald."

"Shall I leave you? The Mountain Rescue is a voluntary service, not an official agency," David asked.

"Of course, you may go if you wish, but if you do stay, we may need your services. However, it could be dangerous, even life-threatening. We're dealing with professional killers," Sven answered.

"If there's a chance I can help, then I'll stay."

"Thank you, David. The same applies to everyone present. There is no shame if you have any doubts. You can leave now."

Nobody moved.

Out of the window they saw a dark grey BMW 3-Series pull up in front of the hostel, and two policemen in civil clothing got out.

At least I hope they're the police, Ebner thought, now unsure of everyone and everything. The car was the type that the Kripo preferred, nondescript but with a powerful engine. He looked at the car antennae; it was longer than average, typical for the vehicles plain-clothed officers used, so at least that spoke for the truth. He went outdoors and shook hands with them. Blushing slightly, he asked to see their warrant cards. He studied them both carefully before returning them.

"Kommissar Otto Beck and Sergeant Lukas Schwarzkopf. I'm sorry about the scrutiny, but you'll understand when you hear everything."

He invited them indoors and led them into the seminar room. "Let's begin by all introducing ourselves."

"Yes, of course. Once again, sorry about the delay. The forest fire wasn't caused by tourists this time, but by a car that someone had set alight! I've not had to deal with anything like it here in Berchtesgaden before. And two dead men. Charcoaled! It will keep us busy for some time. I'm not sure if we'll have the resources to help you as well. I can always request extra help though."

"A car? With two dead bodies, where?" Sven asked breathlessly.

"The car was on a private forest road, just a hundred metres from the main road between Ramsau and Berchtesgaden, about ten kilometres from here."

"That must be Benni and Danny!" Sven proclaimed. "That means that the Argentinian's thugs got to them before our agents did. And our agents were already on their way. How did they find out about them so quickly? And how did they find them?"

"There may have been a tracker on the car," Mark said.

"Yes, but why kill them? They couldn't know that we rescued Ivanna."

"Unless Ivanna is being tapped and traced, too," Tina said.

Sven's face fell. He put a finger to his mouth, signalling everyone to be silent and then motioned with his fingers for Tina and Ivanna to leave the room and go upstairs. Once they'd left the room, he put his hands briefly over his face. "Sorry, I must let Mr. Buchenmeyer know. He'll advise our agents, who are on their way. Benni and Danny may have been killed to stop them talking to us." The telephone was answered immediately and Sven told Mr. Buchenmeyer the problem. He listened carefully before finishing the call.

"I presume I'm talking for all my colleagues here when I say that we are completely puzzled," Ebner said. Sven looked at the blank faces in front of him, but before he could speak, Tina and Ivanna entered the room again. Ivanna was wearing different clothes and shoes.

"There was a tracker on the phone, and it was being tapped, too. I filled the bath, and after stamping on the phone and smashing it to pieces, I threw it into the water. I didn't have time to check the clothes and shoes, but they are all in the bath too. Stupid that we didn't think of this before!"

"My flat was broken into, but nothing was stolen. I didn't think of tracking and tapping devices, but Benni and Danny took my phone from me," Ivanna recalled.

"Whether it was done earlier or later doesn't make any difference. We gave the phone back to you and you rang your cousin. He's in danger! Does he have family?" Sven asked.

"Yes, and I have another cousin in Salzburg, too. They were going to help me, you see. After the police weren't interested in the map. One, Toby, is a caver, and the other, Olivia, said she would take photographs of the treasure if we found it, and then we could have shown them to the police as proof."

"Which one did you ring last night?"

"Toby. We went back to his place and Olivia joined us there!"

"And we picked you up this morning! Ring Toby now! Here, take my phone, it's safe! Tell him to leave his home immediately, without delay. He mustn't stop to take anything with him. Then ring Olivia."

Ivanna's fingers trembled so much that she misdialled.

"The number that you have called is not available…"

"Sorry!" she cried, trying again. "He'll be at work now… Toby, hi, it's me! You're in danger, and Mel and the kids! Leave work immediately and pick them up. Don't go home! Go to…" Ivanna looked at Sven questioningly.

Sven turned to David. "Where can you land the helicopter?"

David hesitated for a second. "The football ground. Not the Red Bull, the Toni-Kronreif stadium in the Plainstrasse. I can be there in fifteen minutes."

"Did you hear that, Toby?"

"Yes, we'll be there. What about Olivia?"

"Don't worry, we'll let her know. Go now!"

"Oh my God!" Ivanna sobbed as the telephone went dead. "If I'd known what we were getting into!"

"It's too late now, ring Olivia!" Sven ordered. Ivanna did as she was told, while Sven hurriedly asked David how many people could fit in the helicopter.

"We'll manage," David assured him. "Where to?"

"Bring them all back here first," Sven decided. "We can think about that in the meantime. Can you take Mark with you?"

"Yes, that would be practical because then I can leave the

helicopter motor running when we land. We'll be quicker."
David and Mark ran out of the door. The group in the
conference room watched them clamber into the helicopter
and spiral away, David speaking urgently into his radio
controls.

For a moment silence prevailed. Ivanna stopped chewing
her nails and asked how long they would need.

"At least half an hour," Sven replied. "I must organise
a safe house for them." He rang Mr. Buchenmeyer again.
Finishing the conversation, he asked Rudolf how he could
reach David. Rudolf gave him a number and soon Sven was
speaking to him. "Change of plan," he said. "After you
pick them up, you're to take them to the Mountain Rescue
Service at Ruhpolding. You can land on the meadow in
front of their station. Two of our agents will be waiting
there and will drive them to a safe house."

"Roger and out," David answered. Only now did Sven
let out a sigh of relief. "Well, presuming he picks up your
cousins on time, they should be safe now," Sven consoled
Ivanna. "Once they've settled in, we'll take you to them."

Before, whilst giving orders, Sven had appeared cold
and ruthless. Now that the issue had been primarily solved,
his voice was softer and full of empathy. Ivanna examined
him closely. It couldn't be easy to make decisions and whip
out commands in a crisis and remain calm. Presumably
that was why he was leading the group of agents. The last
thing one needed, was somebody who panicked and made
decisions without thinking them through properly.

He was quite good looking but not in the conventional
way, she thought. He was tall and slim and obviously
very fit. His eyes were blue and his skin clear, well, apart
from the red bruises he was now sporting. However, he
had a hook nose, his lips were thin and his chin protruded

forwards. He had mousey coloured hair, cut very short. He may not be a director's first choice for an advertisement, but his personality made him attractive.

She couldn't help wondering if he was married, he wasn't wearing a ring. Then she told herself off for even thinking along such lines. Just because her boyfriend of eight years had finished with her four months ago, and now she was twenty-nine and single and her biological clock was ticking, didn't mean she had to eye up every male within a mile, like a randy bitch. Anyway, she had enough other things to worry about on this trip without any romantic diversions.

Chapter Seventeen

2 P.M. MONDAY, 26 SEPTEMBER

"Can you let us know what's going on now?" Ebner asked Sven. "At the moment, nothing that has been happening here makes any sense."

"Yes, certainly, let me begin. For nearly two years now, the BND has been investigating a man named Esteban Vargas, known as 'the Lizard'. He is half Argentinian and half German and possesses dual nationality. He is the head of the presently most powerful drug cartel in Argentina, the Los Ortegas clan, and responsible for the massive increase in drug trafficking to Europe, as well as other drug-related crimes: extortion, blackmail, and money laundering. The BND applied for his extradition to Germany, which Argentina refused. So, we have been investigating his work methods and his contacts here in Europe..."

"Drugs! But what's that got to do with me?" Ivanna cried out.

"Exactly! That's what has been puzzling us. Two weeks ago, our contacts at Buenos Aires airport informed us that the Lizard had left Argentina and taken a flight to Paris. We were surprised, to say the least! What could be so important for him to leave his safe haven in Argentina and risk being captured and imprisoned here in Europe? Our agents, working closely with the French Directorate-General for External Security, were awaiting him at Charles de Gaulle airport and watched as someone in a black limousine met him. The DGSE agents tailed the car and observed it stopping in front of the Hôtel de Crillon. A gentleman got out of the car, but he wasn't the Argentinian. The car was empty save the chauffeur."

"Damn! How did they engineer that?" Ebner couldn't stop himself from interrupting.

"Exactly, that was very unfortunate. We couldn't find him in any hotel in the city and he seemed to have disappeared from the face of earth. Of course, he could have been staying with friends practically anywhere. Luckily, we got another breakthrough a week ago, when our associates let us know that the Argentinian, accompanied by two men, had taken a private jet from Paris-Le Bourget, stating their destination as Munich. Again, our agents were waiting at 'Franz Josef Strauß' airport, but he basically never left the runway. He left the private jet and boarded a helicopter waiting next to the hangar, whose pilot told the tower that their destination was Salzburg. Somewhere over the Bavarian Alps the pilot broke off all communication with the ATC and the helicopter hasn't been seen or heard from since. So once again the Argentinian has slipped through our fingers. However, we are now convinced he is somewhere in this area."

"Why?" Matteo asked. "And what has all this got to do with our training centre here?"

"I was coming to that, but let Ivanna tell you her story first."

"Me? Well, all right, but I still don't understand the relevance. My grandfather was Ukrainian and served in the Red Army in World War Two. In 1941, he was taken prisoner during Operation Barbarossa in Kyiv. After a long march south-west, he was forced to work in a salt mine somewhere near here. Towards the end of the war, a high-ranking Nazi officer visited the mine. Soon afterwards numerous wooden crates began to arrive there. My grandfather, along with his fellow prisoners, were ordered to carefully stow the crates away at the end of the mine. Through chance and luck, my grandfather survived the war. When he arrived home, he became convinced that the wooden chests must contain stolen Nazi treasure. He drew a map of where the salt mine was and wrote an account on the back of it about his time in the war, explaining what I've just told you. Mind you, he said the entrance to the mine had been blown up, so I didn't really think it would be possible to find it.

"My grandfather died in 2005, but my grandmother lived until five months ago. The farm was left to my cousins and me, but none of us wanted to keep it. It's run-down and needs extensive restoration. Besides, none of us are farmers. I live my life in Germany, and two cousins live in Austria. The other three still live in Ukraine, but they all live and work in Kyiv. So, we decided to sell the farm.

"Three months ago, we all met at the farm and started clearing out our grandparent's belongings. I was clearing out the loft. Amongst other junk, there were boxes full of dusty old books. I removed one book from a box and was flipping through it when a piece of folded paper fell out. It was a hand-drawn map of where, supposedly, stolen Nazi loot had been hidden. At first, I considered throwing it away, then I decided to show it to my cousins first. Toby, who is a caver, said it could be possible that treasure really was hidden in a salt mine. He agreed that vegetation had seventy years to grow over the entrance, but he said that it may have been left undiscovered just for that very reason. He added that a professional should still be able to find it.

"None of us wanted to enrich ourselves, but we thought it would be dutiful and beneficiary if the treasure could be returned to its rightful owners. We agreed that Germany was anxious to do the right thing nowadays, regarding returning stolen wartime property, whether to museums or private people, and that I should take the sketch to a police station. We hoped the authorities would be able to give me an address where to send the map. However, when I went to my local police station, the officer in charge wasn't interested. He said the police didn't have enough resources to check all the information that they got every year about possible hidden treasure. Besides, the map wasn't at all conclusive. My grandfather had no way of knowing exactly where he had been. If I could find the mine and take photographs as proof of the actual existence of treasure, then of course the appropriate experts would come and salvage it. And try to find the rightful owners.

"Although, as I said, the policeman at the station in Bonlanden wasn't interested in the map, a few days later I noticed that I was being followed by two men. It scared me. I reported it at the police station. It was the same officer as before. He wanted to know if the stalkers had menaced me in any way, spoken to me in an insulting manner, or harassed me with telephone calls or threatening letters. I answered no to all his questions, but I filed a complaint anyway against the two unknown men. I even described them for the record. I don't think the police actually did much, though, if indeed anything at all.

"A week later, my flat was broken into. The furniture was turned over, books ripped from their shelves, grocery packets emptied. But I didn't notice anything missing. I went back to the police station and filed another complaint. It was the same officer yet again. This time he apologised, but said that if nothing had been stolen, then he doubted whether the police could do anything about it.

"Now I realise that the men must have bugged my flat. They probably put a tracer on my phone and most likely a wiretap, too. I don't know how they could have known so much otherwise.

"I got very worried and nervous and didn't know why I was being followed. My best friend, Alina, was registered for this course. A week before it was to begin, she confided to me that she was pregnant. With our boss! He's a married man with a family of his own. She didn't want to come on this physically strenuous course and risk a miscarriage, but she didn't want to tell her boss that she was pregnant either, not until she had decided what she wanted to do.

"I came on this course myself last year. I remembered that our names were called out from a register, but that our identity cards weren't asked for. So, we agreed that I should take her place. We thought that way I would elude my followers – I didn't realise I was being monitored at the time – and she could skip the course without anyone knowing. I took time off work in lieu of overtime. We had no idea what I was getting into. I'm very sorry about that. And about all the trouble I have caused. I still don't understand what is happening, but no doubt Sven will explain everything now."

"What happened between registering yourself at the car park and walking up to the hostel?" Matteo asked. "You just seemed to disappear, and David found a corpse beneath the Archenkanzel."

"What? I don't know anything about that!" Ivanna cried out.

"I'll explain about that later, but for the moment just finish your story."

"Okay. I recognised the two men as soon as the bus entered the car park. I was so shocked that I decided to run off as soon as they started the hike to the hostel. I think they read my thoughts! In any case, they waited until I set off with Tina and Nicole and then followed us. I ran into the woods to escape them, but they followed me, found me, and gave me an injection of some sort. The next thing I knew I was in the boot of a car.

"Tina, Mark and Sven rescued me. My cousin, Toby, who lives in Salzburg, picked me up and I grabbed a few hours' sleep before they came to collect me, to bring me here. I'm so grateful. They saved my life, because the two stalkers were looking for the map, which I had under the insole of my boot. And once they had it, I'm sure they would have killed me."

"Thank—" Matteo was interrupted as the door burst open, banging loudly against the wall. Freya stood there, face red with anger, feet apart, hands on her hips. Matteo's jaw dropped. "Freya! Oh my God, I forgot all about you!"

"I got an urgent call from Robert, telling me you'd been attacked and were on the way to Traunstein hospital with the emergency services. I was so worried! I dropped everything and drove there as fast as I could. I cursed every red traffic light... and then? You weren't there! 'Never arrived' they said. Didn't you think to let me know? Then a whole hour's drive back again!" Freya sobbed.

Matteo rushed over to comfort her. He took her in his arms. "I'm so sorry, darling!"

"It was my fault," Robert interrupted. "I rang in the first place. I should've thought to let you know."

While Matteo and Robert fussed around Freya, Dennis used the opportunity to stand up. He pointed to his mobile. "It's getting on," he said. "The buses will be arriving soon. I'll go to the kitchen and warm up some soup. I made some sandwiches earlier. Maybe we could take a short break for lunch?"

"Good idea," Beck agreed. "In that case, Lukas and I should start questioning the remaining participants on this course. I hope that somebody can tell us something about Erik Benz. He's still missing as far as we know, and at the moment, he seems to be an unknown factor."

"Robert and I could look to see if he's in the storage building outside," Matteo suggested. "He could be hiding there."

"Fine," Sven answered. "Then let us do that and have a lunch break. I'll ring the technicians and ask them to come and set up computers and safe telephones here in the seminar room, if that's all right with you, Harald?"

"Yes, of course."

"Good. Afterwards, I can explain the rest to you, and we can decide about what to do next."

At that moment Sven's mobile rang. He took the call and held a hand up to stop the others from leaving the room. It was David ringing from the helicopter. The connection crackled loudly.

"Toby wasn't... meeting point." David's voice kept getting cut off, so that the sentences weren't complete. "...waited ten minutes... couldn't risk... longer. ...flying to Ruhpolding. Toby's wife, Mel, really... upset. I've promised... fly back via the football ground... way back to... Kührointhaus."

"But what did she say? Surely, he must have brought his wife and children to the football ground if they were there waiting."

"Yes. ...told her he wanted something from the house... he... back quickly. ...didn't return."

"Is Olivia with you, with her husband and family?"

"Yes, yes, everyone... present. Just Toby ...missing. ... ring back when know more."

"Okay. Thank you." Sven rang off, frowning. He turned to the people in the room and told them the bad news.

Ivanna burst into tears. "What on earth have I done?" she cried.

"There's no point worrying at the moment," Sven said. "Let's have lunch, and by the time we've finished, David might have rung back with better news." He gave Tina a sign to comfort Ivanna.

Matteo saw Freya back to her car, promising to return home early that evening. After she had driven away, Robert joined him to look for Erik Benz in the storage building. "Wait for me," Rudolf called after them. "I'll come with you."

Chapter Eighteen

MONDAY AFTERNOON, 26 SEPTEMBER

Matteo inserted his key into the locked door of the storage building. He eased the door open cautiously, Robert was close behind him. They went inside and looked around. The large room appeared empty of people. "Nothing conspicuous here," he called to Rudolf, waiting outside. "Unless someone is hiding, but we can check more thoroughly and open the toilet cabins."

"Okay," Rudolf called back, and entered the building too, pushing the door wide open. He had his hand on the door handle, wanting to close the door behind him. Suddenly the door slammed back violently into his face. He cried out sharply in shock, barely registering the black figure that dashed from behind the door and ran past him out into the open.

Matteo and Robert turned around in surprise and then sprinted past Rudolf after the figure, who was making for the Unimog parked outside the Kührointhaus. Matteo, capable of running a hundred metres in twelve seconds, raced to the beginning of the winding road, intent on cutting off an escape in that direction. Robert, equally fit and muscular, chased the figure racing towards the Unimog. The person, realising he was being followed and that he didn't stand a chance of making it to the Unimog, took a revolver from his pocket and fired it twice into the air. He didn't seem to want to kill his pursuers, not even hit them, just gain enough time to flee.

Matteo and Robert backed off with their hands up. "It's Erik!" Matteo shouted to Robert. "He has a holdall with him. Careful, I don't know what's in there!"

They watched Erik turn abruptly to his right and start the precipitous, narrow descent down the Rinnkendlsteig towards St Bartholomä.

As soon as he disappeared, Matteo and Robert followed him. They had been up and down this route a hundred times or more and knew they could conceal themselves behind rocks and bushes and so catch up with Erik without him noticing them. They were confident they would be able to overpower him because Erik was overweight and not fit.

The Rinnkendlsteig wasn't a path for beginners. You needed alpine experience for this route, along with a head for heights and sure-footedness. The track was steep with breath-taking views of Lake König. However, there was a constant danger of rock fall, particularly all along the upper half of the track.

The stony path was so narrow that you could only walk in single file. Matteo took the lead and Robert followed. They went down a wooden ladder fixed directly onto the precipitous rock face with iron bolts. Matteo wondered how Erik was managing with his holdall. The ground was dry, and now and again a loose stone fell from the path and down into the valley. It fell for several seconds until it reached the bottom.

Matteo was so close to Erik now that he could see that his face was red and that he was sweating profusely. He hung onto the wire rope that secured the path with his left hand and was struggling clumsily with his holdall in his right hand, and it was slowing him down. He was obviously neither fit nor an experienced climber. Matteo thought he could see his knees shaking. He turned around to Robert and signalled that they should slow down. They didn't want to cause Erik to have an accident. Besides, there was still a long way to go, and they could easily catch up with him, without danger, further down.

Erik stopped suddenly at the end of a hairpin curve on the path. Matteo saw him swing his right arm back, as if to throw his holdall down the mountainside. As he swung his arm forward again, letting go of the holdall, it caught on a button on the cuff of his jacket. The momentum of the toss thrust Erik forward and he lost his footing. With a scream like a cat squawking blue murder in the night, Erik was swept off the path along with his holdall. He fell down a sheer drop of six hundred metres. To his death.

Chapter Nineteen

MONDAY AFTERNOON, 26 SEPTEMBER

Matteo and Robert strode to the place where Erik had fallen and looked down. There was no sign of either Erik or his holdall. "There's nothing we can do here," Matteo said. "We might as well go back and make sure Rudolf is okay. I'll be interested to hear what Erik had to do with this and how it came to such a tragic end. I hope Sven will be able to tell us."

They found Rudolf at the Kührointhaus. He was sitting down with his head laid back against a cushion and a bag of ice on his nose. "Are you all right?" Matteo asked.

"Yes, I'm fine. Nothing's broken. Just a nosebleed. What about Erik?"

"He went down the Rinnkendlsteig and lost his balance. He stumbled over the edge and fell to his death. No way could he have survived a fall like that."

"Oh my God, that's terrible! I hope Sven is finally going to tell us what is going on now. They're searching for the boss of a drug cartel, but what has that to do with your training centre?" Rudolf asked.

*****

The lunch break finished, and Harald Ebner bid farewell to the remaining course participants. He apologised for the circumstances and promised they would go to the top of the list for the next available course. As the buses drove off, there was a moment of peace, but it didn't last long.

Scarcely had they disappeared down the winding road, when several vans rolled up in front of the hostel. A man dressed in jeans and a T-shirt under a black leather jacket got out of the leading van. He entered the common room where Matteo and Robert were rapidly devouring a pile of sandwiches and looked around. Seeing Sven, he waved and approached him.

"Ah, Sebastian, you've arrived. That's great. Come on, let me show you the seminar room." Sven led him away, then returned almost immediately and spoke to Ebner. "The technicians have arrived. They'll set up several workplaces with computers fitted out with the latest antivirus programme and safe telephones. Also, a massive screen at the front of the room that everyone can watch at the same time. When lunch is cleared away, we can push some tables and chairs together to make a large conference table here in the common room. Is that all right with you?"

"Yes, of course, whatever you need."

Finally, Sven was ready to explain the events of the past twenty-four hours. He had hardly begun as the sound of a helicopter approaching resounded through the room. Sven stopped talking and they all went outside to greet David and see if Toby was with him. The helicopter landed, churning up clouds of dust and dead leaves. Gradually the blades stopped rotating, leaving peace in their wake.

Much to everyone's relief, Toby was the first to jump

down from the helicopter, closely followed by David. Ivanna ran to her cousin and hugged him. "Thank goodness you're all right," she said. "I was so worried. Why on earth did you go back to your house?"

"I had some detailed maps of the caves around here at home. I thought they would be useful. I took Mel and the kids to the football stadium and thought if I ran quickly, I would have time to collect them. As I approached the house, I ducked behind some bushes, just to be on the safe side. It was lucky I did, because two men dressed in black jeans and hoodies went up to the front door and rang the doorbell. I immediately rang the police and told them somebody was trying to break into our house. The gangsters went round the side of the house to the back. They broke the glass door to the veranda to force entry. The police caught them inside the house emptying drawers. They were taken into custody and are hopefully still detained at the police station."

"Oh, well done!" Sven exclaimed. "I must ring Mr. Buchenmeyer immediately. He can arrange for them to be taken to Munich for questioning. The more of the Argentinian's thugs we manage to eliminate, the better. I'm sure he has plenty of contacts and enough people at his beck and call, but he'll have to advise and instruct anyone new that he puts on our heels."

Sven rang Mr. Buchenmeyer and waited for the return call. It didn't last long. Mr. Buchenmeyer's call to the police station in Salzburg had been too late. After the gangsters' details had been taken, they had been set free again.

Sven related what Mr. Buchenmeyer had told him. "They hadn't stolen anything, and they didn't have a criminal record, so they would probably only get a fine. He has already checked the details that the gangsters gave the police. As to be expected, they were false as were the passports fake. So, we're back to square one again, I'm afraid." Sven concluded, "I don't think it's going to be easy to get hold of the Argentinian. We'll have to debate how to outwit him. I can use the time while the technicians are busy to fill you in with some more details."

"Tell us about the corpse first," Ivanna begged. "Obviously it wasn't me, but it's a too-good-to-be-true coincidence that a body was found and no doubt bought you some much-needed time."

"You're right," Sven confirmed. "You're quick picking things up. If you ever decide to change jobs, let me know. We're always on the lookout for people like you.

"I'm afraid this is a necessary part of our job, but not one we're proud of. We checked the pathology lab in Munich and found the corpse of a woman who had been in a bad car accident. She had no relations and her face was unrecognisable, so we used her body and placed it on the ridge, knowing it would be found. We wanted Benni, Danny, and the Argentinian to believe you dead. Unfortunately, the ruse didn't work because they were already tracking you."

His confession left the room silent and Matteo thoughtful. Sven hurried to continue his explanations. "As I said before, the BND has been investigating Esteban Vargas, 'the Argentinian', for two years. We know that his father was Gerhard Weckmann, and we are now ninety percent certain that he was the high-ranking Nazi commander who visited the mine where Ivanna's grandfather laboured. He studied art history at the University of Berlin before the war broke out and was in charge of the transport and storage of the stolen fine art, gold, and jewels. Anyhow, from autumn 1943 onwards, Hitler ordered that the most valuable works of art were to be stored in the numerous salt mines in Salzkammergut. The region was part of the so-called Alpine Fortress, the last area of retreat for the Nazi Party.

"After Germany was defeated, and the magnitude of Nazi war atrocities became apparent to the world, many in the party's elite, especially those who masterminded the Holocaust death camps, knew they needed to disappear."

"But how could someone like Gerhard Weckmann not only escape but even remain undetected in Argentina?" Matteo wanted to know. "I mean, the war criminals were persecuted and brought to trial, weren't they? At Nuremberg."

"He left his wife and children in Berlin and changed his name to Felipe Vargas, a common South American name. Once there, we know he underwent plastic surgery and quietly slipped into a new life. He took enough diamonds with him to pay for an extravagant existence. He married an Argentinian beauty from a powerful family and had a son, Esteban Vargas, and two daughters. He lived a life of luxury. Esteban inherited his father's love of fine art and over the years has become one of the most serious art collectors in the world."

"Now I'm beginning to see," Matteo countered, "but was it really so easy for him to escape justice? That's devastating."

"I'm afraid so. It's common knowledge that Argentina was a safe haven for many Nazis after World War Two. Juan Perón spent part of the war working in Argentina's embassy in Italy and openly admired the politics of Benito Mussolini and Adolf Hitler. When Perón became president of Argentina in 1946, he ordered diplomats and intelligence officers to establish secret escape routes, so-called 'ratlines', to smuggle thousands of former SS officers and Nazi Party members from ports in Spain and Italy out of Europe and into Latin America."

"Ratlines? I've never heard of that term," Matteo queried.

"Me neither," Robert agreed.

"In 1946, the Perón government sent word through Argentine Cardinal Antonio Caggiano to a French counterpart that Argentina would be willing to receive Nazi collaborators from France who faced potential war crimes prosecution. That spring, French war criminals, carrying passports issued by the International Red Cross, stamped with Argentine tourist visas, began to cross the Atlantic Ocean."

"What? Are you saying the Church helped Nazis escape justice?" Matteo was outraged.

"The Catholics, yes. Catholic leaders apparently accepted working with the Nazis in order to fight the common enemy of Bolshevism. Numerous Vatican officials aided the escape of Nazi war criminals. Specifically, they provided them with false Vatican-issued identity documents that were then used to obtain passports from the International Red Cross.

"These Vatican papers were not full passports and thus were not enough to gain passage overseas. They could, however, be used to obtain a displaced person passport from the International Committee of the Red Cross, which in turn could be used to apply for visas. In theory, the Red Cross would perform background checks on passport applicants, but in practice, the word of a priest, or particularly a bishop, would be good enough."

"That is absolutely sickening," Matteo burst out. "I didn't know so many escaped."

"The Americans had proof that Gerhard Weckmann, alias Felipe Vargas, was responsible for a lot of deaths, but they couldn't do anything if he was in Argentina. The

Germans applied for extradition, but the country's Supreme Court refused to extradite him because of supposed inaccuracies in the paperwork."

"But what has Felipe to do with Esteban?" Matteo asked. "Presumably the father must be dead by now. You mentioned drugs before."

"Yes, and yes. The father died in 2005. I told you that Felipe married into a powerful family. More precisely, he married Lucia Rodriguez, daughter of the Minister for Foreign Affairs. The ministers were appointed by and served at the pleasure of the president at that time, Juan Perón. One factor that made Argentina an attractive location for processing drugs was its chemicals industry, which supported robust pharmaceutical sectors.

"For years, Argentina was open territory for individuals and groups seeking to import industrial quantities of ephedrine, pseudoephedrine, and other precursor chemicals, used to produce drugs like cocaine and methamphetamine. The country had minimal restrictions on imports of these chemicals, allowing potential drug manufacturers access to a near endless supply of precursors. Illegal synthetic drug production emerged in the country due to the availability of relatively inexpensive precursor chemicals.

"The pharmaceutical companies were some of Perón's biggest campaign donors. He was unwilling to regulate this trade, yet happy to support this welcome source of income, not only for his party but also for himself personally.

"So, Lucia's father, Alberto Rodriguez, was well informed and actively involved in the drug business. He ensured a job for Felipe Vargas in the foreign service, where he was responsible for making contacts in Europe. Felipe Vargas, in turn, procured a good position in the foreign service for his son Esteban. His son stood directly under his command, and learned all that was to be learned, until his father retired, and he took over his position.

"In 1990 Esteban married Bianca Suarez, daughter of Alfonso Suarez, leader of Los Ortegas, one of the most powerful drug cartels in Argentina. Alfonso Suarez insisted that all members of the family work actively for Los Ortegas. Esteban joined the diplomatic service and thus he could send and receive parcels from abroad with a complete absence of border controls. He was responsible for the transport and the distribution of drugs in Europe and made useful contacts here. The Schengen Agreement, a treaty that led to the creation of Europe's Schengen Area, where internal border checks have largely been abolished, made his task a piece of cake.

"In the 1990s, Argentina underwent one of the severest economic crises in its history. The Suarez family, based in Rosario, took advantage of the extreme poverty by picking up unemployed youths from the streets and putting them in 'bunkers', small brick structures, making and selling synthetic drugs. By the early 2010s, Los Ortegas grew bolder, more sophisticated, and more violent. Their success was in no small part due to their strong criminal ties to local police, prison staff, and businessmen. They also managed to establish links with drug producers and distributors in other provinces in Northern Argentina, as well as in neighbouring Paraguay and Bolivia.

"So, Esteban was set up comfortably working in the foreign ministry and was also a major player for Los Ortegas, as his father-in-law demanded from him. He earned masses of money enabling him to finance his hobby, the collection of fine art. Paintings nowadays go for immense sums, even millions of dollars. He had no reason to leave Argentina and risk coming here. The temptation of finding long-lost paintings to possess himself must have been too great. Benni and Danny were ordered to follow Ivanna, and they found out she was coming here. Berchtesgaden is on the border with Austria, in the region of the Salzkammergut. In former years, it had an important salt mine itself. Esteban must have thought that Ivanna was going to look for the salt mine and the treasure. He wanted to make sure he could procure the treasure himself, before Ivanna and the authorities retrieved it."

"But what is the point of having the paintings if you can't show them openly to anybody?"

"He has a ranch in Argentina, between Buenos Aires and Rosario. Underneath the ranch are cellars fully acclimatised for paintings. He stores all his unlawfully obtained treasures there: paintings, antiques, jewels, and only shows them to a very few select people. He cannot lend such paintings to museums or galleries because they are stolen goods. However, there is a huge black market, and he can sell them to people inside certain circles. Then he can buy paintings with documentary proof of origin, thus laundering the money illegally earned in the drug business. Esteban is known in Argentina as a philanthropist... A good, generous man who lends valuable paintings, legally obtained, to galleries throughout the world and donates millions of dollars to charities.

"Business prospered and the group continued to consolidate. That is until 2012 when a shipment of drugs went missing. Alfonso Suarez suspected Jose Moreno. He had been laundering money for the Suarez family through his car dealership and occasionally transported drugs for them. Alfonso had him killed in broad daylight in the centre of Rosario. Eight months after Jose Moreno's murder, Santiago Suarez, Alfonso's son, was fatally shot as he left a nightclub. Santiago's murder generated a wave of indiscriminate violence. Following Santiago's death, his brother, Benicio Suarez, assumed leadership of Los Ortegas, shortly before being killed himself.

"A turf war began on the streets. It was estimated by national news sources that the open warfare between local drug gangs was costing an average of one life every twenty-five hours.

"The public didn't like it and made demands for the police to do something about it. The population that had already endured nearly four years of economic crisis and significant wage cuts wasn't ready to take any more: violent social unrest mired in a deep political, social and economic crisis, financial collapse, a large growth of unemployment, and a massive increase in poverty.

"Mauricio Macri, Law-and-Order candidate in Argentina's presidential election in 2015, promised to clean up the streets, and this helped him win. The new administration moved swiftly to toughen security and drug policies. Investigators cracked the encrypted messaging service Sky ECC, which was popular with criminals, and gathered enough information to investigate Alfonso Suarez thoroughly. Esteban's sister had her cell phone hacked. From the contents of this device, the detectives found a large amount of evidence about the current members and their different roles in the alleged criminal structure. The investigation lasted several years and was based primarily on evidence collected through intercepted phone calls. An intricate felonious network that involved criminal groups, the police, and businessmen, from Rosario, as well as other Argentine provinces was exposed.

"In 2018, in what was widely seen as an historical court decision, Alfonso Suarez was sentenced to twenty-two years in jail on charges of illicit association and homicide. The leaders of other drug cartels were sentenced for drug trafficking, for violent homicides, and for money laundering.

"At first, the Suarez family worked from prison, organising their business from there. But then the corona virus came, and it was no longer possible for them to order organised transport. This was when Esteban took over in Rosario.

"In 2020, the first case of the virus arrived in Argentina. Nearly all transport, by ship or by air, was forbidden, with very few exceptions. Esteban took advantage of the situation and used his immunity as a diplomat to send parcels to Europe. Presently, he is the most powerful drug cartel boss in Argentina."

"If all this is true and he came here because of my map, how did he find out about it? And why did he risk everything by coming himself?" Ivanna asked.

"The police station in Bonlanden sent us copies of the complaints you made. We now know the name of the policeman you spoke to, Jürgen Gross. Zehra is doing extensive background checks both on him and Erik Benz. There must be a connection somewhere. Somebody informed the Argentinian about the existence of the map. The next bit is a bit speculative. We presume that Gerhard Weckmann told his son about the hidden Nazi treasure in the Salzkammergut. Even if Weckmann wasn't the man who visited the mine where Ivanna's grandfather worked, he would have known with certainty that Hitler had ordered the stolen goods to be hidden in the Salzkammergut. The Argentinian will know which paintings are still missing since the war, and the temptation to find and view the treasure first, personally, must have been too great to resist. Of course, he intends to steal it as well, at least as much as he can get out of the country."

"Oh, I understand," Ivanna said. "And the BND want to catch him to destroy his drug cartel in order to stop so many drugs arriving in Europe?"

"Yes, exactly," Sven agreed. "For the last three years, the BND, together with Interpol and several other European intelligence and law agencies, have been observing the increase in drug trafficking in Europe with alarm.

"The BND has already secured more than thirty-five tons of cocaine this year, the majority of which arrived in the port of Hamburg. The drug is smuggled to Europe and other destinations via various South American ports. Due to its geographic location and strong trade ties with European countries, Argentina has become one of the key transit and starting points for Andean drugs headed across the Atlantic. Record amounts of cocaine are being seized in Europe. Its availability on the continent has never been higher, with extremely high purity and low prices.

"Belgium is now gaining a reputation as Europe's cocaine-trafficking hub. In 2021 nearly a hundred tons of the drug were seized in Belgium, more than in any other country in the EU. Law enforcement authorities in six different countries have joined forces to take down a cartel of drug traffickers controlling about one third of the cocaine trade in Europe. Belgium has asked for help in finding out why traffickers are using Antwerp's port and what can be done to tackle drug smuggling."

Several officers present let out gasps of astonishment. Matteo looked at his boss Harald Ebner and gave him a wry smile. "Not *Candid Camera* after all," Matteo said. "Who would have thought that our peaceful town of Berchtesgaden would turn out to be at the centre of an international crisis?"

"Let's hope it has a successful outcome," Ebner answered. "We don't want to be made fun of in the newspapers."

Chapter Twenty

MONDAY AFTERNOON, 26 SEPTEMBER

By the time Sven had finished explaining why they were searching for the Argentinian, the weather had changed dramatically. Since lunchtime, a cold wind had swept under the door and through the cracks in the wooden window frames. Now large snowflakes started to fall. Not just one or two, but masses of them, rapidly developing into a blizzard.

"The weather changes very quickly here," Sven remarked, looking out of the window. "To think that earlier we had twenty degrees." Thunder rumbled and lightning flashed over the Alps.

"Yes," Ebner answered. "It's typical of this region, but I'm not surprised, the weather reports forecasted snow. Don't worry, though, it won't stick to the roads. The ground is too warm for the snow to hang around for long. It could be different on the Watzmann, though."

"Well, I've finished my report, I think," said Sven, "unless anyone has any questions?"

No one spoke, and after a short silence Ebner remarked

that it had been a lot to digest and that questions would probably crop up later.

Sebastian came from the seminar room into the common room. "We've finished setting up workplaces with PCs and secure telephones," he announced. "Err, Mr. Ebner, could I have a word in private, please?"

"Yes, come into my office," he said, leading the way.

*****

"Well, there's no more we can do tonight," Matteo said. "It will be dark in a couple of hours, and I promised Freya I'd be home early today. Anyway, I should get some rest for my head, so I will see you soon!"

"Yes, of course, have a good rest. Thank you for your help. The four agents who arrived this morning in the helicopter couldn't do much as the car had been burned out, but they've been checking things over and will arrive here soon. We'll all get onto the computers and then sleep here." Sven withdrew his wallet from his back pocket. "I'm sorry for the mix-up with Freya. Here," he said, holding out a fifty euro note, "please buy her some flowers from me."

"I'm perfectly capable of buying flowers for my wife myself!" Matteo retorted angrily. "Goodnight. I'll see you tomorrow at seven."

Matteo went outside and looked at his mobile. Five o'clock. The flower shop would still be open. He got into the Unimog and drove down into the centre of Berchtesgaden. The windscreen wipers worked furiously against the falling snow, merely managing to push it into the corners of the windscreen. It started steaming up.

His head throbbed and he was in a bad mood. Mainly because he hadn't thought of buying flowers himself. The town was deserted, not surprising in this weather. For the first time in ages, he found a parking space at the bus station. Great, he thought, more cheerful now. He went to the flower shop and chose a bunch of mixed roses that were fragrant, not like the supermarket ones. He wondered whether he should get some ice cream, too. There were several Italian ice-cream parlours in town, but Freya's favourite sort was 'Raffaello', which only one Italian made. It was made with white chocolate, coconut and almond chips. He pulled his collar up against the snow and decided to make a run for it.

As he dashed across the street, a Porsche suddenly appeared from nowhere, driving much too fast and headed straight for Matteo. Shocked, he dived head-first onto the icy pavement, landing painfully on his right hip. The Porsche braked, skidded, and came to a halt fifty metres down the road. Matteo looked after it but couldn't recognise the number plate. All he could tell was that it was black. As he watched, it drove off again, the motor revving unpleasantly loudly. Matteo stood up gingerly and brushed the snow from his trousers. The streets were lonely but an elderly woman walking along the pavement picked up the flowers that had flown from his hand and handed them to him.

"Are you all right?" she asked.

Matteo took a few careful steps and then stood on his tiptoes and went down on his knees.

"Yes, everything seems fine, thank you."

"You were lucky," the woman said. "What a crazy idiot, driving at that speed in this weather. Probably had his summer tyres on too."

"Did you catch the number plate?" Matteo asked.

"No, I'm sorry. I wasn't really looking. But he looked as if he was aiming for you on purpose! Do you want an ambulance? Or should I call the police?"

"No, there's no point. I'm fine, and the police aren't going to find the black Porsche. There are too many of them here."

"Well, if you're sure. Goodbye, then. Have a good evening."

"Thank you. You, too," Matteo answered.

Matteo walked more carefully to the ice-cream parlour, bought the ice cream, and drove home. So much snow was falling that just by going from the car to the front door he was covered in it.

"Hello, darling, I'm back," he called out.

Freya came from the kitchen with a wooden spoon in her hand. "Oh my God!" she exclaimed. "You look like the abominable snowman." They both giggled.

Matteo gave her the flowers and put the ice cream in the fridge. The aroma coming from the oven made him hungry. "That smells nice," he said. "Is there anything I can do to help?"

Freya had put the flowers in a vase on the table, and now that her hands were free, she gave her husband a kiss and a hug. "You could pour us both a glass of wine. I think we deserve it after a day like this."

"Yes, good idea," Matteo answered. "Red or white?"

"I've cooked salmon and spinach tagliatelle, so maybe white?"

"Okay. Which would you prefer? A Riesling? Or we still have a bottle of Sauvignon blanc in the cellar, I think."

"Let's go for the Sauvignon blanc."

"Fine, I'll go and get it. I got some 'Raffaello' ice cream on my way home. It's in the fridge."

"Mmm, fantastic."

The evening at home relaxing with Freya was just what Matteo needed. After the meal he had a hot shower, took an ibuprofen, and decided to make an early night of it. Freya joined him. As she bent over to kiss him, she knocked his hip, and he cried out in pain. Freya threw the sheet back and saw his hip was black and blue.

"Okay, what haven't you told me?" she demanded.

Matteo tried to play down the events of the day, but Freya wasn't fooled. Afterwards, they made love gently and Freya fell asleep straight away. Matteo couldn't sleep. He tossed back and forth replaying the events of the day. Suddenly, he had a thought. Why had Rudolf Hoffmann said that the identity cards were all in order when they obviously weren't? Things just didn't add up. He spent a restless night and finally got up before his alarm blared. His hip was very sore, so he smeared ibuprofen cream generously all over the bruise and took another tablet. He made a coffee and kissed Freya, who was still in bed.

"Goodbye, I'm off," he said.

Contrary to what was usual for this time of the year, a little snow had remained on the ground. The temperature had dropped to just two degrees. Despite his warm clothes, Matteo shivered. He looked at the sky. It was grey and seemed full of even more snow. Mount Watzmann was half-hidden in dark clouds, looking like its nickname, 'Mount Doom'. Matteo drove to the Kührointhaus feeling uneasy.

Chapter Twenty-One

TUESDAY MORNING, 27 SEPTEMBER

There was already a buzz of activity when Matteo entered the hostel. Sven and Toby were pouring over the Ordinance Survey maps that the latter had brought with him.

"My grandfather had no way of knowing exactly where he was," Toby was explaining to Sven. "He never left the salt mine during his time there, so we must imagine we're standing in front of it. From the direction of the sun, he has marked north, south, east, west. Then he's drawn one road in front of the salt mine, which may be larger and more important now, or might have disappeared altogether... who knows what has changed after seventy years?

"His next clue that we can use is the church spire in the distance. The biggest clue, however, is the river with a small island in the middle. That should cut down the possible places for the salt mine to three or four, because otherwise it could be practically anywhere in the whole of the Salzkammergut. Of course, there are geological elements to be considered as well. I shall take everything into consideration. Is there any way I can drive around and search potential locations without the gangsters following me?"

"We could leave them false trails," Matteo butted in. "That way they will have to split up and will be easier to handle."

"Yes, and we still don't know where the Argentinian is staying," Sven said with frustration in his voice. "I'm glad that the additional four agents have arrived to back us up."

"Let's just think of some red herrings then," Matteo suggested, "and decide who should go where."

"Call everyone together. We should discuss this in the seminar room and allocate the various tasks," Sven agreed.

Matteo went to the kitchen to get a coffee and a currant bun for breakfast while Sven gathered everyone up. Dennis was busy chopping vegetables. When Matteo entered the seminar room, he saw Harald Ebner and wondered what Sebastian had wanted to see him about the previous afternoon. He also wondered whether he should speak to him about the identity cards and Rudolf Hoffmann. Rudolf had been in his post for five years now and it was impossible to suspect him of anything amiss. There must be some simple explanation. He decided to keep quiet for the moment and eat his breakfast. Rudolf entered the room, followed by David and Robert, and they all said hello to each other. The technicians left the night before, but Tina, Mark, Nicole, and Zehra joined them, along with Dennis, Toby, and Ivanna.

Sven went to the head of the room to address them all and introduced the four new agents. The most remarkable of the four was Topper. With huge, black-framed, nerd glasses, and acne on his forehead and cheeks, he looked about seventeen, but was actually nearly thirty. He wore wide apple-green trousers that stopped somewhere mid-calf. His socks were blue and yellow with depictions of the Simpsons, pink sneakers without laces, and an oversized orange T-shirt with the word 'peace' written in large letters across the front. His hair was medium length, dyed black, and gelled to stick out in all directions. He had a silver earring pierced through his right nostril. His distinct appearance made him noticeable everywhere he went. Topper went straight to Zehra and stood next to her. Robert, standing on the other side, frowned and inched nearer to her.

"First of all, good morning and thank you for being here," Sven addressed the group. "We are here to discuss how to find the Argentinian. We believe that the best way to do this is to find the stolen Nazi treasure, which he is desperate to get his hands on. We must entice him out of his hiding place."

Ivanna raised her hand. "Sorry for butting in already, but I have a question. If the Argentinian is a diplomat and immune from criminal prosecution, how can you hope to punish him here in Germany, even if you do find and catch him?"

"Mr. Buchenmeyer has spoken to the high justice in the Federal Court and Esteban Vargas's immunity has been lifted."

"Oh, I see. Thank you."

"That's fine. Please, any of you ask questions if they arise."

"In that case, do you know how many men the Argentinian has around him? It would help to know how many we have to go against," Matteo asked.

"I'm afraid I don't know exactly," Sven admitted. "Basically, just that he has plenty of contacts here in Europe from his criminal activities in the drug business."

"Is there any way of finding out, at least a rough number? They must be staying somewhere in a hotel or holiday flat. A man in a black Porsche nearly knocked me down yesterday evening. A witness said he was aiming for me."

"What? Do you mean he tried to run you over?"

"I'm not sure. He was driving too fast, and the visibility was low."

"Did you get hurt?"

"I've got a painful bruise on my hip but otherwise I'm okay."

"Thank goodness for that. Well, we could certainly ring all the hotels and holiday flats in the area yet again and ask about any new arrivals, maybe including Salzburg this time. I don't know if it will get us further, but it can't harm things. Topper, would you take that?"

"Sure thing, I'm onto it right now." Topper sat down, put his earphones on and started typing at an incredible speed into his PC.

"Zehra is still working on Erik Benz and Jürgen Gross. She has discovered that they are in a bowling club together and now she's checking the other members of the club. David has told me that the helicopter sighted a body below the Archenkanzel that fits Erik's description. The helicopter couldn't get near enough to rescue the body, not even to let somebody down on a winch, but there is a ground troop on their way as we speak. We should hear more later. This morning, Matteo made an interesting suggestion, which I would like to put to you. He thinks that if we lay several false trails the gangsters will have to split up and they will be easier to deal with separately."

"I think it's a good idea, and I've been thinking about it," Toby said. "There's a cave beneath the Eagle's Nest that very few people know about. Nobody would find it without local knowledge. Originally, Hitler wanted to build a road through the mountain directly to his house. It was never completed, and in fact it's only about a hundred metres long. It is utterly believable that treasure could be hidden there, and I'm sure that the gangsters would follow us. Of course, it's empty, but only very few people have been inside, including myself, otherwise I wouldn't know about it. You won't find it on any map. The German authorities don't want present-day Nazi followers to make it a place of pilgrimage."

"That sounds ideal," Sven answered. "We shall have to plan it carefully, though. I'll ask Mr. Buchenmeyer to get in touch with Dr. Dieter Roman, president of the Federal Police. We shall need the Special Forces to make the arrests and protect us. If we enter the cave heavily armed it would give our cover away, but who knows what weapons the Argentinian's men will be fitted out with."

"It would be good to lock the gangsters far away, somewhere deserted," Robert said. "Like the Steinernes Meer, for example, or the Ice Chapel. Anywhere away from the civil population. But I haven't thought how to get them there yet."

"What about the Rossfeld circuit?" Matteo threw another idea into the conversation.

"Ah. Matteo fancies himself as a Formula One driver," Robert said, laughing.

"No. But it would be fun to race them around the steep winding corners and then turn off right at the last minute down to Hallein. If a car follows us, then the Special Forces will know who to arrest."

Laughter filled the room. After a minute, Sven said, "All right, let's calm down now. Before I continue, Harald wants to say a few words."

"Yes," Ebner agreed. "Yesterday, Sebastian informed me that the Federal Police IT system was hacked and spyware installed. That explains how the course participants were known to the perpetrators, and they could choose the most suitable, Daniel Berger and Bernhard Mauch, to exchange places with. It also explains why the identity cards were declared valid. The situation is now under control, but the cybercrime unit wants to have all your personal mobiles. They will be returned to you tomorrow. In the meantime, I have new mobiles for all."

Matteo was glad that he hadn't said anything about Rudolf, there was an innocent explanation for the identity cards after all. Ebner waited while everyone put their mobiles in a box on the front table and picked up one of the new ones before he continued.

"I'm sorry to inform you that the two bodies found in a car after the motor accident on the Deutsche Alpenstrasse have now definitely been confirmed as Daniel Berger and Bernhard Mauch. They were on the way to this course. They were our colleagues and died in the course of duty. The police have found skid marks suggesting they were forced off the road and are treating the incident as murder. There will be a memorial service in Bamberg on Saturday, eleventh of October. I would like to ask for a minute's silence now, to commemorate our colleagues." Ebner remained standing and folded his hands together. Everyone in the room rose from their chairs and lowered their heads. After the minute had passed, they sat back down again rather solemnly.

Another minute passed, the only sound being that of computer keys being hammered furiously by fast fingertips and Topper talking quietly into the mouthpiece of his earphones. He put his hand up to signal that the detectives listen.

"Right… You are sure… When exactly did they check in? Really… Okay… Can you let us know when they leave? Ah, I see… A black Porsche… In your garage… And the other two men? Can you send me the car registration number and copies of their passports? Thank you very much, and as I said before, don't mention this conversation to anyone. It falls under the National Security Act. Good… Thank you. I may need to get in touch again… Yes. My name is Thomas Topper." Topper clicked off the phone.

"I think I've found three of the gangsters. They are staying at Hotel Schwabenwirt, just outside the town centre. It's a private hotel and the proprietor was at the reception when one of them checked in. The guest has a black Porsche and reserved a place in the hotel's garage for the next three nights. The other two men arrived separately but they are all staying together in a three-bed room. He doesn't know whether the other two arrived by car or by train. They didn't book places in the garage but there is a large public car park just opposite the hotel.

"The proprietor said that according to their passports all three are Bulgarian. They are large, muscular, tattooed guys in black clothing. He said he wouldn't like to meet them alone on a dark night. Unfortunately, he can't let us know when they leave the hotel, because apart from the main entrance the hotel has a beer garden that leads onto the street. So, it would be pure chance if he noticed one or any of them leaving. They are in the beer garden right now. Two are drinking beer and one is drinking Coca-Cola. They're chain-smoking and fiddling with their smartphones. He said something very interesting though, one of the waiters noticed that they all had a tattoo of a small black lizard on their left thumb. The waiter had made jokes about it."

"Black Porsche and a black lizard… that is one coincidence too many," Sven said. "I don't think the three Bulgarians will be the only helpers the Argentinian has, though. I expect they've split up into several hotels. Good job, Topper. Carry on ringing the other hotels and holiday homes to see who else has newly arrived in town. When the copies of the passports arrive, print them out and bring them to me, please."

"Will do." Topper continued bashing the keys on his computer.

"Can we see a map of all the various locations being mentioned?" Mark asked. "I need to get my bearings."

"Yes, good idea," an agent who had introduced himself earlier as Stefan agreed. He had light brown skin, black oiled, perfectly groomed hair and finely arched, plucked eyebrows. He looked as if he was from the Middle East, but he spoke perfect German with a Berlin accent.

Toby pinned a large, detailed map of Berchtesgaden and surroundings on the wall. It was topographical, showing the enormous differences in height from the peak of the Watzmann at 2,713 metres and the Kührointhaus at 1,420 metres down to Salzburg at 420 metres. He pushed a little flag into the map at the golf club, the Ice Chapel and all the other relevant locations. The agents not familiar with the area stood around the map, studying it.

"Can you show us where some salt mines are? Disused ones of course, or just where it's possible that salt mines could be?" Stefan asked Toby.

"That's a good question," Toby answered. "A lot of salt mines are closed today, including the one in Berchtesgaden. If you mean where I suspect Konstantyn's salt mine might be, then I think somewhere just over the border on the Austrian side. I think the river he drew was possibly the

Salzach. He drew a small island in the river and there is a small island in the Salzach at Hallein. The perspective of his drawing suggests somewhere in the region of Bad Dürrnberg and Scheffau, but that's a large area to search, especially if the entrance is no longer recognisable. Another area is that of the Barmsteine, two rock pinnacles that lie on the border between Austria and Germany. There are many caves there, including ones that were used for the armaments industry during the war. There is also the river Saalach and the river Traun. I can't remember seeing any islands in those rivers though, I would need to drive along them to check."

"Do you think that Konstantyn's secret cave is definitely in Austria?" Stefan asked.

"I'm not sure," Toby replied. "In 1938, Germany annexed Austria, and Salzburg was a part of Germany. In 1945, when Austria was independent from Germany, it became a federal state again. So, the salt mine where our grandfather was forced to work could have been in today's Austria, but there are also several salt mines in Germany on the border to Austria."

Robert had obviously been thinking about Matteo's collision with the black Porsche, and he changed the subject. "Did you see the black Porsche following you?" he asked Matteo.

"No, I was concentrating on the road, the car's windscreen wipers had difficulty keeping the snow at bay."

"Because I was wondering," Robert continued, "how the Bulgarians could know you were there since they no longer have electronic trackers on us. I realise they must know about Matteo and myself and Harald and Rudolf, but what about the four new agents who have arrived here and Nicole and Zehra? Does the Argentinian know how many agents he's up against? Are they watching us, hidden in the forest somewhere, with binoculars? Or is the Argentinian as much in the dark as we are?"

"They know about the Kührointhaus and could be watching us," Sven answered. "They could also be taking photographs of anyone arriving or leaving. Then they will check out our details – it's easy with face identification on the Internet. I think we must reckon with them knowing all about us. I hope that none of you write too much personal stuff on social media."

"Shouldn't we try to find their spy?" Robert asked. "Matteo and I know the area better than anyone else. We could wander around and try to spot the guy, ideally take a photograph of him, or maybe there are even a couple of men out there. David could support us from the air with an infrared camera, so we know roughly where to look."

"That's a good idea but just keep an eye on him or them, don't attempt to arrest anyone yet. I cannot emphasise enough how dangerous they are."

"What's this trail here?" Stefan asked. He pointed to a trail that led through the national park.

"That's a disused road that once led from Ramsau in Germany to Weißbach bei Lofer in Austria. Nowadays, the road is closed for public use. There's just a tourist bus that goes along it. It goes up a hill called the Hirschbichl, which is well known because there's a green border there into Austria. The bus continues along the river Saalach to the Vorderkaser Gorge, Lamprecht's Cave, and the Seisenberg Gorge, all popular tourist attractions. The road is particularly popular for hikers and cyclists," Matteo informed him.

"I could walk along that trail, maybe with another person. It might occupy a couple of the Argentinian's men for a few hours and maybe we can take some photographs of them, too," Stefan suggested.

"I'll come with you," Nicole offered. A couple will look less suspicious, and I can pretend to pose for photographs."

"Good," Sven said.

Rudolf Hoffmann said he needed to get back to his office and catch up with some work. Ebner asked if he could accompany him and find out how the ground troops were getting on with rescuing Erik's body.

Ivanna asked if she could stay with Topper and Zehra. "I've really had enough excitement for a while," she added. "I can help them ring up the hotels."

"I would like to drive round the Rossfeld circuit and from there turn off towards Bad Dürrnberg and Hallein. I could take some photographs of possible locations and then ask my friends in the potholing club what they think. If that's all right with you, Sven?" Toby asked.

"Yes, I'll come with you and drive the car," Sven answered. "But I will need to know the names and addresses of any cavers you speak to. If possible, keep the number down to just one or two."

"That leaves just me, Mark, Patrick, and Julian," Tina said.

The last two belonged to the group of the newest agents. Patrick was a slim man in his mid-forties, his fingers were stained with nicotine. He had shaved his hair to within a millimetre of his scalp, possibly to make the rather large bald patch on top of his head less noticeable. He looked so ordinary that he could easily melt into the background and not be noticed. Julian was in his mid-thirties and looked extremely fit. He was tall, at least one metre ninety, and wore sporty clothing. He looked like fifty per cent of the holidaymakers in Berchtesgaden. "How can we help?"

"I would like Patrick to go to the Hotel Schwabenwirt and observe the Bulgarians, if they're still there. Otherwise, wait until they return and of course try to photograph them," Sven said. "Mark, I know you can paraglide. Julian, what about you?"

"Yes, I have my certificate," Julian answered.

"Great! Then you and Mark could take the cable car up onto the Jenner and fly down to Brandnerfeld. From there you can get the bus back to Berchtesgaden and one of us can meet you there with a car."

"You can borrow my paraglider if you like," Matteo offered.

"And I have one, too," Robert added. "Mine is here, in the storage building."

"Mine is at home, but if we drive you both to the valley station for the cable car, we can stop at my flat on the way and pick it up. We can return here afterwards and explore the forest."

"What if somebody follows us?" Mark asked. "They will find out where you live, and your wife will be at risk."

"I expect they already know where I live," Matteo answered. "But it's a good point. I'll ask Freya to go to her mother's for a few days until this business is over."

"Won't she mind?"

"I think she'll understand. She's already seen that I've been injured twice, and she gets on well with her mother. She doesn't live far away. In the same town, actually. So, it won't make any difference driving to work."

"Good, we cannot be cautious enough," Sven answered.

"What about me?" Tina reminded him.

"I thought you might enjoy a boat trip on Lake König," Sven replied. "You can get on the tourist boat at the harbour, and I would like you to leave it at St. Bartholomä pilgrimage church, have a look around the church and grounds and then hike up the Rinnkendlsteig to the Archenkanzel and back here."

"Alone?"

"If anyone follows you, they won't try anything on the boat or at St Bartholomä, there will be too many tourists around. Once you get to the Rinnkendl trail, your climbing skills will exceed anything the gangsters are capable of."

Tina's face lit up at the compliment. "Right, it sounds like a nice trip out," she said, pleased.

Chapter Twenty-Two

TUESDAY MORNING, 27 SEPTEMBER

The Federal officers and other team members readied to leave on their various assignments. Just ten minutes later, Ivanna, Zehra, and Topper were left alone in the seminar room.

"After the buzz of activity before, it seems very quiet in here now," Zehra remarked. "It's just as well because I'm still busy checking out the backgrounds of all the members of the bowling club. I had to make some phone calls before and I could hardly understand the person on the other end."

"I've finished ringing all the hotels in Berchtesgaden apart from the Kempinski. I'll ring there first and then start on the hotels in Salzburg." Topper replied.

"What should I do?" Ivanna asked.

"Could you ring up the holiday flats in Berchtesgaden?" Topper asked.

"Yes, of course," Ivanna answered.

*****

"Hello, is that the Kempinski Hotel?" Topper asked.

"Yes, you are talking to the switchboard, how can I help you?"

"I'd like to speak to the manager, please."

"Just a minute, I'll connect you." The telephone rang several times before the manager's secretary answered. At first, she didn't want to connect Topper with the manager and said he was busy. After saying that he was a BND agent and that obstruction in a criminal enquiry was a criminal offence, she put him through straight away.

"Claus Wiederkehr," a voice barked down the telephone, "The manager, Kempinski Hotel. What's so important that you find it necessary to threaten my secretary?"

"This is a criminal investigation, and we need to know the whereabouts of an Argentinian called Esteban Vargas. It is very important. If he is staying at your hotel, we need to know, and if he is accompanied by any other guests."

"It's not the hotel's policy to reveal any information about our guests and they value our discretion." The manager had shouted down the phone but now he hesitated, becoming a little uncertain. In a calm voice he asked, "However, um, just out of interest, what if this man is travelling with a diplomatic passport? Not that I'm saying that the man you are looking for is staying in this hotel," he hurried to add.

"Well, just out of interest, a German judge has lifted Vargas's immunity. If it would ease your conscience, I can send you a copy of the judge's decision."

"That would be helpful, yes."

Topper ended the call and sighing, stood up to fetch a copy of the judge's decision to lift Vargas's immunity. After scanning it, he emailed the document to the manager. A short time later, the manager rang back, falling over himself to be helpful. He told Topper that the Argentinian had been staying with them since the previous Friday. He was accompanied by four men, and they occupied the presidential suite and an adjoining room. They didn't have a car but had sometimes used taxis. They had arrived via a helicopter which had landed on the Kempinski's helipad. He had added rather snottily. Vargas had paid for a week in advance with cash. The manager promised to send Topper copies of the passports by email and to let him know if any of them checked out early.

"Sven will be pleased with you," Zehra said. "You should send him an email to let him know and forward the copies of the passports when they come."

"Good idea," Topper answered. "It might cheer him up a bit, although the passports will probably be one of several they'll have."

"The photographs should at least show a likeness though," Zehra answered. "I've been successful, too… at least I think so. One of the members of the bowling club, Detlef Riek, known as Didi, is an antiques dealer, and I suspect he's our missing link. He's been in trouble with the police a few times for handling stolen goods. He was in prison for six months once. Erik Benz could have heard about the map from Jürgen Gross and then told Didi, who presumably has contacts outside the *legal* antique business. I'm going to get permission to check their finances now. I doubt this is the first time that Erik has given Didi a tip, and he won't have done so for nothing."

"Well done," Topper praised her. "Shall I let Sven know in my email?"

"No, I would prefer to wait until I know more. How are you getting on, Ivanna?"

"I may have struck lucky, too," Ivanna answered. "I rang Alpenhotel Weiherbach. They have seventeen holiday flats and serve breakfast. I spoke to the proprietress, a Mrs. Plenk. She was awfully nice and very helpful. She told me they had nobody staying with them with a foreign passport, at the moment, but there was a young German couple who spoke Turkish with each other. They looked Turkish, too. Of course, there are lots of Turkish people with German passports, but Mrs. Plenk was still surprised, because Turkish people of that age are usually second-generation immigrants and have grown up in Germany, and gone to German schools, have German friends, and basically feel more German than Turkish. So why were they speaking Turkish together? It may mean nothing, but after breakfast they asked her if she had a map of the caves in this area. She told them about Lamprecht's Cave, thinking they meant tourist attractions, but then they were rather rude to her and left in a bit of a strop. I asked her to send me copies of their passports, just to be on the safe side, and she promised to do that. She also gave me their car registration number and said they had left the hotel half an hour ago.

Before Zehra or Topper could utter a response, the front door banged open with a deafening crash. The force of it sent a shockwave through the air, freezing the three in their seats. Before they could react, another door burst open— this time, the seminar room. Benni and Danny stood in the doorway, guns gripped tightly in their hands.

Ivanna's face turned ghostly white. A strangled gasp escaped her lips—then, agony. A Taser crackled, electricity surging through her body. Every muscle in her body locked up in a tight contraction. She collapsed, her body a lifeless heap on the floor. The moment of silence that followed was shattered by the sound of a gunshot. Ivanna turned her head, the world around her blurring. Zehra lay sprawled beside her, a crimson stain spreading across her chest.

Ivanna sucked in a sharp breath, her scream breaking the air. Another shot. She turned towards Topper, who also lay on the floor. A large patch of blood stained his orange T-shirt a darker shade, and more blood was seeping onto the linoleum. Numbness swallowed Ivanna whole—an eerie void that rapidly gave way to fury. Fire surged in her veins. She sat up, wild-eyed, just as Benni and Danny loomed over her.

Rough hands yanked her up. One arm each, they dragged her out of the seminar room, away from the carnage, into the common area. A chair scraped against the floor. She was shoved down onto it. Rope coiled around her wrists and ankles, binding her tight.

Ivanna glared at her captors, her body trembling but her gaze unyielding. "You're supposed to be dead," she spat. "Sven said you died in that forest fire. You were in the burnt-out car! How did you escape? Who the hell are the dead corpses?"

Benni's lips curled into an indifferent smirk. "Where's the map?"

Ivanna hesitated. "I don't have it. It's not here."

"But you've seen it."

A heartbeat of silence. Then, barely above a whisper, "Y-yes."

Danny dropped a piece of paper in front of her, a pen clattering beside it. He levelled his Glock at her head. "Draw it."

Ivanna sneered. "Then untie me, genius."

Danny yanked at the ropes, unbinding her. As soon as he leaned in, she spat directly into his face. Danny didn't flinch. He merely wiped his cheek with the back of his hand, unfazed. "Draw."

Ivanna grabbed the pen, her hand trembled violently.

Tears streamed down her face. "Why?" she screamed. "Why did you kill them? Zehra and Topper had nothing to do with this!"

Her captors ignored her. The cold muzzle of Danny's Glock pressed harder against her temple. Ivanna swallowed the lump in her throat. The pen scratched against the paper. A river. A church. Buildings. Mountains. A road. A pitiful, skeletal version of the real map.

Benni scoffed. "That's it?"

"My grandfather never knew the exact location," Ivanna stammered. "He could only speculate. No names. No coordinates."

Benni's eyes darkened. "That's not good enough." A gunshot split the air. The bullet embedded itself in the ceiling, raining dust and plaster.

Ivanna flinched, her breath hitching. "Please! I don't know anything else!" Another shot. This one closer. The bullet whistled past her ear. Ivanna jerked sideways, terror clawing at her chest. "Wait! Okay, okay! Let me think!"

Benni cocked his gun again.

"My cousin thinks it was in Austria! Somewhere in the Salzkammergut!" she blurted.

"That's a big area," Danny sneered. "Not good enough."

"I swear! That's all I know! He planned to drive around and search."

Danny exhaled sharply. "She's useless. Let's end this."

The howl of sirens suddenly tore through the afternoon. An ambulance, approaching rapidly. Benni's face twisted in rage. "What the hell? Who called them? Who else is here?"

A shadow shifted in the kitchen doorway. A voice, low and lethal, cut through the tension. "Drop the gun."

Dennis stepped forward, his own Glock steady in his grip. His eyes flickered to Danny, who moved his arm, ready to shoot, —too slow. A shot rang out. Danny shrieked, clutching his calf as blood poured between his fingers. His gun clattered to the floor. Gasping, he reached for it, but another bullet cracked through the air, tearing into his hand. He screamed, writhing in agony.

Dennis kicked the gun away. His aim never wavered as he turned to Benni. "Hands up."

Benni hesitated, then slowly raised his hands.

"Gun. On the table. Now."

Benni complied, carefully placing the weapon down before stepping back.

Dennis took some spare cable ties, that Sebastian had left in the kitchen, and   tied Benni's feet and hands together, then he went to Danny and did the same. He scooped up the guns and slid them into his waistband, keeping his own trained on the captives. "Don't get any ideas," he warned. "I'm just itching for a reason to kill you two motherfuckers."

Ivanna sobbed, her body wracked with exhaustion and relief. Dennis strode to her, his voice gentler now. "Stand up." He handed her the two confiscated guns. "Go to the kitchen. Lock the door." With trembling hands, Ivanna obeyed, disappearing behind the door and securing it behind her.

The front door banged open again—this time, paramedics rushed in. One moved toward Danny, but Dennis held up a hand. "No. There are more urgent casualties in the seminar room. Is another ambulance coming? When I rang, I said there were two injured."

"Yes, one is right behind us, and the doctor on duty will be arriving any second now." As if on cue, the doctor entered the room, and as with the medics before, he made a move towards Danny.

"No," Dennis repeated. "My colleagues in the seminar room are worse off." The second ambulance arrived, and shortly behind it, Matteo and Robert stormed in.

"What's going on?" Matteo asked. He broke off as he saw Benni and Danny. He turned chalky white. "I thought you were dead," he said. "Who are the bodies in the car?"

Neither Benni nor Danny answered.

"Topper and Zehra are in the seminar room," Dennis said. "They've been shot."

Robert paled. "Zehra?" His voice cracked. Without another word, he sprinted into the seminar room.

Matteo turned to Dennis. "What about Ivanna?"

"She's in the kitchen, badly shaken but physically uninjured. If you stay here and keep an eye on these two, I'll go and calm her down."

"Yes, go ahead," Matteo answered. "Thank God you were here. Danny and Benni must've forgotten all about you."

Dennis smirked. "People tend to underestimate a cook."

Matteo chuckled, shaking his head. "Guess they didn't know you used to be Angela Merkel's bodyguard."

Dennis's grin was razor-sharp. "The fewer that know, the better." He knocked on the kitchen door. "Ivanna, it's me. Open up."

A moment later, the door unlocked. Ivanna stumbled forward, tears still streaming. She threw herself into Dennis's arms. "Thank God," she choked. "I thought—I thought—"

Dennis gently untangled her. "It's over. Matteo's here. The thugs are secured. The police are on their way."

Ivanna wiped her eyes, her breath shaky but steadying. "Dennis… I'd forgotten all about you."

Dennis smirked. "Yes. So did they."

Chapter Twenty-Three

TUESDAY AFTERNOON, 27 SEPTEMBER

Two medics passed Matteo with a stretcher from the seminar room. The local funeral home had been informed and was waiting in front of the Kührointhaus with a hearse. They would bring the body to the pathology in Traunstein. Robert followed them. His face was pinched, and Matteo could see that he was finding it hard to keep a hold on himself. He, too, felt saddened and, glancing at Benni and Danny, extremely angry. He gritted his teeth. Speaking to them would only provoke a sneering answer, causing him yet more pain.

He rang his boss and told him the devastating news. Ebner was shocked. "What about Topper?" he asked.

"He's fighting for his life. The doctor rang for a helicopter to take him to the University Hospital in Munich. They are best equipped there. At the moment he's being stabilised for the transport."

Ebner said he would ring Mr. Buchenmeyer so Topper's next of kin were informed and brought to the hospital. Zehra's family must also be notified. He would organise that with the police. He would ask Mr. Buchenmeyer to arrange for Benni and Danny to be picked up and taken to the high-security prison in Straubing. Then he would ring Otto Beck to let him know that the two corpses in the burnt-out car were not those of Benni and Danny. Finally, he would ring Sven and report to him and then he would come to the Kührointhaus himself.

Matteo was grateful for the support. Already he could hear the helicopter landing and waited patiently for the noise to stop and the doctor and the medics to come indoors. He directed them straight to the seminar room and soon afterwards Topper was rolled out on a stretcher, accompanied by the new doctor and the two medics. One of the men was holding an infusion bag, and the first doctor was hurriedly reporting Topper's injuries and vitals to the doctor who had come in the helicopter and would accompany Topper to Munich. When the helicopter left, the doctor and the medics returned indoors to wash their bloodied hands.

Scarcely twenty minutes later, a second helicopter landed, and four heavily armed agents jumped out. Matteo's phone rang. One of the agents asked about the indoor situation. Matteo assured him that Danny and Benni were secure, and they could enter without force. They entered and arrested Benni and Danny. Barely five minutes later their helicopter took off and peace was restored in the Kührointhaus.

Dennis opened the door from the kitchen carrying a tray full of coffee mugs, milk, sugar, a packet of biscuits, and a bottle of schnapps. He put it down on a table in the common room. Ivanna came to sit down with Dennis and Matteo, and the doctor and the medics joined them. "How is Topper?" she asked the doctor.

"He is stable for the moment. The bullet didn't hit any

vital organs. However, he has lost a lot of blood, so I'm afraid his condition is very serious. I'm not sure if he'll make it."

"And Zehra?" Ivanna asked. Her fingers were trembling, and Dennis, sitting next to her, took one of her hands in his. He stroked it tenderly.

"She was already dead when we arrived. There was nothing we could do for her. A straight shot through her heart."

Ivanna's eyes filled with tears. There was nothing anyone could say, and nobody felt like talking, either. They sat in silence, sipping coffee. Dennis stirred three heaped teaspoons of sugar into Ivanna's mug and made sure she drank it.

Eventually, Matteo stood up and brought some small glasses from a cupboard. He poured himself a measure of schnapps and knocked it back. "I don't usually drink this stuff," he apologised, "but I must admit that did me good. I think I should go outside now and look for Robert. He's absolutely gutted. I think he was falling for Zehra."

"Shall I come with you?" Dennis offered. The three of them had known each other since they had begun their police training fifteen years ago. They had been in Libya together and were as close as brothers. It was there that Dennis had lost a leg and could no longer be in active service. He enjoyed cooking and said he didn't mind taking a step back. He didn't fool Matteo or Robert but there wasn't much they could do about it. Despite his leg prosthesis, Dennis was remarkably fit, and many people never noticed that he had one. He could even ski, and Matteo and Robert often went on tours together with him.

Matteo looked at Ivanna. He didn't want her to be left alone, and the doctor and medics would be departing soon.

"No, it's better you stay with Ivanna until the others get back. I'll manage."

Matteo put on his jacket and went outside. He found Robert sitting on the damp ground next to a tree behind the high ropes course. His knuckles were bloody. It looked as if he had been beating the tree. Matteo sat down next to him and put his arm around Robert's shoulder. They sat there silently for a while.

"All right, I'm ready now," Robert said, standing up. "Let's go back inside. We have work to do."

Chapter Twenty-Four

TUESDAY, LATE AFTERNOON, 27 SEPTEMBER

When Matteo and Robert entered the Kührointhaus, Ebner, Sven, and Toby were already there. Dennis shared that after hearing the two gunshots, he had rung first for an ambulance and then Matteo, whom he knew would be the nearest to the hostel and the quickest to arrive to help. It had all happened so quickly.

Ivanna nodded. "Yes, all of it happened within a few seconds."

"Did you find any places where the cave could be?" Matteo asked Toby.

"Yes," Sven answered for Toby, "but let's wait until the others get back so they can tell us how they got on as well. I've rung them all and asked them to make their way back here. Patrick is bringing pizza. We may not feel hungry now, but after a tragedy like this, our bodies need carbohydrates to keep our energy up. I don't know about you, but I am more determined than ever to catch and punish these damn criminals. Otto Beck will be arriving with his forensics team at any moment to take photographs and fingerprints.

I know it sounds heartless, but when they've finished, let's mop up the blood from the floor and tidy up the chairs and desks. I'm sorry, but we need somewhere to work. In the meantime, help yourself to drinks and let's lay the table."

One after the other the agents returned. The forensics team worked in the seminar room while Ebner stayed in the common room, looking gloomy. His short hair was still sticking up at the back. He wasn't sleeping well and had forgotten to shower or changes clothes. His wife had died from cancer two years ago and he lived alone. Matteo wondered whether he should say something, but then he thought that it didn't really matter, there were more important things to worry about.

By the time everyone found their way back to the hostel, eaten pizza, and cleaned the seminar room, it was eight o'clock. The forensics team had driven away. Otto, Ebner, David, and Rudolf joined the Federal Policemen and the BND agents in the seminar room. They were all quiet.

"Let us start with a minute's silence for Zehra," Ebner began. He waited a while and then continued. "You will be glad to hear that the bullet was removed from Topper's chest. It missed his heart by less than a centimetre... he was very lucky on that score. The operation went well, and Topper is now in ICU. The doctors say that his vitals are strong, and they do not expect any complications. If his condition continues to improve so rapidly, he can probably be moved to a normal ward tomorrow and leave the hospital within the week." Instantaneous clapping filled the room. The agents sat up a little straighter in their chairs and looked slightly more cheerful.

Robert appeared very determined. "Let's catch the bastards," he cried out. "We owe it to Zehra, and our unknown colleagues, Bernhard and Daniel, killed on their way here."

Toby told the room that he was sure he had found the cave. Standing in front of it, the view matched Konstantyn's map exactly. He had taken some photographs and sent them to a potholer friend who, like him, belonged to the county of Salzburg's potholer club. The friend, a guy called Marvin, agreed that the entrance looked very promising. It had been blocked by misshaped rocks and was covered in vegetation. "We will need an excavator to move at least some of the rocks to allow access to the cave," Toby continued full of excitement. "But as far as I'm concerned, if somebody can organise an excavator, we can begin straight away tomorrow morning."

"Wow, that's brilliant!"

"Fantastic."

Toby's enthusiasm was catching, and all the agents and policemen wanted to be present the next day when the excavator started to work. Sven grinned so broadly that Matteo was afraid his face might split. "I would never have guessed that a cave was there," Sven admitted. "I was there, but I didn't see it."

"Where is it?" Matteo asked. "Come on, tell us, don't keep us in suspense!"

Toby went to the map on the wall and pencilled a little cross along the road past Bad Dürrnberg but before the crossroads to either Scheffau or Hallein. "Here it is. I hope I'm right and we find the right cave at our first attempt. It would be so amazing to find long-lost paintings or gold."

"It's very exciting and will need good planning," Sven added, "but first we need to deal with the Argentinian and his accomplices. I rang Mr. Buchenmeyer earlier. He was very pleased that we had pinpointed the Argentinian at last. He said he would speak to the control room in St. Augustin to organise the GSG 9 Forces and establish an operational plan to arrest the Argentinian and his four bodyguards. The Kempinski Hotel stands by itself on top of a hill and should be easy to encircle and to block any attempt at escape. He is hoping to arrange an arrest for tonight, so if all turns out well, we could really order an excavator for tomorrow. If the Argentinian and his men are imprisoned, I doubt that his other accomplices in this area will stick around for long."

"Tonight? Can they get here that soon?" Matteo asked.

"Yes. They have Super Pumas at their disposal and won't need long to fly down here." Sven's mobile dinged. It was Mr. Buchenmeyer calling, and judging by Sven's grimace, he had bad news. Sven clicked off his telephone and looked at his colleagues with a sombre face. He breathed out, uttering a sort of exasperated 'huff'.

"The Argentinian and his bodyguards left the hotel this morning after breakfast and haven't been seen since. They didn't check out and their luggage is still in their rooms. They were wearing sports clothing and the bodyguards had backpacks with them. They didn't order a taxi and the receptionist at the front desk presumed they were going on a hike.

"The receptionist was a little wary when they didn't return for dinner. They usually ate dinner together in their suite and the kitchen had rung the front desk to ask whether the Argentinians had ordered their meals yet.

"When Mr. Buchenmeyer rang to let the manager know about the forthcoming operation, the receptionist told him that the manager had already gone home leaving he himself in charge. He had ordered the whole hotel including the spa and outside grounds to be searched. There was no sign of them. The receptionist promised to let Mr. Buchenmeyer know as soon as they returned.

"Ten minutes later he rang back. Not because the Argentinian and his men had returned, but because the manager was missing. The receptionist had rung him up at home to let him know about the turn of events and his wife had told him that her husband hadn't got back yet. Normally, the receptionist wouldn't have thought much about it... it could easily be that the manager had something to deal with before going home. However, as the other men were missing too, it was unusual and he thought he should report it."

"I saw the Argentinian and one of his bodyguards," Tina called out. "They made no secret about knowing who I was. They boarded the pleasure boat with me in Schönau. When I sat on a bench at the front of the boat, they were dead cheeky and sat right next me, one on each side, pushing up uncomfortably close to me. I recognised the Argentinian immediately from the photographs, and he called his companion Rollo. Rollo smirked at me. 'Now then,' he said, 'what's a pretty girl like you doing all alone?' He was so cheesy! What a creep!" Tina shuddered at the memory. "My pulse was racing like mad. I got up, easing myself from between their sweaty bodies and moved to sit next to a family with two children. Luckily, they left me alone after that, and I had time to calm down. When I got off at St. Bartholomä there were masses of tourists taking selfies in front of the church. I thought, what the hell, and quickly shot a photograph of them both together. They noticed and were absolutely furious. I smirked at them and watched with pleasure as the Argentinian held Rollo back.

"I went to a large information board," Tina continued, "with a detailed map and various hiking tours highlighted. I wanted to gain some time to get a head start up the steep Rinnkendl trail. I didn't want the Argentinian and Rollo following me, waiting for an opportunity to push me off the perpendicular edge. I had already descended the trail once with Sven and Mark and remembered several dangerous places.

"At that moment, lots of hikers from the boat were heading in the direction of the trail to the right, past the pilgrimage church in a north-westerly direction along the lakeshore. And then, after a hut, left into the forest where the Rinnkendl trail begins. At this point, I sprinted quickly and pushed past the people in front of me, so that by the time I started the single-file ascent, there were at least twenty people between me and my two pursuers. The path climbed via numerous hairpins through mixed forest on the precipitous slopes of the Kleine Watzmann. Here, within this forested area, I had to complete a short section secured with a wire rope.

"I looked back several times to my pursuers, who were not only overcoming the incline with ease, but to my dismay had already somehow managed to push past and overtake two climbers using Nordic sticks, who were struggling a little.

"After leaving the forest, I crossed several exposed sections secured with wire ropes. Then I came to metal steps that ascended approximately fifty metres. I had to wait until the people in front of me had finished climbing the ladder, one after the other.

"My heart was beating fast. I risked a look down to my pursuers and my stomach lurched in shock as I saw them pushing past the queue of hikers, ignoring their protests. Finally, it was my turn, and I shot up the steps at a run, two steps at a time. The track led to the right, passing a wide gully to a small hill. Here I broke into a run and passed several people. From there, a long path led, partly descending again and over to a narrow gully – the so-called Rinnkendl – and through this up to the high wooded plateau that leads to the Kühroint meadow. Reaching the top, I raced at full speed to the hostel. I was so worried that my pursuers might catch me up that I didn't notice the police cars and ambulances until I almost ran into them."

"Well done," Sven praised her. "So that accounts for the Argentinian and Rollo until about four p.m. I'll let Mr. Buchenmeyer know. Toby and I were followed around the Rossfeld circuit by a black Porsche with two occupants. They could have been two of the bodyguards."

"I don't think so," Patrick interrupted. "When I got to Hotel Schwabenwirt, the three Bulgarians were still in the beer garden. I sat down next to two other occupied tables, ordered a coffee, put on my mirrored sunglasses and began to fiddle with my smartphone just as they were doing. When my coffee arrived, I stood up and began to take photographs of Mount Watzmann, which was clearly visible from the beer garden. I also took some good shots of the three Bulgarians, and they never even noticed. They didn't pay any attention to me either. I sat down again, took a sip of coffee and waited.

"Not much time had passed when the phone of one of the Bulgarians rang. He answered and then talked quickly to his companions. One of them left the beer garden with him and I saw them drive off a minute or two later in the black Porsche. The third Bulgarian signed for their drinks and then also left the beer garden onto the street. He crossed the bridge over the river Ache, and I could still see him at the bus station on the other side of the bridge. I was wondering what to do because there's also a train station there, when I saw him get onto a bus. The bus drove straight past the beer garden. It was number 843, which goes to the cable car valley station for Mount Jenner.

"I stood up and quickly removed their glasses from the table where they had been sitting, before the waiter beat me to it. Then I went to reception and spoke to the proprietor, who permitted me to take the glasses. I have already given them to Otto Beck and presumably they are already at the forensics laboratory."

"Great, I'll ask them to send the fingerprints to Berlin and maybe they can identify the men. That means that Toby and I were followed by two Bulgarians and the third one must have been looking out for Mark and Julian. So, we have no account about three of the bodyguards in the Kempinski. Mark, how did you and Julian get on?"

"After Matteo and Robert dropped us off at the cable car station, we travelled to the top of the Jenner," Mark began. "We didn't notice anybody at the station paying any attention to us. It was just the usual mix of tourists, hikers, a couple of families and a paraglider. We had a gondola to ourselves, and when we got to the last station, we went to the area where other paragliders were. We looked around and even waited, but nobody came who seemed particularly interested in us.

"Anyway, we took off and circled through the air a few times before landing at the designated point in the Brandner field, about a hundred metres from the cable car valley station. There, finally, we saw a man hanging around and looking at us. We pretended not to notice, and I'm afraid we didn't take a photograph, but just came straight back here. Luckily, Patrick took a photo in the beer garden."

"Yes, and Patrick seems to be the only one not on the gangster's radar. Let's try to keep it that way, it could be useful," Sven added.

Chapter Twenty-Five

TUESDAY, EARLY EVENING, 27 SEPTEMBER

"Maybe Stefan and Nicole can tell us about their day now. We need to get rid of most of the Argentinian's men. They are all criminals. So, if possible, I would like them identified, arrested, and sent to Straubing. Hopefully, that way we will learn more about the transportation and the distribution of the drugs," Sven said.

"Okay," Stefan answered. "Nicole, do you want to report or shall I?"

"I don't mind. Let me start and you can correct me if I get anything wrong. We took the bus to the town centre, and getting off, noticed that right next to the bus stop was a bicycle shop that rents out bikes. On the spur of the moment, we decided to hire two pedelecs and cycled to the national park. Up until then we hadn't detected anyone following us, so we agreed to cycle along a track that led to a place where the deer are fed in winter. There was hardly anybody about, and we would have spotted it if someone was paying attention to us. We went back to the beginning of the trail and wondered whether to take the alternative track that leads to the Hirschbichl. It's a hill with a green border to Austria, and there is a restaurant there that is supposed to be quite good. But we were worried that nobody had recognised us yet.

"It was nearly lunchtime and crowds of people were getting off tourist buses or arriving on cycles. They were making a beeline for Gasthof Auzinger, famous for its gateaux, situated alongside the road. We opted to join the masses of people sitting outside and managed to grab the last table. We both ordered coffee and rhubarb meringue cake. The slice was absolutely huge and melted on my tongue... I can still taste it now! Hmm, sorry, you didn't need to know that. Anyway, Stefan and I were sitting there in the sun, keeping our eyes open, sipping coffee, and playing the typical tourist. We still couldn't see anyone looking at us. I put my mirrored sunglasses on and started posing for Stefan, who took some photographs.

"After a while we put our cycle helmets and cycle glasses back on. We were a bit anxious that we were so well disguised that anybody following us wouldn't recognise us. Then we started cycling towards the Hirschbichl. The track became a lot narrower and was quite steep. We were glad to have auxiliary motors on our bikes. We stopped for a short break at the restaurant on the border. There we eventually noticed a couple whom we had seen before, but not paid any attention to, looking a bit too long in our direction. Drinking shandies, we flicked through the photographs that Stefan had already taken. We discovered the couple again on a close-up shot of myself, mirrored in my sunglasses. Now that we were certain we had discovered the right people, we wondered how to get a better photograph of them.

"Some people at the table next to us were talking about continuing to a gorge that wasn't far away. It was called

Vorderkaser Gorge, and I remembered Matteo mentioning it. One of the men next to us was telling his companions how spectacular the gorge was… a single track, hewn out of rock, along which tourists could walk and take dramatic photos. He had seen some posted on Instagram. Stefan and I thought it would seem natural if we took photographs there, and as the tourists were in single file, it should be easy to get some good shots of the couple without making it too obvious.

"We cycled on to the Vorderkaser Gorge. We left our cycles locked up at the entrance and went through the gate. It was only possible to go along the path in single file. We both wore our mirrored sunglasses so that our followers couldn't see in which direction we were looking. I think at the gorge, the couple were worried that we might make a run for it, so they followed us closely. We got some very good, recognisable pictures of them."

Stefan had printed photographs from his mobile and passed them around before pinning them on the wall.

"Look!" Ivanna said. "They are the couple who are staying at the Alpenhotel Weiherbach. Mrs. Plenk sent me copies of their passports." Ivanna went to her desk and picked up two prints, then she pinned them next to Stefan's photographs. The agents looked. The likeness was striking.

"Let me tell you a little more about what Toby and I got up to," Sven said. "As I mentioned before, Toby and I were followed around the Rossfeld circuit by a black Porsche with two occupants. We can presume now that they were two of the Bulgarians staying at Hotel Schwabenwirt. It was obvious that they didn't know the road, the driver braked and accelerated continually along the hairpins and then shot past the turning to Hallein. Toby and I had plenty of time to drive to the Barmsteine, park our car nearby and walk back towards Bad Dürrnberg. We saw the Porsche pass down the road, but we thought that, as the gangsters didn't know their way around the area and we were well hidden by the vegetation, we would have plenty of time to examine the crags above the road and take photographs. Toby was brilliant! I didn't recognise any caves but he got very excited and took photographs and samples of rock. As he has already told you, his friend Marvin also found the photographs very promising. As soon as I received the telephone call from Harald, we returned here."

"Robert and I dropped Mark and Julian off at the cable car valley station, came back here, parked the Unimog and had barely taken up our positions in the forest when Dennis rang, and we rushed back here. We hadn't even contacted David to fly a circuit in the helicopter. The rest you know," Matteo said, and shrugged his shoulders.

Sven thanked him and was just about to continue speaking when there was an almighty crash in the common room.

Chapter Twenty-Six

TUESDAY EVENING, 27 SEPTEMBER

The detectives leapt up from their seats and rushed to the door. Matteo, in the lead, tore it open and saw broken glass and a rag on the floor of the common room. Flames burning bright blue and yellow were already spreading rapidly across the floor as seconds later three more petrol bombs were thrown through the windows, crashing through the glass; fire began to devour curtains and to lick up the legs of chairs and tables.

Matteo rushed to the fire extinguisher at the foot of the stairs, ripped it from the wall and extracted the pull pin at the top of the extinguisher, but the pin had already been torn and the seal broken! He squeezed the handles together to discharge the extinguishing agent inside, but it was empty. He swore. "Danny!" He ran to the kitchen, but Dennis was already there holding an empty extinguisher in his hands. He looked at Matteo, eyes wide open, astonished.

They ran upstairs one behind the other, taking two steps at a time, to the third and last extinguisher. As Matteo expected, it had also been sabotaged and rendered useless.

He opened the laundry cupboard, snatched two blankets and rushed to the bathroom to douse them with water. Dennis was standing behind him and did the same. As Matteo raced back down the stairs, he pulled one blanket over his head and shoulders to protect himself, and with the second blanket he started desperately beating the flames surrounding him.

The room was full of smoke and unbearably hot. His eyes stung and he had trouble breathing. He coughed. The smoke made it impossible to see anything, but he became aware of more people in the room, all beating the fire with blankets. He heard fire sirens in the distance and passed out.

When he came around, he was lying on a stretcher outside, wrapped in a gold foil blanket and with an oxygen mask over his nose and mouth. He sat up. He had chest pain and coughed. Bright neon blue lights were flashing from the emergency vehicles. They irritated him and he blinked several times. They lit up parts of the car park, leaving other parts in eerie black shadows. He counted two fire engines and four ambulances. Firemen were spraying foam in the Kührointhaus. Medics were attending to his colleagues, making sure they all had oxygen.

Tina, Nicole, and Ivanna sat in the back of one of the ambulances. A medic closed the doors, and the ambulance drove slowly away. Robert lay on a stretcher inside a second ambulance. He had an oxygen mask over his face. Once again, a medic closed the doors, and he, too, was driven away. Although the lights of the ambulance were flashing, the sirens weren't turned on, so, Matteo thought with relief, Robert's condition was probably not too serious.

Matteo held the oxygen mask close to his face. Squinting his eyes against the ever-changing light, he searched the hostel's car park for the rest of the team members who had been inside. His boss, Harald Ebner, was sitting on a bench next to Rudolf Hoffmann and Otto Beck. Both of his hands were bandaged, and his face was black with soot. He was getting oxygen through a nose tube. Sven and Dennis were lying on stretchers, and, like himself, receiving oxygen. He didn't see the others, but presumed they would be there somewhere, being treated for smoke poisoning or light burns.

A fireman came out of the building and spoke to Harald Ebner. Matteo couldn't hear what he said, but he saw Ebner pointing to him and the fireman approached him with a small package in his hand. "One of my men found this on the Unimog's bonnet over there," he said pointing. He gave it to Matteo, who saw his name written in large capital letters on top of the parcel. Matteo opened it and found a small sheet of paper inside, and a tiny object wrapped in paper. He read the note first, it was written in biro.

> *We did not appreciate the games you played with us today. If you want to see your wife alive again, drive to the Wimbach car park and leave the map below the information board. Come alone and tell no one. If the map is not there by 10 p.m., your next parcel will contain her finger, not just the ring.*

Matteo started trembling violently. He felt nauseous and broke out in a cold sweat. He unwrapped the remaining object in the parcel and found Freya's wedding ring, engraved with his name and the date of their wedding on the inside. He looked at the time on his phone: 9:40 p.m. With trembling fingers, he untied the oxygen mask behind his head. His knees were shaking as he stood up and stumbled towards the Kührointhaus. The house, made of stone, stood intact, but the wooden door had burnt away. As he tried to cross the threshold, a fireman held him back by the shoulders. "Stop!" he said. "You can't go inside; the chief hasn't cleared it yet."

Matteo pushed the man's hands roughly away. "I've got to get something urgently. I won't be a second," he said, and pressed past him despite the man's protests. He went directly to the seminar room, which, contrary to the common room, was scarcely damaged. He steered straight to Toby's workplace and riffled through his papers, finding the map almost immediately. He grabbed it and left the room. He raced outside, sprinted to the Unimog and drove, as quickly as he dared, to the Wimbach car park. Picking up the map beside him, he jumped out of the car, placed it below the information board and then got back into the Unimog.

He would have liked to hang around a bit, but nobody would pick up the map if his vehicle was in the car park. Would they return Freya immediately? He prayed so. She must be terrified. It wasn't fair. She hadn't been trained like himself and his colleagues. She was a secretary for an insurance broker in town. If they harmed her... he couldn't bear to think about it. He had done what they wanted and now they must let Freya go. He started to drive slowly back to the Kührointhaus, still wondering whether to hide the car and go back on foot to see who came and from which direction. The trouble was, there was nowhere to hide the car on this winding road, and he didn't want to risk being discovered before Freya was safe.

He drove back to the hostel and sat down next to his boss on the bench. He told him the whole story, regardless of Otto and Rudolf sitting next to Ebner – they must know the truth, too. "Do you think they will hurt her?" he asked

Ebner, wringing his hands nervously, trying hard to keep his voice steady.

Ebner looked at him, full of empathy. He covered one of Matteo's hands with one of his bandaged hands. "I'm going to be honest with you," he said. "I haven't a clue. I don't think anyone with a clear understanding can see into the minds of these heinous criminals. Give me five minutes. The fire chief has just finished examining the building and declared it safe to enter. I'll ring Mr. Buchenmeyer and inform him of the new turn of events. I hope he'll know what we can do to ensure Freya's speedy return."

Chapter Twenty-Seven

TUESDAY EVENING AFTER THE FIRE,
27 SEPTEMBER

Ebner returned a few minutes later. Mr. Buchenmeyer had let him know that a unit of GSG 9 agents would be flying to Berchtesgaden early the next morning. They would land two Super Pumas at the mountain rescue service in Ramsau, hoping that by avoiding Berchtesgaden they wouldn't attract attention from the wrong people. The twenty-four agents would dress like sporty tourists and split up into groups of two or four to explore the whole area.

They would concentrate on finding Freya, searching deserted buildings where she might be held – several mountain shelters in the higher regions had already been closed now that the hiking season was nearly over, and there were innumerable stone ruins of old shepherds' huts that were no longer used. They would also be looking for the manager of the Kempinski Hotel, because he was still missing. At the same time, they would explore the lie of the ground surrounding the Kempinski, and the area near the Barmsteine, the rocky pinnacles where Toby suspected the cave to be.

Two BND agents in Berlin were busying themselves with research, and thanks to the photographs and fingerprints, they already had the names of the couple from the Alpenhotel Weiherbach and the three criminals in the Hotel Schwabenwirt. They were happy about the photograph of the Argentinian, it was the most recent one they had, and the name of his companion, Rollo, who they knew as the Argentinian's second-in-command. The men had flown together from Buenos Aires to Europe. Mr. Buchenmeyer said he would send Ebner all the information they had gathered about the six gangsters per email, immediately after ending this conversation. Ebner printed the information and gave a copy to Sven.

Two BND agents would be arriving in Berchtesgaden to take the places of Zehra and Topper. They should get to the Kührointhaus at about ten o'clock the next morning. Mr. Buchenmeyer had said that his main worry was that the Argentinian would activate more helpers. He had asked the police to reinforce the controls at all the borders and they had promised they would do their best, but they didn't really have enough personnel. Mr. Buchenmeyer had sent them a list of all the Argentinian's known contacts with photographs. The customs police would copy the list and distribute it. They would also inform the Austrian authorities and ask for support.

While they were talking, Toby approached them. His right arm was bandaged, and he had an oxygen mask, at the moment dangling around his neck so he could speak.

"I'm sorry for interrupting, but I just had a call from Marvin… you remember my friend from Salzburg's potholer club? And, well I think it may be important. I hadn't had time to check the messages on my phone until now, but all the members of the club have received a message from the chairman. A famous potholer from Berlin, Mr. Conrad Neuberg, rang our chairman about an hour ago. He told him that a businessman had offered him a large sum of money if he would help him find a cave situated in this area.

"Mr. Neuberg told the man that it wouldn't be possible, because he didn't have much knowledge of the area. The man had begged him and said that his beloved grandfather had worked as a prisoner of war in World War Two in a salt mine near here. He had died before the end of the war and didn't have a grave. The man was now in a financially secure position and more than anything else in the world wanted to find the cave and pay his last respects to his grandfather.

"So, Neuberg said he would see what he could do, and had rung our chairman to ask if he thought any members of the club would be willing to help him and the man to find the cave. His time and efforts would be generously rewarded. Marvin had read the message and then rang me to ask if I thought there was a connection between the two lost caves. I thought you should know as soon as possible, and I told him I would ring him back after I'd spoken to you." Toby was out of breath after talking for so long and quickly put his oxygen mask back over his face.

"You've done well to tell us," Ebner praised him. "If Mr. Neuberg found the cave for the Argentinian, and of course he now has the map to help them, then I doubt that the Argentinian would let him, or any other helper live. He'll want as few people as possible to be in the know, quite apart from any hidden treasure that still might be in the cave."

"Would you speak to Mr. Buchenmeyer, please?" Toby asked Ebner. "Of course, I could speak to the chairman, but the message will have much more weight coming from Mr, Buchenmeyer."

"Yes, I'll do that immediately." Ebner stood up from the bench, sighing a little at the effort, and went inside again.

As he disappeared indoors, Toby asked Matteo, "Did Harald just say that the Argentinian had the map?" Matteo explained that he had given the map to the Argentinian and why. Toby said that it didn't really matter because he was fairly certain he had already found the right place, and even if it wasn't the correct cave, then he had looked at the map so often he knew it off by heart.

Ebner returned. "I've informed Mr. Buchenmeyer and he's going to call the chairman and ring up Mr. Neuberg personally. He's convinced that any outsider who helps the Argentinian will be disposed of as soon as he's done what the Argentinian wants."

Matteo caught his breath at this last sentence. He was terribly worried about Freya and agitated that he was helpless to bring her back to safety. He rang her number for the umpteenth time, but nobody answered. He rang Freya's mother, who had called him several times. He could only tell her that he had no news about Freya, but that early the next morning police officers, disguised as tourists, were going to scour the whole area.

Time passed and it was getting late. Finally, Ebner's mobile rang. It was Mr. Buchenmeyer. After the call, Ebner told them what he had said. Mr. Buchenmeyer had rung the chairman of the potholer club, and he had promised to send out a second message to all the club members warning them not to answer Mr. Neuberg. Mr. Buchenmeyer had also spoken to Mr. Neuberg, who had been very grateful. They had agreed that Mr. Neuberg would cancel his arrangement with the Argentinian. In case the latter was suspicious, he would say that he had ruptured his knee ligament, and that he was in hospital awaiting an operation. Mr. Buchenmeyer had arranged for Mr. Neuberg to be given a hospital bed for a few days, because he didn't put it past the Argentinian to check on all the details. Mr. Neuberg hadn't really wanted to occupy a hospital bed that somebody else might need, but finally gave way, as it was preferable to being shot.

Matteo looked at his mobile. It was already midnight. "I'm going home," he told his colleagues. "I'm not hungry and I won't sleep, but I'll be there in case Freya comes home. See you tomorrow at six."

Chapter Twenty-Eight

WEDNESDAY MORNING, 28 SEPTEMBER

Matteo watched dawn break through the open window. He was still lying fully clothed on the sofa in the sitting room. He hadn't slept for even a minute, but had tossed back and forth, sick with worry about Freya and what might happen to her. He had cried till no more tears came.

The birds began to sing but the sky remained dark grey. He heard rain falling heavily outside. He listened to every tiny sound, hopeful that Freya might be returned. His mobile showed the time, 4:45 a.m. He got up and put the coffee machine on. Then he decided to have a hot shower to clear the cobwebs and distract him from thinking about Freya for a moment. Afterwards, he dressed in his thermal sports underwear and sports clothing. He drank his coffee in front of the window and looked at the rain, which was still beating down.

His mobile pinged. With trembling fingers, full of hope that it was a message from the kidnappers telling him where to find Freya, he pressed the buttons to open his messages. His heart sank with disappointment as he found a message telling him that operation headquarters had been transferred to the village hall at Ramsau.

Sebastian Meier and his team of technicians had been working all night, rescuing what they could from the Kührointhaus, and setting up workplaces in the village hall in Ramsau. That day a surveyor would examine the Kührointhaus, and experts sent by the insurance firm would also be looking. It was impossible to work there any longer.

Matteo decided to drive to Ramsau. He would arrive a little early, but it sounded like some people had been working through the night.

Sure enough, when he entered the village hall, the first person he saw was Harald Ebner. His eyes were bloodshot, and he was making a visible effort to keep them open. Matteo wondered whether he could send him home to rest. When Harald saw Matteo, he tottered towards him, not quite in control of his movements, like a puppet on a string. "Matteo. Has Freya come home?" he asked.

"No," Matteo replied and changed the subject. "What about the manager from the Kempinski?"

"No sign of him either. The good news is that none of the women, nor Robert, are seriously injured, and they will be released from hospital this morning. We're expecting them later."

Sven joined Harald and Matteo. "The first Puma is landing now," he told them, "And the second one is just ten minutes away."

"Have you got a plan?" Matteo asked Sven.

"Yes, we've been discussing various plans throughout most of the night. I've been in continual radio contact with the leader of the GSG 9 unit. Together we have planned routes that should cover most of the area. We've marked the wall map with highlighter the routes we wish to take. Toby has had a look at it, but I would like you to have a look, too. You might find it advantageous to make a few adjustments. The other thing is that it has been snowing a lot in the higher regions through the night. The leader of the GSG 9 unit, Ludwig Fuchs, says he knows you…"

"Foxy! Yes of course."

"Well, er… Foxy says that with snow on the ground, it can be very difficult in the Alpine regions, and they would prefer to have an expert in his group, particularly one with good local knowledge of these mountains. They want to cross the Watzmann. He wondered whether you would be available? They could also ask Robert, but it depends how fit he is when he returns from hospital. What do you think? I told him you were anxious about Freya and may prefer to stay here in the operations centre."

"No, I would much prefer to be active. I presume you would radio in if you got any news about her?"

"Yes, of course. That's settled then. As soon as they arrive and everyone is equipped, you can set off."

*****

Foxy and his two agents, Emil and Finn, greeted Matteo like long-lost friends, and then they all got into a waiting minibus which drove them to Lake Koenig. The four men took the first scheduled boat, which left the quay at 8 a.m. to St. Bartholomä. It was the only way to get there. There were no roads and not enough room between the trees for a helicopter to land. The journey on the boat to St. Bartholomä took thirty-five minutes. There was nothing much they could do on the boat so they had chatted, catching up with each other's news. Matteo had told them about the Ice Chapel, the first place they wanted to search.

It was about six kilometres from the boat's landing jetty at St. Bartholomä.

"It's the lowest ice field in the German Alps," he informed them. "It lies beneath the east face of the Watzmann. In summer, the snow line is almost two thousand metres higher but this firn ice field persists throughout the year. That's because of the enormous amounts of snow that accumulate during winter and spring, primarily in the form of colossal avalanches descending from the east face of the Watzmann, feeding the firn field. Inside the ice field, there is a spacious hollow space known as the Ice Chapel. Its entrance resembles a glacier snout."

They were the only people to disembark in St. Bartholomä. The boat only had two others on board and they had stayed on it, possibly wanting to disembark at the end station, Salet. Or possibly being discouraged by the rain, they would just take a round trip and return again to where they had set off.

Matteo looked up at the dark grey clouds hanging low and blotting out the vision of the Alps. All he could see were different shades of grey, a fuzzy horizon, and sky resembling dirty cotton wool. The men zipped up their weatherproofs over their chins and mouths and pulled their hoods up over their woollen headgear. Only their eyes and noses were exposed to the elements.

In addition to heavy bulletproof vests, each man had a rucksack weighing thirty kilos containing ropes, hooks, a hammer, emergency rations, a gas stove, a pot, tablets to purify melted snow to make it fit for drinking, flares, a satellite telephone, and all sorts of other emergency objects. A pickaxe was slung across their shoulders, as was a rifle. A revolver and knife were stored beneath the waterproofs. Most men, even fit ones, would struggle to walk a hundred metres with the heavy equipment and clothing, but the GSG 9 agents had been trained to walk, run, and climb thirty kilometres a day or night equipped like this.

The rain beat down incessantly and clouds of midges hung low beneath the trees. "It's not far to the Ice Chapel," Matteo told the men. "It's an easy stretch from here. The difference in height is about two-fifty metres. In other words, the Ice Chapel lies at eight hundred and thirty-four metres. If we're lucky, the rain won't turn to snow before we get there."

The four tall, slim men, clad in black, started walking along the gently ascending hiking trail towards their destination and continued to pursue the track to the left around a scree field. They walked in single file, their heads bent down to thwart the elements. Apart from the rain thrashing onto the ground and their boots crunching on the stones, not a sound could be heard. The path became steeper and led through a forest until they reached the Eisbach river. On a different day, they might have enjoyed the splendid nature of the Alps. Today, their faces were grim, not just because of the task in front of them, but also because of the rain, which was hammering down on them without mercy, dripping off their faces and clothes, and turning the forest floor into a perilous, waterlogged bog.

The riverbed was often dry in summer, but not today. Snow melt was surging powerfully down the mountain slope. The path led alongside the river through rough, rocky terrain. Despite their sturdy hiking boots, each man had to concentrate carefully where to put his feet, to avoid turning an ankle or just stumbling and cutting his hands on the sharp edges of the rocks. The beautiful Alpine panorama was wasted.

Eventually, they emerged from the forest and saw a

field of snow in front of them. Not far inside the snow line, a longish low entrance to a cave was visible. The four black figures, silhouetted against the pale grey background, marched silently towards it, across the boulders, looking like a scene from a Nordic horror film.

Matteo pointed. "There it is, the Ice Chapel."

The Ice Chapel was always at risk of collapsing due to the frequent changes of temperature. A large noticeboard was bolted into the rocky surface in front of the entrance warning potential visitors that it was life-threatening to enter. Matteo had accessed the cave on several prior occasions, and he wanted to be present in case Freya was there. On the other hand, someone must remain outside and notify the operations centre, in case the men didn't return within fifteen minutes. Emil volunteered to wait outside.

Matteo let Foxy and Finn crawl in first and then dropped to his stomach and followed them through the low entrance. He wriggled on his stomach for ten metres until the cave opened up. Inside, there was room to stand and it was lighter than outside. The packed ice reflected pale blue and turquoise light. It was silent and stunningly beautiful. The roof was about fifteen metres high, and from the centre, various shafts, chambers, chutes, and passageways had been created, some of them as much as thirty metres wide.

Matteo looked around himself in wonder. Melted snow had left grooves down the walls in intricate patterns. Foxy started to trace the walls, looking behind nooks and crannies. Matteo had already warned the men not to shout because even loud voices could reverberate and invoke an avalanche. So, it was no surprise when Matteo, looking up, saw Finn waving his arms rather than calling. Matteo made his way cautiously towards him and saw Foxy following him. Finn didn't need to speak. Matteo and Foxy immediately saw the figure of a man lying in blood on the ground. His throat had been slit, and blood covered his outer clothing. His mouth was open in a grotesque grimace and his open eyes expressed horror.

"What on earth…" Matteo began and then gagged as he realised what he was looking at. The man's tongue had been cut out and placed beside his head, looking like a piece of black rubber. He forced himself to look again to make sure he had identified him correctly. Yes, it was the manager of the Kempinski. *Oh my God, what in God's name might they have done to Freya?* He bent over, away from the body, and vomited. "Time to get out of here," he said to Foxy and Finn.

This time he took the lead and scrambled out of the cave as quickly as possible. Finn followed him but Foxy needed a little longer. The oldest of the three had remembered to take photographs before crawling out of the Ice Chapel himself.

Matteo radioed into the operations control and spoke to Sven. "We've found the manager of the Kempinski. He's dead. Can you send some agents to retrieve the body and sort things out?" he asked. "We should really get on our way if we want to cross the Watzmann before it gets dark."

"Yes, of course," Sven answered. "I'll send the rescue boat and four men. Would you prefer to call it a day and come back? You can do the crossing tomorrow; the weather might be better."

"No, on no account!" Matteo replied. "It was a brutal murder, and I'm terrified about what they might have done or may do to Freya. I've spoken to the men, and they've all opted to continue with me, but I asked Finn to stay here and wait for you. We have everything we need for emergencies. Theoretically, nothing can happen, but my heart is hammering like a pneumatic drill. I need to find Freya!"

Chapter Twenty-Nine

WEDNESDAY, LATE MORNING,
28 SEPTEMBER

As Matteo had predicted, on leaving the Ice Chapel, the rain turned to snow and as they gained more height in the journey, more snow lay underfoot until they were stamping through snow thirty centimetres deep. "Our next goal is an emergency bivouac box about five hours from here. I hope Freya isn't there because she's terrified of heights and it's situated at over two thousand metres, but it is a possible hiding place and we need to check it," he told Foxy and Emil.

He put his climbing helmet on, and the men followed suit. Despite some turns and markers, the east face of the Watzmann was virtually unmarked, but Matteo knew the mountain as well as his own sitting room.

He led the men carefully over a ridge, across some steep gullies and along rocky terrain, now slick from the freshly fallen snow. They passed a long traverse that led into a scree field, and having successfully overcome this obstacle, turned right onto a slab ramp. The ramp was icy, and Foxy's feet, despite him wearing the correct boots, slid again and again, downwards towards the bottom. Then he had to fight his way up anew, time and time again. There was nothing to hold on to and he became frustrated.

"Damn fucking ramp!" he swore.

Finally, Matteo tied a short rope around Foxy's belt and pulled him up. Having mastered the brutal ramp, they swung left, their boots crunching on the hard ice covering the jagged ridge steps. Ahead they had to pass across a traverse stretching over a sheer, four-hundred-metre abyss.

"Don't look down!" Matteo warned Emil and Foxy. "The drop can make you dizzy, and you could lose your balance."

They walked slowly. Every step sent pebbles skittering into the void. Then, bracing themselves, they veered left once more, facing the final trial—a notorious black waterfall rock face, slick, treacherous, and waiting to challenge their every move.

"We must climb now," Matteo told the Emil and Foxy. "In this weather it's better we use our ropes." He secured the climb in four rope lengths with some bolts. Ten metres above the crest of the waterfall he crossed sharply to the right to climb over the so-called 'waterfall slab' to a ledge.

From the ledge, Matteo led them initially to the right and then up an almost perpendicular gully to a small saddle. They crossed a snowfield and continued over a slab of rock and another gully before continuing through scree. Then they took a rightward loop through rugged terrain to the bivouac box.

The bivouac box was painted bright orange and stood under an overhanging rock. It looked tiny, although ostensibly there was enough room for ten people to sleep overnight. It was made of what looked like flimsy tin. Two thin, short, stick-like iron rods, serving as legs, were bolted from the floor of the box into the rocky ledge at the front of it. The legs at the back were longer as the rock fell steeply downwards. In addition, there was a rod fixed from the top of the box to the boulder above it. Scarcely had they arrived before Matteo threw off his rucksack and helmet and took a large step through the entrance. He recognised Freya immediately. She was nestled inside one of the available sleeping bags, her knees under her chin. Her chestnut-coloured hair fell over her pale face.

"Freya's here!" he yelled to his companions.

After Matteo's initial joy at finding his wife, a deep frown etched his forehead. An icy vice clutched at his heart. He couldn't breathe. She didn't respond to his presence and was trembling like a fragile bird that had flown into a windowpane. The bivouac box was too low to stand. Matteo crawled over to her and touched her gently on her shoulder.

"Freya! It's me, Matteo," he whispered softly. He stroked her hair away from her face, and Freya crossed her arms over her face to defend herself.

She screamed, "Leave me alone! Go away!" She beat her fists against Matteo. He moved to lie down next to her and take her in his arms, but as he did so, the bivouac box lurched violently downwards towards the precipice. Usually calm, Matteo screamed out in shock. The legs broke away and the bivouac box began to gravitate slowly downwards. Matteo turned white and broke out in sweat. He froze and tried to think – any movement could be disastrous.

Foxy and Emil had sat down away from the bivouac to have a break. Matteo had been leading them at a breathtaking pace and their feet were burning. Suddenly they heard Matteo scream, and turning their heads, they watched in horror as the bivouac box slid slowly downwards across the rocks towards the precipice. Foxy took a huge leap from his sitting position to the bivouac and grabbed hold of the frame around the entrance. He dug his heels into the pebbles below him. He couldn't stop the box from sliding, but it slowed down a little. He felt Emil slip a rope through his belt and then start pulling. The box stopped sliding, but it already hung almost a foot over the precipice.

"Matteo, we've got you, but not for long! Get Freya out, then come yourself, but slowly, don't make any sudden movements!" Foxy cried.

"Freya's in a bad way. She can't move herself. I'll try to push her out. Someone must help her on your side."

Matteo got hold of Freya's sleeping bag and tried to push it towards the entrance. She screamed and shouted but Matteo ignored her.

"Hurry!" Foxy called urgently. "I haven't got a good grip; I can't hold on much longer!"

Matteo realised the futility of his task. Freya, although weak, was battling against being removed from the bivouac box and Foxy was frantic. He pushed past Freya and exited the box. He got a good hold of the frame and dug his heels into the pebbles. Now Foxy could release his hold and get a decent grip of the box. Emil wrapped the rope around his fists several times so he could support Foxy better.

"Ready?" Matteo asked.

"Yes, ready!" Foxy answered breathlessly.

Matteo, anchoring his heels into the ground as best he could, inserted his arms and torso into the bivouac box. He got a good grasp of Freya's sleeping bag and pulled. Freya tried to hold onto the box frame, but Matteo was stronger. He pulled her out and collapsed on his backside. Foxy let go of the bivouac box and Emil released the rope. Both men climbed carefully down to Matteo and helped him pull Freya up, in her sleeping bag, to safety.

Simultaneously, the bivouac box slipped over the edge of the rocky precipice. The men heard it bump down, hitting some rocks a couple of hundred metres below them, then there was another noisy crash and then nothing.

Matteo's heart was hammering painfully as he tried to make Freya comfortable on the rocky floor. She was feverish and delirious, tossing her head back and forth and crying out again and again, "No! No!" Carefully he unzipped her sleeping bag. He caught his breath. He could feel his pulse drumming fiercely in his neck. He clenched his fists and forced himself to stay calm. Freya didn't need him ranting. He took her gently in his arms. This time she didn't fight but lay in them motionless.

"Her ankle is broken. It's an open fracture, the bone is sticking out through the socks," Matteo told his companions. "She's wearing a snowsuit, but it's torn. It's not hers and doesn't fit properly. The gangsters must've borrowed it somewhere without knowing her size and she's only wearing normal underwear, suitable for the office but not for up here. She's got socks and boots on, but the boots are much too large. She is seriously under cooled. Her whole body is covered with cuts and bruises, and I think she may have pneumonia." He didn't tell them that her panties were torn and her abdomen and thighs full of blood.

"Oh my God, I hope you're wrong. I have ibuprofen in my rucksack," Foxy offered. "Unfortunately, nothing else of any use."

Emil went pale but remained silent. Nothing he said could help in a situation like this.

"I'm going to ask David to take her to hospital with the helicopter. She needs urgent professional help," Matteo answered. He was already opening his rucksack to remove his phone. His mobile didn't work because they were in a dead spot with no mobile reception. At least it had finally stopped snowing. He tried again, this time with the satellite telephone. Robert answered his call, and without offering any explanations, Matteo asked if David was there. Robert connected him without further ado. Once on with David, Matteo asked if he could get the helicopter up to the bivouac box. "It's Freya," he explained. "She needs to be transported to hospital as soon as possible. You'll need a rescue bag. She's seriously injured, has a high temperature and is delirious. It's stopped snowing here. What's the weather like at your end?"

"It's raining, but don't worry, I can be with you in ten. I'll get a doctor on board."

"If it doesn't delay you, yes. Otherwise just come."

"The duty doctor is hanging around here somewhere. We're on our way."

Matteo turned his attention to Foxy and Emil, who were examining the bolts of the bivouac box legs.

"They've been fiddled with, all of them. They were unscrewed and the legs were just balancing on top," Foxy told Matteo. "It was a trap, meant to kill you and Freya."

Matteo wasn't surprised. He had thought as much. He had stayed overnight in such bivouacs on several occasions. They were sturdy and safe, despite looking the opposite.

"The evil of the Argentinian and his men has no boundaries. Lucky no one else came by before us. The helicopter will be here in ten minutes. We need to transfer Freya over there," he said pointing, "where it's easier for the helicopter to let down the winch, that is, the colleague with the winch can get closer to whoever is on the ground. Can you help me carry her?"

The ledge was narrow with a sheer drop to one side. As the men began to manoeuvre themselves somewhat cumbrously around Freya ready to lift her, they suddenly heard a deep rumbling. They stopped in the middle of what they were doing. There was a grumble again and a boom.

"Is that an..." Foxy began.

"Avalanche, yes," Matteo confirmed. "The bivouac box falling probably initiated it."

"But that was.... a couple of minutes ago," Foxy finished lamely, realising that two minutes was nothing. But it had seemed like half an hour ago.

Matteo listened carefully. "What in the name of suffering!" he said with emphasis. "I think it's going towards the Ice Chapel."

"Finn! We've got to do something!" Emil called out.

Matteo was already on the satellite phone to let the operations centre know. They said that Sven and his team were on their way, and they would inform Finn immediately.

The men continued their job at hand, and lifting Freya gently, began to shuffle their way to the designated point. "A helicopter can't land here!" Emil said.

"No, someone with David will come down on a winch with a rescue bag."

"Even so, it looks very dangerous. The helicopter can't get close. The rotors will clash against the rock," Foxy pointed out.

"David is a genius. I just hope the weather is going to hold," Matteo answered. He held onto Freya's hand continuously and studied her face to note any change. He looked at the time and put his headphones on. "He should be here soon," he told Foxy and Emil.

He had hardly spoken when he heard a crackling in his ears as David radioed in to let him know that he was on his way with the duty doctor, Dennis, and Robert. Robert had insisted upon coming, and to be let down on the winch to rescue Freya. Freya knew him well and would be less anxious than with a stranger. Matteo strained his eyes to watch for the helicopter arriving. He heard it first before he saw it.

David flew confidently to the point where Matteo, Foxy, and Emil were waiting. The helicopter hovered in the air above them to the right. The door slid open and Dennis let Robert down on a winch with a red rescue bag. As the winch line became longer, Robert swayed further and further back and forth. David corrected the position of the helicopter to get Robert nearer to the three waiting men, but Robert couldn't set down near the deployment site. There was nothing to hold onto and the weather conditions were too dangerous. Robert tried to get close enough for the men on the ground to grab hold of him, but he remained just out of their reach. A chilly wind started blowing along the mountain wall. The men saw David struggling to control the helicopter.

"I'll give it one more go," David told Matteo, "Then I'll have to break it off and try again later."

"All clear," Matteo answered. David was already risking his life by taking the helicopter up in these conditions. No doubt he would have to answer to his superiors later in the day.

The helicopter circled above them, getting very close and trying to swing Robert in the direction of the men. "I've got the line!" Foxy called out. Matteo and Emil rushed to help him. Together they got a good hold, and Robert was able to be let down the last couple of metres to join them.

Robert quickly removed the rescue bag from his backpack, unrolled it to release the vacuum pump, and let it blow up. The bottom was sewn with high-strength diagonal belts to provide even weight distribution.

Matteo and Foxy lifted Freya carefully into the bag and Robert put an immobilisation collar around her neck before closing the bag with additional padding and fixing the ten high-strength fibre suspension ropes. The wind caused by the helicopter rotors was nearly blowing Matteo and his friends off the mountainside. They sat on the ground and held onto each other. Robert gave a thumbs up to Dennis in the helicopter, who hoisted the winch up, and Matteo could see the bag, together with Robert, being stored safely inside, before David flew quickly away.

As the helicopter disappeared, peace was restored to the men's rocky outcrop. Matteo let go of Foxy. The adrenaline that had been surging through his body since Freya's kidnapping sizzled out like helium from an airship. He sat on his backside, with his knees under his chin and his head in his hands. He had done all he could. David would fly Freya straight to the helipad at Traunstein hospital. The doctor would let his colleagues there know what to expect, and they would be awaiting her, and be prepared to operate if necessary.

Chapter Thirty

WEDNESDAY, LATE AFTERNOON, 28 SEPTEMBER

It was slowly getting dark. Matteo, Foxy, and Emil, sitting on an exposed ledge of the east wall, felt the full brunt of the icy wind sweeping along the east face.

"It's not the best place for a break but eat a power bar and drink something while I try to contact the operations centre. The quickest way back is to climb to the summit and then descend to the Wimbachgries valley. It will take about an hour to reach the summit, but we must overcome a challenging eight-metre wall first. After that, it gets easier and we can have a proper rest."

Matteo rang the operations centre but there was too much crackling and interference to make himself understood. After two attempts he gave up. "No luck, I'm afraid," he told his companions. He looked up at the sky. "It looks like more snow; we'd better get going."

As before, Matteo took the lead. The sight of the south summit, the first part of the ridge, was intimidating. There was a knife's edge arête stretching before them with eight hundred metres of sheer drop to the right and left. The wind howled across the exposed rock, robbing Matteo of his breath. He began to move, stepping carefully to the left where the exit chimneys loomed. Turning back, his voice cut through the icy air.

"Watch your footing! Loose debris under the snow. I'll stop at the ridge step before the hardest part."

Ahead, an eight-metre wall of raw, unyielding rock reared up, slick with ice and utterly devoid of natural handholds. However, bolts were already driven into the rock to allow for securing handholds. Matteo fastened the rope, testing its hold with a firm tug before he began his ascent. Hand over hand, he climbed, his muscles burning with the strain. The moment his fingers scraped over the top, he heaved himself up and flattened onto his stomach. He stretched out his arms, bracing for the others.

Foxy motioned for Emil to go first. Emil hoisted himself up with the help of the fixed rope. His style wasn't elegant, but it was efficient. Foxy followed. Matteo exhaled in relief as he finally reached them.

After that, the climb was steep and narrow and exposed to the elements, but no longer life-threatening. "The view down to the Wimbachgries valley is awesome!" Foxy called out, "but scary, too."

"Don't look down!" Matteo warned.

And then – it happened. A low, ominous rumble echoed from above. A shower of small rocks dislodged, skittering down the chute. Foxy looked upwards. One of the rocks struck him on his face and he cried out in surprise. His footing faltered and losing his hold, he tumbled down the steep rock face, his hands grasping into thin air.

The rope securing him jerked and Matteo lunged, the rope snapped taught before he could react, wrenching him forward. Only Emil's split-second reflexes stopped Matteo from being dragged over the edge after him. Emil had thrown his weight back and wound the rope around his wrists. A heartbeat passed. Then another. Silence.

"Foxy!" Matteo's voice was desperate. There was no response.

Matteo secured himself with a harness and rope. He hammered a bolt into the ground next to him, threaded his rope through it, and instructed Emil what to do.

"I'm going to look for him. Let me down slowly."

Emil lowered Matteo down metre per metre. Matteo strained his eyes – searching – but there was nothing. No movement nor sound. "There's not much rope left," Emil's voice was distant. Matteo was forty metres below Emil. He looked downwards but still couldn't see Foxy or even any sort of rocky outcrop where he might have landed. "Keep going," Matteo yelled back. The length of rope ran out. Matteo unhitched himself. "I'm going to climb down a little further. Wait fifteen minutes. If you don't hear anything from me, descend to the Wimbachgries valley and let the operations centre know."

Matteo hammered bolts into the rock face and, using a second rope, climbed backwards down the sheer precipice. Finally, he saw a rocky outcrop and a figure lying on his back, motionless. He scrambled down as quickly as he could and looked worriedly at Foxy's waxy face. He dropped beside him and reaching out, pressed his fingers to Foxy's neck. There was nothing. He tried again, his figures trembling. There was no pulse. There was nothing he could do for him.

A loud gasp escaped his lips. Foxy! His vision blurred, the wind wailed around him, as if crying in grief. His family would be inconsolable. What a waste of such a good man. He was so full of life, so close to the summit. Gone. Just like that. A wave of rage clawed Matteo's chest. He clenched his jaw, pushing back the rising tide of grief. This wasn't over. Matteo felt more determined than ever to bring the Argentinian and his men to justice.

A voice shouted his trance. "Matteo!" The sound of Emil calling jolted him back to the present. "I'm coming," he called. "Wait for me."

Matteo climbed back to where he had unharnessed himself, and with a debilitating effort, secured himself again. His fingers were numb, and his strength sapped. "You can help me now," he called to Emil. "Pull!"

Reaching the top, he collapsed onto his back, his chest heaving.

"Didn't you find him?" Emil asked.

"Yes, I did. No one can help him now. Someone will recover his body tomorrow."

Silence. Emil was shocked. "Only just below the summit, and only a few steps from the end, he whispered.

Matteo closed his eyes. "Yes," his voice was rough. "The rock that hit him wasn't large and probably didn't even hurt him, but it distracted him. Just for a second. That's all it took, one second."

The weight of it pressed down on them both. But there was no time to grieve. Not yet.

"We have to go." Matteo's voice was steel now. "We should return as soon as possible."

They climbed the last couple of metres to the summit of the south peak. It was broad, with enough room to sit down, have a rest, and savour the extraordinary views. The whole karst plateau of Steinernes Meer stretched out in front of them. But in silent agreement they continued their subdued descent to the Wimbachgries valley.

It grew dark very fast now, and with the last of the

twilight they turned their headlamps on. There was some fog around, and the Watzmann, lying in deep shadows, looked menacing. The first part of the descent was mostly unsecured. The route zigzagged, winding down steep ridges, some short rocky steps, small chimneys and chutes, with nothing to hold onto. Matteo led Emil confidently over narrow notches in front of fierce and wild-looking rock spires. The descent was about twelve hundred metres, and from the first to the very last step it was necessary to pay attention to the terrain. Matteo and Emil scrambled and skidded awkwardly downwards. The trail disappeared and they found themselves in a mixed terrain of rocks and meadow.

The air was freezing cold, and an icy rain bit like thorns into their faces. They dipped into an area of dwarf pines and joined the trail again. Matteo's eyes glazed over. He was walking automatically now. He knew the trail well, but he realised he should stop before another accident happened.

"I can't go on," he told Emil. "The risk is too high, for me, but for you, too. We can rest here in the forest for an hour, until we get some energy back."

Matteo sat on the ground and leant his rucksack against a tree trunk. He wasn't hungry but he forced himself to eat a couple of power bars and drink some sickly, strongly sugared and caffeinated pop. He removed the satellite phone from his rucksack, stretched his legs out, and rang the operations centre.

Mark answered. "Matteo, thank goodness you're safe. We were worried because of the weather conditions and the avalanche. We've heard from David; Freya is stable and Robert is staying at the hospital with her. Dennis has returned here, waiting to pick you up and drive you straight there."

"Hello Mark, Emil and I are safe, but Foxy lost his footing and fell a couple of hundred metres. I managed to get down to him, but there was nothing I could do. He was already dead." Speaking the words out loud seemed to make the reality worse. Matteo couldn't continue speaking. Mark was silent, too, perhaps hoping he may have misheard or misinterpreted Matteo's words. Finally, he asked, "Where are you now?"

"In the dwarf pine area. We couldn't carry on, we had to rest., It was just too much."

"Dennis is going to drive to the end of the supply road, then he'll start walking to meet you."

"Thank you," Matteo answered, unhurriedly and exhausted. "How is Finn? Did Sven find him?"

"Yes, he's fine, thanks to one of those new avalanche airbags he was carrying."

"Thank goodness for that. I'll tell Emil, he's been worried."

Emil had been listening as best he could. "Did I hear right, is Finn okay?"

"Yes, he's fine. Dennis is driving out to meet us at the end of the supply road. There's still a long way to go. Let me rest another fifteen minutes and then we can set off."

Matteo watched the trillions of stars between the wavering tree tops and occasional clouds in the inky blue sky. He massaged his feet and calves and then stood up and stamped his feet on the ground. He hoisted his rucksack onto his back and set off with Emil along the knee-grinding descent, looking forward to meeting Dennis.

They continued on, crossing several huge scree fans and between rocky outcrops, until after half an hour they reached the Wimbachgries. The Alpine valley was gloomy-looking and cold. In the dark, the hike seemed twice as long as normal.

"Not much further now," Matteo encouraged Emil. "We'll reach the Wimbach springs soon. In the daylight it's a beautiful canyon. The water running through the thick layers of scree come to the surface here and then rush through the Wimbachklamm before the creek flows into the Ramsauer Ache. The valley stretches for seven kilometres from the western end of the Steinernes Meer between the huge rock faces of Mount Watzmann to the east, and Hochkalter to the west, down to the Wimbach Bridge. The supply road comes down to the trailhead. We can start looking out for Dennis soon."

Sure enough, in just another half an hour, they saw a small light bobbing up and down. "There he is!" Matteo called "That's his headlamp."

Dennis greeted them both cheerily, giving each of them a short embrace and clapping them on their shoulders. "Glad to see you both," he said. "You had us worried."

"It was a fateful climb," Matteo answered. "It's left us mentally wasted. Have you heard anything new from the hospital?"

"The doctor wouldn't tell us much as we aren't related to Freya. They operated, I think, to stop some internal bleeding, and her condition is stable now. If she stays stable overnight, they want to operate on her ankle tomorrow. Let me take those." Dennis grabbed the mens' rucksacks and together they marched the last couple of kilometres to Dennis's car.

First, he drove Emil to Alpenhotel Weiherbach, where he and several of his colleagues would be staying as long as they were needed in Berchtesgaden. Next, he put his foot down on the gas pedal and sped off to Traunstein where Freya was hospitalised.

Chapter Thirty-One

4 AM, THURSDAY, 29 SEPTEMBER

"Wake up!" Dennis nudged Matteo, who had fallen asleep in the car. "We're here. Come on, I'm not going to carry you in."

Matteo awoke suddenly and sat upright. "That was quick!" he said. "I hope you don't get too many speeding tickets."

Dennis smiled. "I'll pass them on to you. Hurry up, Robert is waiting."

Dennis directed Matteo through the labyrinth of hospital corridors and elevators. He headed straight for a family room, where Robert was snoring in an armchair. "I'll go and get some strong coffee," Dennis offered and left the room.

Matteo decided against waking Robert, there wasn't really much point in it. He would wait until Dennis returned with the coffee and then announce himself to the night nurse. He wondered whether he would be able to speak to the doctor. Someone must be on duty, he supposed, but maybe he was busy with other patients. Unsettled, he opened the door and stuck his head out, looking along the corridor to see if he could see Dennis.

He saw a light on in a glass-panelled room halfway down the corridor, and thinking it must be the night nurse's room, walked stealthily towards it, not wanting to disturb her in case she was resting. Coming nearer, he could hear two women's voices. Without wanting to, he caught snippets of their conversation.

"Tragic... She'll never get over it... The husband will be devastated... If something like that happened to me, my Josef would murder the monsters responsible..."

Matteo turned on his heels to retreat and nearly bumped into Dennis. Scalding coffee spilled out of the three paper cups balanced between Dennis's hands. "Hey, careful! Ouch, that's hot! What are you doing here? I only left you a minute."

"Sorry!" Matteo hastened back to the family room. His hands were shaking. Had the nurses been talking about Freya? They must have been. Had something happened that he didn't know about?

Dennis hurried to put the coffee cups on a table, then he shook his hands to free them from the scalding coffee and wiped them clean with a tissue. Robert stirred in his armchair, stretched his arms, and then, noticing Dennis and Matteo, woke up quickly. "Mmm, coffee!" he exclaimed.

Matteo's face was strained. "What did the doctor tell you about Freya?" he asked.

Robert looked at him, serious now. "Not much, I'm afraid. She had some internal bleeding, which the doctors stopped, and then they put her in an induced coma, as her body needs rest, and they didn't want her to wake up and get upset. For now, she's stable, and if she passes the night well, then her ankle will be operated on. The doctor told me to inform him as soon as you arrive. Shall I go to the night nurse and tell her, or do you want to go yourself?"

"I'll go," Matteo replied and left the room quickly.

The night nurse rang the doctor in his presence. "I'm to show you to his room," she told Matteo. "He'll be along in a couple of minutes."

Matteo sat down in a comfortable upholstered chair. It wasn't long before a white-coated doctor with a grave face entered the room and shook hands with Matteo before sitting down opposite him.

"Mr. Stocker, I'm Dr. Marzoll, the consultant on this ward and responsible for Freya's well-being," he started. "I know you will be anxious to see your wife, but it is better that I speak to you first. When she arrived here late yesterday afternoon, your wife had a temperature of a hundred and two and she was delirious. Her blood pressure was over two hundred and her pulse a hundred and thirty-five. She was losing a lot of blood from her vagina. Despite her broken ankle, our main concern was to find out where the bleeding was coming from and to stop it. Mr. Stocker, I'm very sorry but we couldn't save the baby."

"Baby? I didn't know... Freya didn't tell me..." Matteo trailed off.

"It was very early on, just seven weeks. She may have been waiting for an appointment at her gynaecologist to confirm it."

"Yes. You sound as if that isn't everything."

"You're very observant. I don't know if you saw the state of Freya before she was put into the rescue bag?"

"The ripped clothes and the bruises? Was she raped? I've been worrying about it every minute since I saw her."

"I'm afraid so." Dr. Marzoll took Matteo's hands in his. "We found traces of three different samples of semen and DNA..."

"THREE! You mean...? THREE men?"

"Yes. I'm very sorry."

"God, I'm going to kill those bastards! No wonder she was ranting, and didn't want me near her! Now I understand. Oh, poor Freya. I wasn't there to protect her. I'll never forgive myself."

The doctor waited silently before speaking.

"Your wife's body needs complete rest. If she gets upset and thrashes out, which would be a normal reaction, may I add, then she will be putting her life at risk. The men injured her severely. We have secured their DNA. If they are arrested, we can prove their guilt. We have put your wife into an induced coma. We are hoping to operate on her ankle in the morning. It has been X-rayed, and the orthopaedic surgeon has examined it carefully. He wants to pin the bone together and use two plates for stability. He is confident that in six months from now it will be as good as new. He will be here in the morning and can explain the operation in detail to you, if you wish."

"Can I see Freya now?"

"Yes, I will take you to her and you can stay with her as long as you like. I'm not your doctor, but you look exhausted, and there is nothing you can do for her. Once you have seen her, I suggest you go home and get some sleep and then return in the afternoon. Your friends have been very supportive. Will one of them drive you home?"

"Yes, I expect so."

"Good, you are in no state to drive yourself at the moment."

Dr. Marzoll led Matteo to the intensive-care unit. He opened the door to a single room with white walls, bare of any decoration. It was full of beeping and flashing electronic equipment. Freya lay in the middle of a bed that looked too big for her. Her face was as pale as a frosty winter morning and she was covered with white sheets. She had a thick tube inserted into her mouth and down her throat, leading to a monstrous-looking machine. She was receiving some sort of infusion that was hanging on a hook over her bedside and more tubes trailed across the mattress onto the floor.

Matteo put his head in his hands. "Oh Freya, what have they done to you?" He gasped. He went to her bedside, picked up her hand and pressed it to his lips. Her hand lay limp in his. "Can she hear me when I speak?" Matteo asked the doctor.

"Maybe," he answered. "We recommend friends and family talk to the patient. If all goes well, we shall wake her from the coma in the morning and then operate on the ankle. After recovering from the anaesthetic Freya can be transferred to a normal ward."

"Will you tell her about the baby immediately?"

"Not necessarily. Not unless she specifically asks. She will have enough to deal with her ankle for the time being. Any other questions will come soon enough."

"I don't think she will want anyone to know about the rape."

"That is natural, at least at first. Our psychiatric doctor will visit her in a day or two. She will need help dealing with the trauma. The details of her medical condition are confidential. It is up to you what you tell her friends and relations."

"Oh Freya, I'm so sorry, I'll never forgive myself." Tears ran down Matteo's cheeks and the doctor handed him a tissue.

"It is good to cry and to be mad and furious but try to get it out of your system before you visit Freya tomorrow.

She needs you to be calm, loving, caring, and most of all, positive."

"Yes, I can do that in Freya's presence, but there's also one thing that I can guarantee you, I'm going to catch those monsters and I'm going to make sure they rot in prison for as long as they live!"

Chapter Thirty-Two

THURSDAY, EARLY MORNING, 29 SEPTEMBER

Matteo returned to Robert and Dennis, who were still waiting faithfully in the family room. They stood when Matteo entered. He gave them both a brief hug and thanked them for being there for him. He told them that Freya was resting and that the doctor had ordered him to go home to get some rest.

"I haven't slept for two nights, so I agreed. I need my strength for Freya now. I just want to ring Sven and ask what the situation is, and then, as far as I'm concerned, we can get going."

Sven was pleased to hear from him and receive the update on Freya. He told Matteo that GSG 9 agents had circled the Hotel Schwabenwirt four hours ago and arrested the three Bulgarians. The men had been completely surprised and offered no resistance. Not a single shot had been fired. They were now on their way to the high-security prison in Straubing, near Munich.

"That's good news," Matteo said. "What about the others? Have you found them yet?"

"No. Neither the couple from Alpenhotel Weiherbach nor the Argentinian and his four companions. But don't worry, in another hour it will be light, and the agents will continue to comb through the whole area."

"What about Benni and Danny? Have the police in Straubing interviewed them yet?"

"Yes, but they've only confirmed what we already knew, that the drug cartel is receiving inside information from employees of the Port of Hamburg. We know that it is the same in Rotterdam and Ostend. Over six thousand people work directly for the harbour in Hamburg. We need some names but they both claim they don't know any. The officer in charge tends to believe them. They are merely hired thugs to do the dirty work, and there would be no reason to give them that sort of information."

"The employees won't have parted with information for nothing. Have their bank accounts been checked?"

"Yes. The BND has been checking and double-checking the employees for months now. The Argentinian isn't stupid, either he has paid them in cash, or he has bribed them in a different way, threatening their families or exposing secrets. There are innumerable possibilities. The trouble is that even if one employee is caught; he simply replaces the person with someone else.

"We need to get to the men at the top, and that is the Argentinian. He was extremely mistaken to come to Europe. He knows that and is probably regretting it already. Now that he is here, though, we believe he is determined to stay until he gets to the treasure. If we haven't caught all five of the gang we know about, plus Rollo and the Argentinian, then Mr. Buchenmeyer is coming to Berchtesgaden on Friday and will oversee the entrance to the cave that Toby found. Our men will access and open the cave."

"That's quite a bit of news. I'm driving back to Berchtesgaden now with Robert and Dennis. I'll tell them about it on our way home."

*****

Sven and his agents had been discussing the fact that neither the Turkish couple nor the Argentinian and his men seemed to be staying in any of the hotels or guesthouses within a twenty-kilometre perimeter.

Harald had told him that there were innumerable holiday homes in the area that stood empty year-round until the owners decided to go on holiday in summer or go skiing in winter.

"Most of them have alarm systems, but someone with a little knowledge of electrics could probably disconnect the alarm. However, they will still need food and drink, which they must buy somewhere."

"That's a good point." Sven said. "Rudolf, if we print flyers with the gangsters' photographs, could the police distribute them to all the supermarkets in the area?"

"Yes, and anywhere else that sells food, too. There are lots of kiosks in the area. We'll do that as soon as you have the flyers printed."

"Good, that won't take long."

Chapter Thirty-Three

THURSDAY, MORNING TO EVENING,
29 SEPTEMBER

Henry Steger was a seasoned fifty-year-old mountain guide who worked for the National Alpine club in Berchtesgaden. He was good-humoured and complacent. Nothing could make him lose his fuse. He had seen it all. For that reason, he was well liked, and thanks to mouth-to-mouth propaganda, his tours were always fully booked.

On Wednesday he had been accompanying a mixed group of enthusiastic, but wildly overconfident middle-aged hikers on a five-day trek along the Berchtesgadener Höhenweg. One woman in particular, Anja Kohl, had been a nightmare. Instead of breaking in her hiking boots beforehand as specifically advised, she had obviously bought brand-new ones for the tour and was wearing them for the first time. The result was painful blisters the size of cow pads.

Every kilometre, the group was forced to stop so she could, painfully slowly, sit on a bench, remove her boots and socks, and slap on yet more antiseptic cream and another layer of plasters. Her fellow hikers stood around, growing increasingly mutinous. After six hours of this slow motion disaster, she had had the audacity to complain that they hadn't reached their shelter for the night yet. "The tour description *clearly* said no more than six hours per day!" she had huffed.

In fact, it lasted another two hours until they reached the small wooden hut that was private property of the National Alpine Club. Mentally exhausted from Anja's irritable squabbling, but relieved that they had reached their goal for the day, Henry unlocked the entrance and told the participants to choose their rooms and get cleaned up before they prepared a simple meal together. Henry went to his own room and dumped his rucksack on the floor next to the bed. He was just about to wash his hands when he heard a loud commotion coming from the guest rooms. He picked out Anja Kohl's loud indignant voice and groaned. He left his room and nearly bumped into her generously proportioned body. "There are two people in my room. Sleeping in my bed!" she protested.

"What do you mean? I said you could choose your rooms. Couldn't you agree with each other? The rooms are identical," Henry asked.

"No! I mean *other* people! Not in *our* group," she added, as if talking to an imbecile.

Henry pushed past her and went to look for himself. In the meantime, the four male participants of the group were in the common room, holding on to the two culprits who were struggling to get free.

"You see," Anja said triumphantly. "You can't expect me to sleep in their beds. I'm going to make a complaint and demand a refund!"

For the first time on one of his tours, Henry nearly lost

it. He wished that he could tell her to go and roll down the mountain. As it was, he ignored her.

"Who are you and what are you doing here?" he asked the man and the woman who were still struggling to get free. They didn't answer. "How did you get in?" Henry asked. The couple shrugged their shoulders as if they didn't understand German. "Hold onto them," he told the four males. "I'll have a look around."

At the back of the hut, he found a broken window. He returned to the common room and told the participants, "I'm sorry about this, they've broken in. Let us sit them down in a chair and tie them up to keep them here. I'll ring the police. They can be here quite quickly. No doubt they will take them to the station, check their identities, and find a translator if necessary. They will have to pay for the damages they've caused. Anja, I'm sorry about your room, but if you give me ten minutes, I'll change the sheets and bed clothing."

"What about my bathroom? I can't use it after they have."

"Yes, I will clean that too and open the window to give the room a good airing. Now, let me ring the police, and once that's settled, we can begin to prepare a meal."

*****

Sasha Berger was eighteen years old. His parents owned a petrol station with a small shop attached. Sasha often worked there before or after school to earn pocket money for he was saving up for a motorbike. His parents were terrified at the thought of their son on a motorbike, but they couldn't forbid it, he was of age. They thought that if he had to pay for the bike himself, then he would treasure it more, and specifically drive carefully so as not to damage it.

On Thursday evening, he relieved his mother at 6 p.m. He had just said goodbye to her, when two men on foot, clad in black, entered the store and filled two shopping baskets with bread, milk, margarine, and anything else resembling food. They paid cash and left. The shop was empty, and Sasha wondered why they hadn't gone to a proper supermarket or grocery store. Then he remembered the police bringing in a notice with seven black and white mugshots of people in the area for whom they were searching. He opened a drawer, and taking out the flyer, examined the black and white photographs. He wasn't a hundred per cent sure, but he thought that he recognised the two men who had been in. He lifted the receiver and rang the police. He secured the shop videotape and then rang his parents.

*****

Friedrich Horn was walking through the Klausbach valley, picking blue gentian flowers. He did this every autumn, and when he had enough, he would take them to the local distillery where gentian schnapps was made, a local speciality. He was eighty-three years old and had lived all his life in Berchtesgaden. He knew everybody who had lived in the area for at least five years and even some regular guests who had second homes. He knew every tree and every grass stalk.

When he wasn't occupying himself with activities to improve his meagre pension, he could be found at the regulars' table in Bier Adam in the town centre. There he exchanged gossip and, in the main part exaggerated, stories with similarly situated men. Basically, there wasn't much he didn't know about, and if anybody wanted information about something, then they always went to him first. He particularly enjoyed collecting the gentians because the distillery always gave him, in addition to his pay, a bottle of schnapps.

On Thursday evening he continued to walk along the valley path until dusk began to fall. He was about to call it a day when he noticed a light on the other side of the valley. There was only one single chalet there. It belonged to Victoria Beyer, the rich heiress of an industrial family. Friedrich was surprised because Mrs. Beyer usually only came in winter, to enjoy the skiing. Maybe she had lent it to someone, he thought, although she had never done so before. It was a bit strange. Hopefully no one had broken in to have a party or burgle it. He would ask Margit, the housekeeper. She would know, and if no one was expected, she would have a key and could check it out.

On Friday morning, Friedrich was sitting with his cronies outside Bier Adam, enjoying a beer and watching the goings on at the market. He saw Margit with a basket over her arm, full of vegetables. Ah, he remembered and strolled over to her.

"I saw a light on at Victoria Beyer's place last night," he told her. "I didn't know she was in the area so soon this year."

Margit frowned. "She isn't, not that I know of anyway, and she would have told me. I'd better go and look."

"I'd take a policeman with you, if I were you. There are all sorts hanging about nowadays."

"No, it'll be a couple of teenagers fooling about. But I'll check anyway. Hopefully they haven't caused too much mess or damage. Thanks for letting me know."

"Well, be careful. Don't forget those gangsters that the police are looking for. There are flyers all over the place." Friedrich returned to his chair and his beer but his conversation with Margit bothered him. She was a good woman who worked hard. He wouldn't want anything to happen to her. He wondered whether to ring the police himself and asked his cronies what they thought.

"Well, it wouldn't hurt, would it?" one of them answered. "It'd be better than reproaching yourself afterwards if anything did happen."

Chapter Thirty-Four

FRIDAY, MORNING TO EVENING, 29 SEPTEMBER

Matteo had spent all Thursday afternoon with Freya at the hospital. Her ankle had been operated on and now lay bandaged between two splints, slightly raised on her bed. She was still drowsy from the anaesthetic and from the painkillers she was receiving. Luckily, she had no memory of what had happened since she had been kidnapped. Matteo merely sat next to her to comfort her.

Inside, however, he was broiling: angry about what had been done to her and worried that her memory may come back. By the time he had driven home in the evening, he was so exhausted that he simply dropped, fully clothed, onto his bed. He put his alarm on for half past twelve the next day and just managed to kick his shoes off before he fell into a fitful sleep. The events of the last five days sped through his brain like the Bernina Express, only to circle around and complete a few more circuits. At some time, he must've fallen into a deeper sleep, because when his alarm rang, he needed a couple of minutes to orientate himself.

He showered and drank two cups of coffee, looked out of the window at the miserable weather, then opened the fridge and found it empty. He had arranged to meet Freya's mother at 2:30 p.m. – plenty of time yet – so he decided to walk into town and get a decent meal. Afterwards, he would go to the supermarket to stock up with groceries and to the florist to buy Freya some red roses.

Matteo dressed as if he were going on an expedition to the North Pole; it was unbelievably cold for this time of year. It had snowed in the night and the fresh snow on Mount Watzmann came down to eight hundred metres. He crossed the river Ache and walked through the town's pedestrian zone, heading for Bier Adam, where you could still get good Bavarian food in decent portions and at an affordable price.

Most restaurants were Italian these days, and there was only so much pizza and spaghetti that he could eat. He had forgotten that it was market day and lost a little time weaving between the shoppers and saying a quick hello to the many people he knew. By the time he reached Bier Adam, he had talked about the weather at least twenty times and felt himself going crazy. Finally, he reached the pub, nodded to Friedrich Horn and his cronies, who were sitting outside not wanting to miss anything, despite the Arctic temperatures and lethal wind, and disappeared indoors.

He sat down next to a tiled oven radiating a pleasant warmth. Matteo didn't need to look at the menu, he had already decided on what he fancied eating. The waitress came over, a menu in her hand. He knew her from frequent visits to the pub.

"Hi, Sandra," Matteo greeted. "I'd like the spinach dumplings, please."

"Okay, and to drink?"

"Just a Coke, please. I will be driving later."

"Good. How's Freya? I heard she's in hospital."

"Yes, in Traunstein. That's where I'm going. She broke her ankle, and it had to be operated on."

"Oh, I'm sorry to hear that. Give her my best wishes when you see her."

"Will do."

Matteo had just started eating when Friedrich Horn came indoors, had a quick look around, and seeing Matteo, came to his table and sat down next to him. Matteo cursed inwardly. There was nowhere to escape. He was trapped.

"Now then, Freddie, what's up?" Matteo asked. He smiled friendly enough but chewed on his food pointedly.

"Don't let me disturb you eating, just carry on. I've got a bit of a problem I'm not sure what to do about. I was just wondering whether to ring the police when I saw you come in, and I thought you would know what to do."

"What sort of problem?"

Freddie explained in great detail about the empty chalet, the light, and about Margit wanting to head out there alone. He concluded, "I'm a bit worried, you see, what with those gangsters hanging around that you're searching for. Margit is a good maid but as stubborn as a goat. I know she'll go out there on her own."

"Good job you told me. I know the officer who's looking out for the men. I'll give him a ring and I'm sure he'll check it out. What's Margit's second name and do you have an address for her? We'll send someone to stop her going alone."

Freddie thought for a while, chewing on his lower lip. "You know, I don't think I do know her surname, she's just Margit. She lives here, in the Schornbad Lane. I don't have the number but it's the house with the red door on your right. I just saw her, about fifteen minutes ago, shopping at the market."

"That's great, thank you. Look, I've got to go now, but here's my number," he   scribbled the number on a paper napkin and gave it to Freddie, "and for your trouble," he added, taking a twenty euro note from his wallet, "just in case you notice anything else."

Freddie looked at the twenty euro note as if he had never held one in his hands before now. "Aw, no need for that," he said a bit dolefully.

"No, keep it!" Matteo assured him. "You might need to call me." Matteo stood up quickly, went to Sandra and handed her a few banknotes. "Sorry, I'm in a rush," he muttered. "See you another time."

Chapter Thirty-Five

FRIDAY, EARLY AFTERNOON, 29 SEPTEMBER

Matteo had left the pub so he could telephone in peace without Freddie listening in to every word. Outside, the market stalls were being cleared away but there were still masses of people around. He looked at his watch: only an hour before he was due to meet Freya's mother, damn! He decided to ring her first and ask if they could meet a bit later.

"Why? What have you got to do that is more important than visiting your wife?" she asked. It was a constant reproach from his mother-in-law, and it ruined his relationship with her. She was always complaining that he was more interested in his work than in Freya. She was like a verruca, always niggling and jabbing. He regretted having asked her, he should have known better. Freya never complained. They had lived together for two years before getting married and she had known what she was getting into.

"Nothing, I'm just running a bit late, that's all. I wanted to fill the fridge up and go to the florist to buy Freya some flowers."

"Well, I can get some flowers, if that helps you," Freya's mother offered.

"Oh yes, that would be great. I wanted to buy her a big bunch of dark red roses, the fragrant sort from the florist."

"Right, I'll do that and see you in two hours then."

If he left the grocery shopping until that evening, then he would just have time to drive to Ramsau and speak to Sven personally, Matteo thought. He broke into a jog, crossed the river Ache, and pressed on his remote car door opener.

Sven was a little surprised to see him but listened happily to what he had to say. "It was a good idea to hang those posters up everywhere. We've had more help from the people around here. They're much more observant than people in the city." Sven commented.

"Oh, yes. Berchtesgaden is a bad place for hiding secrets. What have you found out?"

"Brilliant news! We've caught the Turkish couple. They're on their way to Straubing now. They had broken into a wooden hut belonging to the local Alpine hiking club, and when a group arrived for the night, they found them sleeping in one of the beds!"

Sven couldn't help chuckling and Matteo joined in. "Sounds a bit like Goldilocks," he said. "So that just leaves the Argentinian, his second-in-command, Rollo, and the three bodyguards?"

"Yes, exactly. Maybe they are hiding in the chalet that Friedrich Horn was talking about. We got another call, too, from a young lad in a petrol station, with an adjoining shop that sells a few groceries. Two men came in to buy food and the lad wondered why they were on foot. Apparently, they sell overpriced snacks for journeys and the men came in at a time when all the normal supermarkets and bakeries were open. So, if they weren't travelling, why were they buying groceries there? If you show me exactly where the chalet is, then we'll be able to see if the petrol station is anywhere nearby."

Matteo went with Sven to the large, detailed map on the wall. He marked a small black cross where the chalet was.

"Oh," Sven said a little disappointed, "it's miles away."

Matteo remembered the time. "Shit! I've got to go," he said. "Look, whatever you do, don't forget Margit. I promised Friedrich not to let her get into danger. By all accounts she's a diligent housekeeper and may be on her way to check the chalet already. I'll try to come back this evening after visiting Freya."

Matteo put his foot down all the way home. He was just five minutes late, but Freya's mother was already standing on his doorstep looking as if she were sucking on a lemon. He let her indoors, apologising.

"Where are your groceries then?" she asked suspiciously.

"I'll get them while you're packing Freya's things," he answered, hoping it sounded like they were in the car boot. "What do I owe you for the flowers?" he asked, changing the subject.

"Twenty euros," she answered.

"I'll put the money on the table next to your handbag," he said, thinking she couldn't have got many roses for that price at the florist. He heard drawers opening and closing upstairs. "Can you find everything? Shall I come and help you?" he called.

"No, I think I've got everything now," she said, returning to the kitchen with a small suitcase. "Right, as far as I'm concerned, we can set off."

The journey to the hospital was uneventful and passed mainly in silence. Matteo told Gisela, Freya's mother, that he had to concentrate on the driving. As they arrived on the ward, the nurse told them that they could only visit one at a time and for just ten minutes each. "You go first," Matteo told Gisela. "I'll see if I can find a vase for the flowers."

"Oh, right," she answered, and gave him a sorry-looking bunch of red carnations. Matteo stopped short. While Gisela disappeared into Freya's room, he looked at the wilted blossoms wrapped in see-through plastic. Freya hated carnations. She said they reminded her of funerals. Surely her mother must know that. A price tag was stuck on the outside of the wrapping – €2.99 was crossed through and replaced by €1.99. Typical supermarket ware, unbelievable! He threw them into a trash bin and tried not to be annoyed, there were more important things to worry about.

The ten minutes were soon up. The nurse brought Matteo to Freya's room and asked Gisela to leave. Matteo sat next to the bed, picked up Freya's hand and pressed it to his lips. She turned her head on the pillow to look at him and gave him a weak smile. "Hi," she whispered.

"Oh, my darling." Matteo's voice cracked and a tear trickled down his cheek. "I'll never forgive myself for leaving you alone. How are you feeling?"

"As if a wild animal has chewed me up and spat me out again. And I'm tired, so terribly tired. Whenever I fall asleep, I begin to dream of dizzying heights and terrifying abysses. Then I wake up covered in sweat. What happened? I remember leaving work and something evil smelling being put over my nose and mouth, but then nothing more until I woke up here." Freya's complexion was pale and blue veins shone through her clear skin.

Matteo looked at the ceiling and blinked back tears. Hadn't the doctor spoken to her yet? He didn't feel up to breaking the news himself. He couldn't. "Maybe the nurse can give you something to help you rest and the doctor will talk to you about your injuries soon." He was a coward. He reproached himself as the nurse entered to ask him to leave. "I'll be back tomorrow," he promised Freya.

*****

Ten GSG 9 agents crept along the Klausbach valley, the crunch of their boots muffled by the soft earth beneath. The air was unnervingly still, not a bird call or rustle of wind to break the silence. As they neared the chalet, the trees thickened, closing in until they were no more than ten metres from the house. Their movements were seamless, every agent slipping between the trunks and bushes with practiced stealth. Each pair of eyes trained on the building, infrared glasses flicking over its walls and windows, confirming what they already suspected—the chalet was empty.

A quick glance at their surroundings confirmed the eerie quiet of the place. The agents fanned out and encircled the chalet. They checked the door, the windows, and the inside. It was clear that someone had been here, but they were long gone. An unmade bed, the faint smell of leftover food in the kitchen, a few articles of clothing carelessly abandoned in the hallway. It spoke of a hasty departure, as though the occupants had left in a rush, or perhaps out of fear.

One of the agents, kneeling near a jacket discarded by the door, bagged it quickly, while others took samples of food scraps and fingerprints from surfaces. Their findings would soon be sent to headquarters for DNA analysis. As they moved toward the front door to exit, the commander's sharp eye caught something. A faint glimmer at the edge of the doorway—a wire, almost invisible against the dark wood. His heart raced, and he signalled the team to stop.

"Booby trap," he muttered under his breath, eyes

scanning the doorframe more carefully now. The wire ran from the door, almost too subtle to notice. If one of them had opened it without looking… the thought was enough to freeze his blood. The agents backed away slowly, their exit now more cautious than before. A deadly trap, barely visible, had been set—too close for comfort.

*****

Matteo drove Gisela home and then went straight to Ramsau to the operations centre. He looked around and saw Robert, David, and Dennis chatting to each other. Ivanna and Toby were also there, consulting with Marvin, Toby's potholer friend. Sven was talking to Harald Ebner, Otto Beck, the Kripo CSI, and the head commissioner of the regional police, Rudolf Hoffmann. The rest of the company was also there: the BND agents Tina, Nicole, Mark, Julian, Stefan, Patrick, and lastly Sergeant Lukas, who was standing next to his boss, Otto.

Matteo went to Sven and asked him if they had checked the chalet yet or explored the area round about.

"Ah, Matteo, you're back," Sven stated the obvious. "Yes, we have, unfortunately without success. But before I tell you more, how is Freya? Is she any better today?"

"She is a little better, thank you, yes. She cannot remember anything between leaving work and waking in hospital. It may be good for the moment. She is very tired and needs a lot of rest," Matteo answered.

"Yes, yes of course. It'll take time," Sven replied. "To this afternoon, first off, Tina went to Berchtesgaden and found the house where Margit lives. She was just on time as Margit was about to set off to the chalet. Margit needed a lot of persuasion not to go to the chalet, and unfortunately, she insisted on ringing up the owner, a Mrs. Beyer. Mrs.

Beyer said that no one should be there, and although Tina asked her not to telephone, we think she must have. The Argentinian and his men were probably expecting us, and we can only think that Mrs. Beyer rang the number in the chalet, and merely by that, the gangsters were pre-warned that they had been sighted. By the time the GSG 9 agents got there, they were already gone."

"So, what now?" Matteo asked. "Have you figured out a new plan?"

"Mr. Buchenmeyer is flying here very early tomorrow morning. He still thinks the best way to catch the Argentinian is to open the cave that Toby has found."

"How does he want to go about it? Does he think the excavator just needs to remove a few rocks so that the cave can be entered, and that the Argentinian will then simply turn up and let himself be arrested?"

"No, to the contrary. Yesterday Mr. Buchenmeyer obtained definite confirmation of what he suspected all along. The Argentinian owns a small private army of mercenaries, well equipped with modern weapons, three helicopters and two Cessnas."

"Bloody hell! How are the GSG 9 supposed to fight against that? How many mercenaries are in the Argentinian's army?"

"We don't know exactly. However, the whole area inside a radius of ten kilometres of the cave is being cordoned off at two a.m. and will stay so until the situation is resolved. The roads will be closed. The German army has been notified and will situate themselves inside the ten-kilometre cordon early tomorrow morning. The Austrian army will closely guard the whole length of the Salzach river up to and including Salzburg, to prevent the Argentinian escaping across the border. The Austrians are cooperating with us so long as the fighting remains on German soil. They have no jurisdiction to arrest the Argentinian or his men as they have not broken any law in Austria."

"I could go and hide in the area now, along with Robert. We are both trained snipers and the Argentinian is bound to send scouts to explore the lie of the land and work out how best to attack. As you said at the beginning of this week, the more of the enemy we can knock out before it comes to the showdown, the better."

"It sounds like a good idea, and you do know the area better than anyone else, but it's very dangerous and I don't know whether Mr. Buchenmeyer will approve of your plan. Why don't you go and speak to Robert while I ask him?"

"Yes, I'll do that now." Matteo strolled over to Robert.

Chapter Thirty-Six

FRIDAY EVENING UNTIL SATURDAY AFTERNOON, 30 SEPTEMBER-1 OCTOBER

Mr. Buchenmeyer spoke to Matteo and Robert personally before approving their plan. "As soon as you give us the coordinates of your positions, we shall try to protect you, but I'm afraid there is no guarantee. Please wear your full protective clothing and don't take any chances. There is no need for you to shoot the enemy and disclose your presence to them, just let us know their positions. Good luck!"

Matteo and Robert looked at the map again and discussed where to take up their positions, about a hundred metres from the entrance to the cave. Then they put on their bulletproof vests, camouflage clothing, and collected their sniper rifles, assault rifles, Glocks, and grenade launchers. Sven drove them to Scheffau, dropped them off, wished them luck, and returned to Ramsau. It was midnight and the tension began to rise.

Matteo could see the lights of Hallein shining below him. They stretched along the Salzach river, in the shadow of the Untersberg massif, close to the border with Germany. Reflecting colourfully on the river's surface, the lights twinkled brightly, competing with the stars in the currently dark midnight blue sky. The moon stood high amongst them, on the wane. It wasn't difficult to understand why Franz Xaver Gruber had composed the carol 'Silent Night, Holy Night' in just this spot.

Robert took leave of Matteo to take up his position as agreed. Matteo darkened his face and hands with the peaty soil and then scrambled down the mountain slope until he was about eighty metres below the cave.

The ground was dotted with shrubs and rocks among knee-high grass that was now pale brown, dead, and partly flattened from the recent rain.

Matteo crouched behind a metre-high rock, flanked by low shrubs. He was wearing night-vision glasses and chose a few more rocks and bushes where he could take short zigzagging runs to change his location whenever necessary. Then he removed the sniper rifle from his back and tested the range and various angles, resting it on the rock in front of him in different places. Satisfied that his position was good, he radioed Robert so he knew his exact location. Robert was behind the entrance to the cave. Although Matteo was ready for a long wait, he didn't stop scanning the area surrounding him even for a second. He was hyped up, but at the same time, deadly calm, determined to make sure Freya's rapists and his colleagues' murderers were brought to justice.

The minutes ticked by and turned to hours. Nothing stirred. The only sound was a low rumble of traffic on the motorway far away in the distance. At 4:30 a.m., a few birds began to sing and flitter from one bush to the next. At 5 a.m., it began to drizzle. Finally, at 5:30 a.m., he recognised the blurred shapes of Mr. Buchenmeyer, Sven, Ivanna, and Toby. They came along the road by foot, so they must've left the car in Scheffau. Dawn began to break and low rain clouds hung between the hills, making visibility poor. It was also cold. Not freezing, though. Matteo had spent colder nights at twenty-two below zero in frozen snow, but this was an unpleasant wet kind of cold that seeped into one's bones.

Matteo was becoming impatient, when he noticed a bustle of activity. It wasn't so much that he clearly saw men arriving and taking up their posts, rather that the numerous bushes began to sway back and forth like waves in the sea. He called in to Sven, who confirmed that the German army had arrived. They were just waiting for the GSG 9 agents to also take up their positions before calling for the excavator that was waiting in the village of Scheffau.

As they were talking, Matteo noticed new movement coming from the east. He quickly interrupted Sven. "Now. Three perpetrators forty-seven degrees, forty-two minutes north, thirteen degrees, three minutes east." He saw Sven looking through binoculars and then passing them to Mr. Buchenmeyer. "I have a clear aim at number three. Asking for permission to act," Matteo said urgently.

"Aim to incapacitate, not kill – permission given," Sven replied. Matteo had a clear view with no obstacles in between. He took a shot and heard a yelp as the bullet hit the man's right hand, which was holding an assault rifle. The rifle dropped to the ground and the two men in front of their colleague turned around to see what had happened. Matteo fired two more shots rapidly one after the other. He had also hit the other men on their right hands. He hadn't had time to ask for permission, but Sven's voice crackled down the radio in sheer amazement. "Crikey, those were three helluva good shots!"

Matteo, crouching low, ran in a zigzag line to change his position to behind a different rock a few metres nearer to the cave. A bullet pinged off the rock close to where he had been hiding seconds before. He estimated the coordinates of the new sharpshooter and radioed them through to Sven. Just then, the heavy excavator came into sight as it slowly rumbled down the road from Scheffau and stopped in front of the cave. All eyes watched as it began to manoeuvre its dipper arm and bucket to remove shrubs that had grown among the rocks in the last seventy-five years.

Swinging the driver cabin around back and forth, the excavator emptied its bucket again and again, releasing the contents down the hill. Bare rocks became visible. Some rocks were so large they didn't fit into the bucket. Instead, the driver used the excavator's bucket cylinder to drag the rocks from the top left corner of the cave entrance onto the ground in front of the entrance. The driver used the bucket to drag down more rocks and shove them out of the way so that the entrance became clear. A small hole became visible in the top left-hand corner and Ivanna and Toby scrambled rapidly through the opening.

As if on cue, three enemy helicopters appeared out of the low rain clouds and to the amazement of the onlookers, six skydivers jumped out of the open cabins. They looked like gigantic black vultures swooping down for the kill. Unfortunately, they were too far away to get a good shot, and they continuously changed their angles to the ground. Matteo aimed and fired, but his sniper rifle didn't have the range, and the shot landed short.

The events raced. Within seconds of sighting the skydivers, two Cessnas were spotted following the helicopters, and at least eight men jumped out of the rear of the planes, releasing parachutes as they fell. Simultaneously, they threw bundles of smoking dynamite to the ground below them, which exploded erratically, causing the German army officers to jump up, disclosing their locations. The skydivers had rid themselves of their skydiving suits and were shooting their way towards the cave. The men with parachutes had landed and were following them, shooting in all directions.

The German army and the GSG 9 agents started firing back. Matteo lost the overview of who held the winning hand. Mr. Buchenmeyer had clearly said to aim to injure but not to kill. The enemy army had no such scruples. The Argentinian's private army seemed to grow by the second. About a hundred men had arrived from goodness knows where and were dodging between the rocks and the shrubs. They used grenade launchers to cause explosions in all directions, and from ground level, all Matteo could see was smoke. It was total chaos. It was impossible to determine which soldiers and agents belonged to the Argentinian army and which were their own.

Changing his position again to try to find a better place to recognise the enemy, Matteo saw two black figures climbing like spiders into the cave. To most of the home army they were invisible, as the enemy army had once again thrown smoke bombs to confuse the situation.

Matteo thought that one of the figures was almost certainly the Argentinian and wanted to follow them. At this very moment, an enemy shot the excavator's driver and climbed into the vehicle himself, threw the driver to the ground, took over the steering wheel, and accelerated along the road straight towards Sven.

The enemy driver scooped the astonished Sven up into

the bucket and dumped him over the side of a hairpin curve straight down the mountainside. It happened so quickly, Matteo's mouth opened in shock. He was still fifty metres further down the mountain slope than the road where the majority of the fighting was taking place, and probably in the best available position to rescue Sven. He scuttled sideways to the west like a crab, and after several hundred metres found Sven lying on a rocky outcrop on his back about fifty metres below the road.

"I'm here, where does it hurt?" Matteo asked.

"I'm a bit winded, but otherwise it's just my left leg. It must've caught on a rock somewhere or maybe a branch."

"I'm going to get help for you," Matteo reassured him.

"No, don't worry about me, I'll be all right. Make sure the others are okay," Sven replied.

Matteo was already on the radio and speaking with David. "Only if you're sure," he said. "It'll be a hell of a risk. As soon as the enemy sees you, they will shoot. But if you stay above the rain clouds until the last minute and let me know when you think you're here, then I'll shoot a flare into the sky. Once you confirm, I can launch a dozen smoke grenades while you let down a winch. A stretcher will take too long, but Sven says it's just his left leg. I'll grab the winch, and he can hold on to me." Matteo gave David their coordinates.

"Right, give me seven," David said, meaning seven minutes.

"Did you hear all that?" Matteo asked Sven. "You're going to have to hang onto me like crazy. As soon as I give David the sign, he'll fly away with the winch still hanging. Someone will haul us up, but it might take a couple of minutes until we're inside the helicopter. Are you ready?"

"Er, I guess so," Sven answered.

"Good, he'll be here pronto."

Just a few minutes later, Matteo received David's radio message. Matteo shot a flare into the sky. David confirmed via radio, and his colleague in the helicopter cabin started to let the winch down. Matteo launched smoke grenades into the sky one after the other until he could grab the winch. Stupidly, he decided against putting his harness on, to save time. He knew the enemy were just waiting for the smoke to clear. He got as close to Sven as he could. Sven wrapped his arms tightly around Matteo's chest and Matteo checked.

"Ready?"

Sven nodded and Matteo tugged the winch line twice to signal to their colleague in the helicopter to haul them up.

The helicopter sped away, diving sideways and downwards out of the line of enemy fire. The winch jerked and Matteo and Sven were dragged off the rocky outcrop. They hung in the air above the forest a hundred dizzying metres below them. The winch line was long and swung back and forth despite the weight that was supposed to prevent just that. Bullets whistled past Matteo's ears, barely missing him. But over time the winch became shorter and the bullets fewer.

Suddenly Matteo's jacket ripped, and he felt Sven slipping. The air was wrenched from his lungs. He wrapped his legs tightly around Sven's body to stop him falling. Sven snatched Matteo's belt with one hand. Matteo's hamstrings were burning; he couldn't hold on much longer. Adrenaline raced through his body. Sven seized the belt with his second hand as the winch line became shorter.

Matteo had laced his feet around Sven's legs, but they were trembling with the effort. He looked upwards to the open cabin door and recognised Julian. The helicopter roared as it picked up speed, slicing through the stormy sky. Julian's heart slammed against his ribs as he spotted Matteo—dangling precariously, without a harness.

"Hold on!" Julian shouted over the deafening rotor blades, yanking the winch control to full throttle. Wind howled through the open hatch as he dropped onto his stomach, arms reaching desperately into the void.

Sven was first—his fingers barely brushing Julian's before he lunged, grabbing hold and dragging him into the cabin. No time to catch his breath. Matteo was next. With one final surge of strength, Julian grasped Matteo's wrist and heaved him inside, just as the helicopter jolted upward. The hatch slammed shut, sealing them away from the abyss below. Safe—at last.

Matteo lay on his back, breathing heavily. "You should have put the harness on," Julian reprimanded him. "It's a miracle you didn't both die."

"Two seconds longer on the ground and the enemy would have shot us," Matteo retorted. "But of course you're right. It was lucky you got us into the cabin in time."

Matteo looked at Sven's leg. There was a long deep gash in his thigh where the leg must've caught on the branch of a tree or on a rock as he fell from the excavator's bucket. "It will need stitches," Matteo told Sven. "What about otherwise? Have you any other pain? Can you move your limbs without any trouble?"

"I'm fine, and the thigh isn't too bad. You shouldn't have risked your life and David's and Julian's to rescue me. I could have waited until the fighting was over. Thank you though. Thanks to all of you."

Matteo refrained from answering that the enemy would have shot Sven at the first opportunity, and, as with Sven and Julian, took a seat in the helicopter. They fastened their safety belts and put headphones on so they could communicate with one another.

"How bad are the injuries?" David asked.

"Not bad at all, but I need some stitches. Can the local hospital in Berchtesgaden do that? I want to get back to the operations centre as soon as possible," Sven answered.

"Yes, that won't be a problem. I'm over Ramsau now. I'll land here, then someone can drive you to outpatients in Berchtesgaden." David radioed the heliport and landed. They all got out of the helicopter, happy to be safe and alive. Sven was limping and looked pale.

"Let me take you to outpatients," Julian offered. "You look as if you've lost quite a lot of blood. Let's not waste time."

Sven agreed and Matteo gave Julian the keys to his Unimog. David was examining the outside of the helicopter, running his hand gently along the outer panelling and talking to it as if it were his girlfriend.

"Any damage?" Matteo asked.

"Very little. There are two bullet scrapes on the landing skids, that's all. We were lucky."

"In that case I'm going to the operations centre to find out the latest. The fight is over for me. I can hardly return to Scheffau now. I've been up all night, so I'll grab a bite to eat and then lie down for an hour or two."

"Good idea, if you wait a minute I'll join you."

Chapter Thirty-Seven

SATURDAY MORNING, 1 OCTOBER

Ivanna and Toby scrambled up the rocks towards the small entrance that the excavator had cleared. Ivanna was in the lead, but before she crawled through the hole, she paused and turned around to Toby. "Do you want to go in first?" she asked. "After all, you discovered the cave."

"No, you go first. If you hadn't found the map, we wouldn't be here."

Ivanna crawled through the hole, which was only a metre wide. In front of her was an open space the size of two tennis courts and roughly five metres high. The temperature was cool but warmer than outside. The air smelled of petroleum or rather burnt diesel. It overlaid the faint aroma of salt-saturated air, but there was something else, too, something unpleasant, similar to sulphur. She stepped aside to make room for Toby and called to him, "Come on, it's amazing!"

She climbed down to ground level looking all around her, conscious of the fact that she was the first person to enter the cave for seventy-five years. She wore a steel helmet with a headlamp but now she also switched her power torch on. She touched her GoPro camera hanging around her neck to make sure it was still there. Toby came down to her and they stood in silence, in awe of the enormity of their discovery.

Ivanna pointed to one side of the cave. "Look! There are still some old tools there." She went around the cave, taking photographs and marvelling at old pickaxes, spades and wheelbarrows. Some rugs and tattered dirty clothing also lay on the floor. The tools looked as if they had been barely serviceable, even seventy-five years ago. The spades were full of dents and the blades chipped. Together they went around the cave, picking up some of the items and documenting everything on Ivanna's camera.

They had immediately noticed the passage at the far end of the cave, and now, satisfied that they had seen everything in this part of the salt mine, they walked along the passage. They had only walked a few metres when they came to a flight of steep wooden steps leading deep down further underground. Ivanna and Toby looked at each other, nodded, and went down the stairs backwards.

"If the prisoners had to move crates of plunder down here, it must've been very difficult. Maybe we've found just an ordinary salt mine, without any treasure," Ivanna commented, a little disappointed.

"Well, they would've had ropes and the opening is plenty large enough. With enough men it could've been feasible."

"Don't forget they were starved and many of them ill."

"Yes, but to have survived that long, they must also have had an innate will to live. Anyway, we'll know soon enough now," Toby replied.

At the bottom of the steps there was a small cavern a quarter the size of the upper one. Another set of wooden steps, longer, narrower and even steeper led once again down into the depths. Ivanna raised her eyebrows but went down the steps without a comment. The smell of petroleum intensified. Toby followed her. They found a long wide passageway, at least three metres high and with many more passages leading off to either side as far as the eye could see. All along the roof of the passages were strong black hooks, some with a lantern still hanging from them.

"We should've brought paraffin with us," Toby commented.

Without their headlamps and torches the passages would have been as dark as black holes in space. The air was damp and cold. They were cut off from any outdoor sounds and the silence was intimidating. The atmosphere was sinister, and Ivanna shivered thinking of the poor prisoners of war who had been forced to work here. Ivanna made herself busy taking photographs, then she asked, "Which passage shall we begin with? And how can we make sure we don't get lost?"

"Let's just start with the first one and see how we get along," Toby suggested.

As they got nearer to the first passage on their left, Toby saw the Roman numeral 'I' engraved on the rock to the left of the entrance. "Look, they're numbered!" He shone his torch exactly on the number to show Ivanna. Then he went along the other passages and found more numbers. "We'll be okay," he told Ivanna. "They're all numbered. Come on, let's get a start on passage number one!"

This time Toby took the lead. He appeared excited and his mood caught on with Ivanna. They had hardly walked twenty metres when they saw yet more passages leading off from this passage.

"Oh no! It's labyrinthine," Ivanna uttered full of dismay.

"No. Look here!" Toby shone his torch on an old,

roughly made wooden frame. Inside the frame was a piece of typed paper. The ink was faded but still readable. "Dental gold, Dachau." Toby entered the cavern and faced three walls all full of medium-sized wooden crates stacked on top of each other from floor to ceiling. He tried to move one, then, realising the weight, called to Ivanna, "Come and help me pull this crate to the floor," he requested.

Ivanna hesitated. The words 'dental gold' filled her with dread. What was she to expect? Did the Nazis pull the gold teeth of the inmates of the concentration camps before they were gassed or afterwards? Tears came to her eyes. Would there be thousands of gold teeth in the crates? She felt unable to move.

"Come on! I don't want to drop the crate and let the contents spill on the floor," Toby said.

That would be even worse, Ivanna shuddered. She braced herself and went to help Toby. They lifted one crate from the top of the stack to the floor, surprised at the weight. Toby removed a crowbar from his rucksack, which he had brought with him, along with other tools, in anticipation of what might be needed. He eased the lid of the crate open. It was full of gold bars. How many thousands of teeth needed to be melted down to produce one bar of gold? While Ivanna was grateful that the contents hadn't been scarier, Toby took a mental scan of the number and size of the crates. He wanted to roughly work out the value of the crates, but after a moment's contemplation, he gave up.

Ivanna took pictures and then they went from one cavern to the next, photographing the wooden frames and typed contents list. The whole passage was full of crates filled with gold bars, although not all from teeth. She also photographed each cave full of crates, but they didn't open any more wooden boxes. Instead, they went to passage number 'II'. Once again it was labyrinthine, but this time the caves were full of jewels, diamonds sorted by size and clarity, rubies, emeralds, pearls and sapphires. Finally, there was a small cave filled with crates full of jewellery made and designed by famous jewellers throughout Europe. In one crate there was a wedding dress made from Bruges lace and studded with pearls. How sad, Ivanna thought. Had the bride even seen her wedding day? They opened a crate in each room and Ivanna took her time documenting everything. She went back to the cave with the diamonds together with Toby.

"Look!" she said to Toby, "I'm going to take one diamond with me, you are my witness. It's proof in case anything happens to me or my camera. Do the same. This is too big to leave here empty-handed. It's taking too long to photograph and document everything. Let's just see what is in the other caves and then let's get out of here."

Toby agreed. He had no idea how long they had already been there, but it would take months if not years to categorise the contents of the salt mine. He had read a book about the Altaussee treasure and seen photographs. The Rothschild family coin collection, paintings, and other heirlooms had been found there. He guessed that the discovery of this mine was in an even higher league. It must be left to the experts. Together they rushed now, finding two passages with sculptures and another with fine arts and paintings.

Ivanna took one last photograph and then said, "Okay, let's get out of here!"

They walked briskly back to the beginning of the passage and Ivanna had her right foot on the bottom step of the wooden stairs when they heard loud voices and footsteps coming down the first flight of stairs. Toby put a finger over his mouth, and taking Ivanna's hand pulled her backwards and raced back down the passage where they had come from. The crates with designer jewellery were the lightest, and entering the cavern, he pushed a line of crates a little away from the wall. He pushed Ivanna into the space left between the wall and the wooden crates and then followed her. "I hope the intruders will be so in awe of their findings that they won't notice the gap," he whispered.

"But they'll know someone's been here," Ivanna protested quietly. "We left so many crates open."

Toby shrugged. "Maybe it's not so important. There's so much loot here, enough for a whole army."

They could hear one man running along the passage, and from the sound of his feet, probably taking a fleeting glance in each cavern. He entered their cave, uttering loud whoops of joy. He pulled some crates onto the floor, letting them break open and spilling their contents on the floor.

Ivanna could see the man through a tiny gap between the crates in front of her. She recognised him immediately from the photographs she'd seen; it was the Argentinian! His teeth were stained brown from nicotine. What a stupid thing to notice, she reproached herself. He continued opening crates like a wild man, his gleaming eyes flashing madly. He unfastened some of the small leather cases inside the crates. There were necklaces, tiaras, bracelets, brooches, rings, and much more.

The Argentinian ran his hands through the valuable plunder, laughing giddily. He removed the rucksack from his back and started filling it with jewellery. For a moment he looked straight into Ivanna's eyes, and she was terrified that he had discovered her presence. She held her breath and was relieved as she heard his steps exit the cave.

"That was close!" she whispered to Toby. He nudged

her to be silent as a second man now entered the cavern. Once again, she recognised him from the photographs. It was Rollo, the Argentinian's second-in-command. He too filled his rucksack with jewels, but he didn't stay long before following the Argentinian.

Ivanna and Toby stayed where they were, waiting for the two men to disappear. They heard the Argentinian again and again uttering cries and hollers of joy.

"He must be in the cave with the paintings now," Toby told Ivanna in a low soft voice. The cave's walls were bare and so deep underground that they could hear every single sound echoing back-and-forth. Ivanna and Toby could hear the Argentinian's voice as clearly as if he were standing next to them. He was swooning over a painting by Claude Monet, *Manet Painting in Monet's Garden*. It wasn't hard to imagine him cradling the painting like a new-born child. Rollo wasn't so impressed by the painting itself, but he was interested in its value. The Argentinian told him to fill his rucksack with diamonds. The gold bars would be too heavy to carry and the paintings impossible to sell.

The Argentinian continued to unwrap the paintings. They heard him name *Five Dancing Women* from Edgar Degas, *An Angel with Titus' Features* from Rembrandt van Rijn, and *Picadors with Bulls Before a Tower* from Francisco Jose de Goya y Lucientes. The two cousins heard the Argentinian cursing that the last painting was too large to take with him, but there were many more. He ordered Rollo to help him turn the paintings over gently, remove the canvasses from the frames, roll them up and place them in his rucksack.

As the Argentinian and Rollo passed the cave where Toby and Ivanna were hiding, the Argentinian told Rollo, "I'm just going to fill the rucksack and my pockets with diamonds. It is almost full already and yours looks full too. We can't carry any more... must be satisfied with what we have."

"But what about the cousins, they must be here somewhere? Surely you don't want to let them go free?" Rollo protested.

"Why not? They won't be armed, otherwise they could have shot us already. They can't stop us escaping, that's the main thing."

"But..."

"Enough! I've spoken."

Ivanna and Toby had been listening with bated breath, now they started breathing again, relieved. "Let's wait until they've well and truly gone," Toby suggested. "I'll feel safer that way." They remained behind the crates, just in case the Argentinian's words had been a ruse. They pricked their ears, trying to catch every sound.

They were soon rewarded. The Argentinian must've been near the exit, where mobile radio reception was possible. He was speaking to someone via radio, telling him that he was finished in the cave and that they should provide smokescreens and confusion for five minutes to allow him to escape. After that, his army should retreat without delay and go to the previously arranged pickup point, a private airport, where they would be flown out of the country in a variety of small aircraft.

Scarcely had he finished speaking than there was a huge detonation and the sound of a rock fall.

Chapter Thirty-Eight

SATURDAY, 1 OCTOBER

The Argentinian had left Rollo filling his pockets with diamonds and run away swiftly, climbing up over the rocks to the exit. He had spoken rapidly with the commander of his army and then removed a bundle of dynamite sticks from his pocket, lit the fuse, and thrown the bundle behind him into the cave. If he couldn't have the treasure, then nobody else should either. As he climbed through the small hole to the outside world, he heard a huge explosion behind him and the sound of falling rock. He hoped Rollo would die – he had been getting too big for his boots – and as for the two cousins? Well, they deserved no better, and they had served their purpose now.

Taking advantage of the shooting and chaos in front of the cave, the Argentinian managed to slip away unnoticed, over the hill behind the cave and then westwards. His escape route had been meticulously planned for weeks. First, he would visit friends who had a ski lodge just outside of Kitzbühel. From there, his friends would drive him to Liechtenstein, where he would leave the contents of his rucksack in his safe deposit box in the LGT Bank in Vaduz. The paintings and jewels could stay there safely for several years until the initial interest about the theft died down.

Of course, he knew the Germans would reopen the cave now it had been found, but on the other hand, he doubted that they would know exactly what was missing. If he was lucky, he could retrieve the paintings next year. After Liechtenstein, he had arranged to stay with friends on their 'masseria', a fortified farm, several centuries old, in the hills of Lombardia. He would stay there for several weeks, before boarding a luxury liner leaving Genoa and heading for Buenos Aires. He hoped he would soon be presumed dead, but if customs were still looking for him, then he could change his appearance and he had a supply of various passports.

He had chosen to travel through Austria to Liechtenstein, rather than Germany, as the Austrians had no jurisdiction to search for him or arrest him. Now he just needed to cross the border into Austria.

Ironically, he was less than a kilometre from the border now. But he knew that the German and Austrian border police would be patrolling every centimetre of the banks of the Salzach river. Luckily for him, the German agents, they were so stupid, had already shown him an alternative route via the Klausbach valley.

*****

Friedrich Horn had spent the morning collecting gentian flowers again. The season was ending, and his basket was only half full. He was close to Gasthof Auzinger, and it was lunchtime, so he decided to have a break. They offered a low-priced lunch. Despite the cold, he sat out of doors, because he wanted to smoke. He had just ordered and was settling down with a beer when he saw a man dressed in black walk by.

Had the man been wearing normal hiking attire, Friedrich wouldn't have given him a second glance. As it was, the black clothing was unusual, and Friedrich, as always curious, examined him attentively. Scarcely had the man passed, when Friedrich took the flyer out of his inside jacket pocket and studied the photographs. My God! He was right. It was the man they called 'the Argentinian' and was, supposedly, extremely dangerous.

With trembling fingers, he took his phone from his pocket and the paper napkin on which Matteo had written his telephone number. He dialled.

*****

The operations centre had installed a few cubicles complete with field beds for agents needing a rest. Some of the team members had long hours of duty during the night. Matteo had lain down half an hour ago but found no sleep. He lay on his back, his eyes wide open, and when his telephone rang, he sat up immediately to answer it.

"Freddie! What a surprise, how are you?"

"Don't bother about that now. I've just seen that man you're looking for, the dangerous one, the Argentinian."

"What? Where? Are you sure? Where are you now?"

"It's him all right, there's nothing wrong with my eyes. All dressed in black, he is. Sticks out like a palm tree on the Watzmann. Not a very good disguise. If he's supposed to be in hiding, I mean."

"Where are you?"

"Gasthof Auzinger. Waiting for my lunch."

"And the Argentinian is there, eating lunch?" Matteo asked incredulously.

"No, dumbass! He's just walked past, heading for the Hirschbichl."

"The Austrian border, of course! Quick, we must stop him crossing!"

"How do you expect me to do that? Anyway, my lunch will be arriving soon."

"Did you see which route he took? Low, middle or high?"

"High, strangely enough. Made me wonder, that."

"Blessed be the heavens... he'll need longer that way. He probably wants to avoid meeting anybody. Look, forget your lunch, I'll make it up to you. Follow him now, quickly, but take the road. Have you got your binoculars with you?"

"Yes, of course, I always do."

"Fantastic. Then go as quickly as you can. I'll come immediately. Try to keep an eye on him."

Matteo left the cubicle and hurried to put his jacket on. David, who'd been in the neighbouring cubicle, rushed out after him.

"I heard that. I'll fly you to the Gasthof. I can land on the field opposite, and it'll save time."

"Great, thanks. Do you fancy coming with me? Sven will still be at outpatients and Julian will be with him. Robert is near the cave."

"Sure. Better still, I'll get the commander to fly us out, then he can bring the helicopter back here. We'll need some weapons."

David struggled to put his jacket on while telephoning his commander, who was in the hangar. Matteo unlocked the gun cupboard and took out a couple of Glocks and two sniper rifles, before running outside with David to the helipad. The commander was just climbing into the mountain rescue helicopter. They took off within seconds and landed just a few minutes later. Matteo and David jumped out of the cabin and, without waving goodbye, set off running along the so-called 'high' path through the Klausbach valley.

At first the path was broad with a flat, even surface. It was pleasant for running, although it went continually uphill. Matteo's telephone rang. It was Freddie.

"I can see you. And I can see the Argentinian as well. You're about twenty minutes behind him."

"And how far is he from the border?"

"About fifteen minutes."

"Ah, shit! Keep on going if you can, Freddie."

Matteo rang off and told David, "We must turn up a gear. He's twenty minutes ahead of us."

*****

The Argentinian had no idea that he was being watched, nor that he was being followed. In fact, he was quite happy that he had met no one along his way. However, he didn't want to dawdle and strode out briskly. For the last two kilometres, climbing up above the Bindalm, a summer meadow pasture for cattle, over a thousand metres high, the path had become much narrower and much steeper. There was a sprinkling of snow, and the air was very chilly. The trail was flanked by dense forest on each side. Suddenly, in the middle of the path, just thirty metres in front of him, he saw a large black something that he had never seen before. He slowed his pace, advancing carefully. As he came closer, he recognised that it was a capercaillie.

He had never seen one in real life before, but ironically enough, he had seen one in a painting. Amazed, he took out his phone and wanted to photograph it. As he shot pictures, one after the other, he abruptly realised that the bird was coming towards him. It had spread out its wings, which were a metre wide, as wide as the path, and it seemed to be standing on its toes. With its neck stretched high and its beak turned towards the sky, it was screeching in a bloodcurdling manner. It came right up to the Argentinian, its head reaching halfway up his chest. The Argentinian was terrified. He let his telephone drop and started walking backwards. The capercaillie followed him. The Argentinian increased his pace, stumbled on the root of a tree and fell backwards onto his backside. He screamed.

*****

Matteo and David had been running quickly, continually catching up with the Argentinian. When they heard a scream, they sprinted as if their life depended upon it. Coming around the bend, they saw the Argentinian sitting in the middle of the path, a capercaillie towering above him. They both approached the enemy, Matteo grabbed his hands and pulled them behind his back, while David took a rope from his rucksack and tied them together as tightly as possible.

Matteo and David held hands and made themselves wide, wider than the path, and tall – they even stood on tiptoes. The capercaillie that had been defending its stomping ground saw Matteo and David as one person, and considering the size of its new opponent, fled back into the forest. The Argentinian looked at Matteo and David and the fleeing bird open-mouthed. With hardly any resistance, he let his legs be tied, his pockets emptied, and his rucksack removed from his back.

Matteo rang up the operations centre and gave them the news. They informed him that the fighting around the cave had ceased and that six GSG 9 agents would be sent immediately to pick the Argentinian up and accompany him to an armed vehicle that would take him to the high-security prison at Straubing.

Matteo gave the operator their coordinates and confirmed that he and David would wait until the agents arrived. Then he rang up Freddie, telling him the story, embroidering it a little, well knowing that Freddie would embellish it even more when telling all his friends. A few shots of complementary schnapps were guaranteed.

Chapter Thirty-Nine

SATURDAY, 1 OCTOBER

Ivanna and Toby heard the detonation followed by the rock fall. Startled, they both ran from their hiding place into the main passageway. They were met by clouds of thick dust billowing their way down the wooden steps into the passage and into the caves.

"Stay here," Toby told Ivanna. "I'll go up and see what the damage is." He climbed tentatively up the wooden stairs, poking his head out of the opening before going further to the next flight of stairs and doing the same. As he looked into the large, main cave, he clamped his hand quickly over his mouth to smother his scream. The cave, previously as large as four tennis courts, was now half full of fallen rocks. He looked to where the entrance should have been, but it was blocked with rocks up to the ceiling. His heart sank. Remembering the Argentinian and Rollo, he examined the fallen rocks carefully. He felt a quick shot of adrenaline as he discovered a white hand sticking out between the rocks.

Trembling, he called out, "Hello," but got no answer.

The man was surely dead, he thought. However, his conscience persuaded him to go to the body and feel the wrist for a pulse. There was none. It would be pointless to try to uncover the body. He had a feeling he would be needing his energy for other things.

Toby climbed up the rocks to where the entrance had been and dialled Sven's telephone number. It didn't ring, and Toby was still so on edge from the detonation, rock fall and dead body, that he presumed they had no mobile reception. Nervous about the fate that awaited him and Ivanna, he hastily climbed back down the rocks, not paying as much attention as before. He slipped and fell backwards onto the hard rock floor of the cave, knocking the back of his skull with a hefty crack. His fall loosened more rocks on the pile, and they came tumbling after him, one of them hitting him full on his forehead.

The fall wrenched all the air from him. He lay on his back for a minute wondering if he was still alive. Warm fluid ran across his forehead and backwards through his hair and into his ear. He could feel it and realised that he was indeed still alive. The rock hitting his forehead had obviously caused a bump, but it had split open and was bleeding, which was a good sign, much better than causing internal bleeding. He wondered about the cracking sound the back of his skull had made when hitting the floor; he didn't seem to be bleeding there. He tried to move his head very slightly from right to left. It was possible and his thoughts were clear, so he must be all right, at least for now. He remembered Ivanna and, using his elbows, tried to sit up. He immediately felt sick and dizzy. His vision spun and his head throbbed. He let himself down again and felt better.

He must've then fallen asleep, because when he opened

his eyes again, he saw Ivanna kneeling beside him and looking very concerned.

"How are you feeling?" she asked.

Toby smiled weakly. "As if I've been run over by an excavator."

"Well, don't worry, help is on the way. Are you comfortable?"

"Yes, my head… Did you put something under it?"

Ivanna smiled and answered, "Yes, one of the rugs that the prisoners of war used. Don't worry, I shook the dust out and the back of your head isn't bleeding, so no bacteria can reach your bloodstream."

"What are we going to do? I know that no help is on the way. There's no need to lie to me, to comfort me. I saw myself, before I fell, that we have no mobile reception."

"What makes you think that? The connection was bad and kept breaking up, but they know we're here, and that you're injured and I'm alive and well. The fighting has ceased outside, the Argentinian's army has withdrawn, and as we speak, the excavator is shifting rocks to make a new entrance. I've even spoken to a doctor and described your injuries. He told me to make sure that you stayed lying down and that you drank enough. Talking of which…" Ivanna removed a bottle of water from her rucksack. "Here, have a sip." She supported Toby's head, and he drank greedily. "Slowly now, just one sip at a time. We don't know how long this bottle must last for."

"Have you seen my rucksack? I brought a bottle of water with me, too. Don't forget to drink something yourself. How long was I asleep for?"

"I'm not sure, not long, maybe an hour. When you didn't come back, I climbed the steps to come and look for you. I saw you straight away, of course. Your pulse was steady at ninety-two. I stayed with you while I dialled the operations centre. They told me about the fighting having ceased and connected me with the doctor. They also said that Matteo and David have caught the Argentinian, so I told them that our dead body must be Rollo. They were as pleased as punch, but then they didn't believe my description of the treasure, so I sent them a couple of photographs, just three, but I've a feeling that they're partying already!"

"No, they wouldn't dare to start without us."

Ivanna laughed. "You won't believe what else they told me. A mercenary killed the driver of the excavator and then, driving it himself, scooped Sven up in the bucket and dumped him over the mountainside!"

"Oh my God! Please don't tell me he died. So that's why his telephone didn't ring."

"You rang Sven? Wait until you hear the rest. Matteo saw it happen and went to rescue him. He had fallen onto a rocky outcrop and wasn't seriously injured. Then David and Julian flew the helicopter to where they were and let down a winch. They were rescued and flew to Ramsau. Julian took Sven to the outpatients at the local hospital in Berchtesgaden. I can't wait to hear the whole story. But even if Sven lost his mobile, it should have rung when you dialled."

"I don't know. Maybe he didn't lose it but turned it off in the helicopter."

"Didn't you get a message, you know, the one that says that the receiver isn't available."

Toby blushed a little. "Maybe I didn't wait long enough. I was nervous, seeing the amount of rock fall and the dead body."

"Well, it doesn't matter now, and it wouldn't have made any difference anyhow."

"What about the excavator? You said a mercenary stole it."

"Oh yes, of course, I forgot to tell you. After dumping Sven, the mercenary continued driving the excavator up the road towards Scheffau. Then, but this is just speculation from Nicole at the operations centre, he probably realised that the road was too narrow for him to turn the excavator around. Presumably he didn't want to drive to Scheffau, so he just left it there and went back to his commander.

"After the fighting was over, a mechanic checked the excavator. There were several bullet holes in the metal panelling, but the motor was in order, as were the caterpillars. In other words, it was battered but serviceable. Can't you hear it now?"

Toby listened. "Now you say so, faintly yes."

"Hmm, I can hear it quite clearly. Maybe your hearing has suffered. Now, listen! A helicopter is landing, probably on the road outside the cave. Can't you hear it?"

"Yes, yes. I can hear it well."

"Ah, thank goodness, it can't be too bad then."

The cousins waited, chatting away to pass the time and listening to the comforting sounds of the excavator removing boulders. About fifteen minutes later, Ivanna's mobile rang.

"Hello?" she said.

"Hello, Dr. Reiter here. Am I speaking to Ivanna?"

"Yes."

"Ah, good. How is our patient doing?"

"He's woken up and is chatting coherently. He drank some water and kept it down. When he sits up, he feels dizzy, and so I've kept him lying down."

"That sounds quite good. When we get to you, we'll give him a neck brace and transport him. Once he's in hospital, we can give him an MRI and then we'll know exactly what the trouble is. He may have fractured his skull or, if he's lucky, just have concussion. How much water has he drunk?"

"Not a lot. I was saving it, not knowing how long we would be in here for."

"Well, don't save it, we should be able to bring you fresh water within the next quarter of an hour. And don't forget to drink yourself. There are about twenty people here helping to remove stones and small rocks with their bare hands. The excavator is pulling and pushing the larger boulders away to one side. There is a man in charge, a Mr. Stadel, an expert engineer for this type of thing, and he is being very careful to avoid any new rock fall. However, he has ensured me that they will soon be able to make a hole large enough to pass water, medicine and food through. If your cousin is in a lot of pain, I can give him something for it. Will you ask him for me?"

"Yes, of course. Toby?" she asked, still on the phone, and on loudspeaker so that Dr Reiter could hear her. "Do you want something for the pain?"

"No, not now, thank you. I can bear it," Toby answered.

"Did you hear that?" Ivanna asked the doctor.

"Yes, that's fine. Now don't forget to drink. We'll be seeing each other soon."

Ivanna gave Toby water to drink and drank herself until both bottles were empty. They continued to talk, particularly, Ivanna wondered whether they had made the right decision to show the authorities the map. So many people had died. She supposed that the paintings and sculptures would be returned to the various museums all over Europe, but what about the jewellery? Were the Jewish families from whom they had been stolen still alive? And the gold? And the dental gold? She shuddered at these last words and Toby held her hand to comfort her.

"Don't forget that if the Argentinian has been caught, then one of the world's largest drug cartels will be shattered." Toby tried to console her.

"But then won't a new one rise up?" Ivanna asked sceptically. "Anyway, I certainly don't want a reward for finding the treasure. I could never find peace with myself for profiting from the massive injustice done to other people."

"I wouldn't either," Toby replied. "But we're a long way from that yet. I suppose there are a lot of worthy causes we could donate to."

While they had been discussing the tragic topic, Ivanna had been keeping an eye on the top right-hand corner of the original cave opening. Although the sounds of scraping came nearer, at first, she couldn't see any daylight. Then suddenly there was a glimmer of light. "There, look!" She pointed to the middle of the cave at the top. Someone was pushing a bottle of water through a small hole. "I'm coming!" Ivanna called.

"Be careful!" Toby called after her disappearing figure. "Don't stumble and fall, like I did."

Ivanna, more cheerful now, scrambled up the rocks and took several bottles of water and apple juice being reached through the hole, along with power bars and fruit. A male voice told her, "Hang on, we'll need two hours at the most, and then we'll get you out of there."

The man was true to his word. Ivanna and Toby ate and drank and watched the hole become larger and larger. An hour and a half later, a man started crawling through the space.

"Hello, I'm Dr. Reiter. I'll be right down." He turned around and took his medical bag that someone had pushed in behind him. Then he climbed down the rocks and shook Ivanna's hand. "And this is the patient?" he asked in the sort of cheery voice that only doctors have. "This is my first house call in a cave. I didn't realise people still lived in them." As a reward, he received a weak smile from Toby, as he expected. "Nothing wrong with your mind then, good, good. If there had been any internal bleeding in your brain, then it would be showing its effects by now. So, I'll ask the medics to come with a stretcher and we'll get you out of here. Now then, young lady," he said to Ivanna. "I've been told to tell you to crawl back through that hole where I've just come from."

"I can't leave Toby alone," Ivanna protested.

"He won't be alone. I'm here and the medics will come just as soon as you're outside. Come on now, the helicopter is waiting."

Ivanna scrambled up the rocks on all fours and then crawled through the exit hole. She blinked her eyes to get used to the daylight and only then became aware of the sound of clapping. She looked around and saw a blue federal police helicopter on the road behind the excavator, and all around her, standing on rocks, about thirty men and women, pausing from their work and applauding her. She called out a thank you, took a little bow, and then scrambled down the rocks to the safe surface of the road.

In the meantime, several medics had entered the cave with a stretcher, and within fifteen minutes they reappeared with Toby lying on the stretcher with a collar brace. He was pushed into the rescue helicopter and it took off towards Traunstein hospital.

Chapter Forty

SATURDAY AFTERNOON, 1 OCTOBER

Ivanna watched the helicopter as it flew away. She stood on the road suddenly feeling empty. She had completed what she had originally come to Berchtesgaden for, finding the cave and documenting proof of the treasure, but at what a cost! So many people were dead or injured. She looked at her mobile; it was 3 p.m. on Saturday afternoon. She couldn't imagine going back to work on Monday morning and carrying on as usual. So much had happened in the last five days that she felt she would need at least another four weeks' holiday just to process all the events.

She looked around her. The GSG 9 agents had disappeared. No doubt they had gone back to wherever they had come from now the action was over. There were a few men and women in army clothing helping to remove rocks from in front of the cave, but most of the helpers wore civil clothing. Maybe they were volunteers from Scheffau. Five white plastic tents were erected in different locations, presumably covering corpses, she realised. Those killed in the fighting between the Argentinian's army and the Germans. She must ask Sven how many Germans had been killed or wounded. Hopefully no one she knew personally. Several members of the forensic team, all dressed in white overalls, were busy bagging up evidence, taking measurements and photographing.

She felt at a loss and completely out of place. She wondered what to do and decided to ring Sven to ask him if he could send a car to pick her up. Her luggage was at the operations centre in Ramsau, and before she went home, she needed to pick it up. Then she realised that she hadn't rung Toby's wife, Mel, yet, to let her know that Toby was at the hospital in Traunstein. She decided to do that first.

For as long as Mel, Olivia, and Olivia's husband, Hannes, and the four children had been in the safe house, their mobiles had been confiscated. Now the Argentinian had been arrested, they would be going back home and presumably their mobiles had been returned to them. Hopefully, they wouldn't be too cross with her for putting them in danger. There was no way she could have foreseen what had happened. In fact, none of the consequences after finding the map.

The lack of drugs available on the streets and the number of deaths from overdoses or even just the number of teenagers beginning to experiment with drugs, would counteract the deaths of Daniel, Bernhard, and Zehra; although their families would no doubt see that differently. She rang Mel's number but only got the voicemail. Hmm, strange. Oh well, she thought, and tried Olivia's number. Once again, she only got the voicemail. Now she was irritated and rang Sven.

"Hi, Sven, it's me, Ivanna."

"Ivanna, hi! How are you?"

"Fine. I wanted to ask you if someone could pick me up

and bring me to the operations centre. I need to pick up my luggage before I go home."

"Yes, of course. I'd come myself but... a new situation has cropped up. I'll ask Dennis, if that's okay with you? I presume you're outside the cave now. Is Toby with you?"

"No, sorry. I thought someone would've informed you. He fell and knocked his head in the cave and now he's been flown to Traunstein for an MRT. The doctor is sure that he's okay, though. It's just a precautionary measure. By the way, aren't Mel and Olivia home yet? I tried to reach them on their mobiles but just got their voicemails. I wanted to let Mel know about Toby."

"Look, I've got to go now, sorry. Dennis will be right with you and can explain everything on your way here." The line went dead. Ivanna looked unbelievingly at her mobile. What was up now? Why was Sven so peculiar on the telephone?

Chapter Forty-One

SATURDAY AFTERNOON, 1 OCTOBER

Toby's wife, Mel, and their children, and his cousin, Olivia, her husband Hannes, and their children, had been flown to Ruhpolding, met by two BND agents and taken to a safe house that stood isolated about two kilometres out of town. After the excitement of flying in a helicopter and exploring the new house had died down, the children soon began to get bored. Their parents played board games with them, read them stories, and let them watch more TV than usual. It was all right for two days but then the squabbling began again. The problem was that it was forbidden to go out of doors, and the children had too much pent-up energy.

The agents took turns to shop the groceries and the mothers tried to occupy the children with crafts, but by Thursday, everyone concerned was desperate for the imprisonment to end. On Friday after lunch, Hannes, still in his pyjamas, decided that if he didn't get a break from the children, he would go mad.

"I need a bath," he told his suffering wife and disappeared

up the stairs before anyone had a chance to stop him. He entered the bathroom, locked the door and started running water into the bath while he brushed his teeth. He climbed into the bath, relaxed in the warm water and closed his eyes. Peace at last, he thought.

*****

After arriving at the high-security prison in Straubing, the responsible officer charged the Argentinian with murder and drug trafficking. His details were written down, a photograph taken, his fingerprints and DNA procured. He was medically examined and given prison clothing to wear. When they had finished processing him, the Argentinian demanded to be allowed to make a telephone call. He knew his rights and he knew that one phone call was permitted. He rang Mehmed Dragovic, the commander of his army. "Organise a lawyer," the Argentinian ordered and put the receiver down. The prison warden was listening in to the call and wondered why the Argentinian hadn't just rung the lawyer himself, but it wasn't his business and so he ignored it.

Unfortunately, the call had been too short to trace. In fact, the message had been a code for Dragovic, arranged two days previously. It meant that the Argentinian had been arrested, and that the commander was to storm the safe house and take Toby's wife, cousin and children as hostages and to use them as an exchange for the Argentinian's freedom. Had the Germans really thought that he would give in so easily? His agents had found the safe house the same day that the women and children had been taken there. As ordered, they hadn't done anything other than inform the Argentinian. He didn't do anything either. It was always good to have a trump up your sleeve.

After receiving the call, Dragovic made all the necessary arrangements and with four further mercenaries drove with two cars to the safe house. Soon after lunch, after seeing that the area was quiet and nobody on the street, they circled the safe house. Without waiting, the five combat soldiers stormed into the house, two through the front door and three through the back door which led straight into the kitchen. Two BND agents were leaning against the sideboard watching Mel and Olivia playing Monopoly with the children. Dragovic shot the two agents in the middle of their foreheads without hesitation and before they had the slightest chance to react.

The women shot up out of their chairs and grabbed their children in their arms; they all screamed at once. Four mercenaries violently pulled a child each from their mothers and lifted it up in their arms, ignoring the screaming, kicking, and biting. Dragovic poured chloroform onto four cloths and gave one each to the mercenaries, who pressed the cloth over the children's mouths and noses. The children passed out, but their mothers continued screaming, crying, and pleading. Dragovic told them, "Shut up or I will shoot the little bastards, the youngest first. Now, follow us quietly and don't cause a fuss. If you follow orders nothing will happen to any of you and tonight you can sleep in your own beds."

The women shut up.

The soldiers carrying the children filed out of the back door, followed by the women and finally Dragovic. They got into the two cars they had arrived in and, accelerating, drove off into the distance.

*****

Hannes had relaxed in his bath for a good thirty minutes. He felt much calmer, and thought he had better get dressed now before he got into trouble from his wife. He immersed his head completely underwater, came up again and rubbed in shampoo. Then he sank his head underwater again. He heard two gunshots and sat up abruptly in the bath. Had he really heard gunshots? Now he heard a lot of shouting and screaming from downstairs. He got out of the bath quickly and slipped into his bathrobe. The screaming had stopped. What the devil? Instead of running, he descended the stairs with trepidation. He heard a man speaking but couldn't decipher the words. It wasn't one of the agents though, the voice was different. He heard the back door closing. He poked his head carefully around the corner and saw the two BND agents lying on the kitchen floor with a bullet hole in their foreheads.

Hannes stifled a scream and ran outside the back door looking left and right, in case he could see something, before rushing to the front of the house. On reaching the pavement he just managed to see a black car swerving around the corner and disappearing. He squinted his eyes to get the number plate and then ran back indoors to write the number down before he forgot it. Only now did he kneel by the BND agents and check their pulses. Before, when he had glanced at them, they had appeared dead. They were indeed dead but now he had certainty. I must ring the police, he thought, but he didn't have his mobile and there was no landline in the house. God forgive me, he thought, as he felt one of the agents all over to find his mobile. The agent's phone was in his trouser pocket. Hannes removed it and turned it on. Shit, it demanded a password! He remembered that new mobile telephones allowed an emergency call even if the battery was empty. Did it work without passwords, too? He dialled 112 and the telephone rang. Thank goodness!

Chapter Forty-Two

SATURDAY AFTERNOON, 1 OCTOBER

Ivanna sat on a rock waiting for Dennis to turn up. Now and again, she tried her cousin's number but, as before, only got the voicemail. What could possibly be wrong now? she wondered. The Argentinian had been arrested, and as far as she knew, his agents, too. His private army had retreated, but she didn't think anyone had expected to arrest the whole army. Anyway, what did they have to do with the safe house? Nobody knew where it was, not even herself.

Finally, she saw Dennis striding down the road towards her. She gave him a wave, stood up, and started walking towards him. Of course, she realised, the road would be closed until the forensics were finished. They met and Ivanna held her hand out, but Dennis ignored it and hugged her, holding on to her a little longer than usual.

"I'm so glad you're okay," Dennis gushed. "I was really worried when I heard about the explosion, but the potholing experts wouldn't let me try to get to you. Everything had to be examined first, for safety reasons.

These damn regulations drive me crazy! But hey, here's me chatting away – you must be starving and thirsty. Would you like to go for a meal first, before we return to Ramsau?"

While Dennis had been talking, they had been walking uphill to his car. "No, that is yes, but first, I'd like to know what's up with my cousins. Sven was strange on the telephone and said you would explain everything," Ivanna said.

"Oh, he didn't say anything to me, and I thought you already knew," he answered, wrinkling his forehead.

Ivanna could hardly bear the suspense. "Please…" she begged. Her heart began to hammer. "*What's happened?*" she repeated. She had stopped walking and turned towards Dennis, hands on hips.

"Oh gosh, how am I going to tell you this? Mel, Olivia, and their children were abducted from the safe house early this afternoon."

"What! How was that possible? Nobody knew where it was! Even I didn't know! What about Hannes? Why didn't you mention him? Oh God, please don't tell me he's been shot." Ivanna was out of her wits. She was almost screaming at Dennis and looked at him accusingly.

"Hannes is fine. For some reason the kidnappers didn't know he was in the house, and he was upstairs in the bathroom. Your cousins, the children, and two BND agents were all in the kitchen. The agents were shot and died instantly. Hannes heard the gunshots and came downstairs, but he was too late. The agents were dead, and your cousins and children had been driven away in two black SUVs. Hannes managed to get the number plate of the second car and rang the police."

"And now? Have the cars been found? Are my cousins safe? Who kidnapped them and why?"

"Slow down, I'm coming to that, I will tell you everything I know, I promise. The Argentinian was allowed one phone call in prison. He rang the commander of his army, a Bosnian called Dragovic. All he said was 'organise a lawyer', but Sven and Mr. Buchenmeyer think it must've been some kind of code that meant he was to kidnap Toby's family. Less than an hour after Hannes had rung the police, the prison received a fax with ransom demands. The Argentinian was to be reinstated with his diplomatic status. He was to be given a passport, a first-class ticket to Buenos Aires, his rucksack complete, with contents, and fresh clothes suitable for travelling. At the moment, these demands are being organised."

"But I thought ransom demands to release hostages were always declined by the government? Otherwise, it would encourage more people to do the same."

"Officially, yes. Unofficially, millions of euros are spent every year to free hostages. It's just never admitted."

"But if Esteban Vargas is allowed to return to Argentina, then the whole purpose of the operation, and all the people who died or were injured… it would have been for nothing!"

"Let me continue. The following agreement has been reached. The Argentinian will be given some travel clothing and driven to Frankfurt Airport. There, he'll be escorted through departures and onto the Lufthansa jumbo jet that is due to leave Frankfurt at 21:40 tonight. It's a direct flight, without any stops, to Buenos Aires. He'll be seated in first class, and only then will he be given the document that certifies his diplomatic status, his passport, boarding ticket and the rucksack. He will be given the opportunity to check that everything is in order. Then he will be handed a mobile phone and obliged to ring up Dragovic, in the presence of the escort, and tell him to release the hostages. The escort will then leave the plane, taking the mobile telephone with him."

"But…"

"Wait, I haven't finished yet. Dragovic must bring the hostages to the nearest police station and give the police officer Sven's number to ring. And before you ask, yes, Dragovic has already been given Sven's correct telephone number. Once the police officer has rung Sven, then theoretically the plane will be given permission to take off. Of course, Esteban Vargas will first be escorted off the plane and brought in an armoured car back to Straubing."

"But the Argentinian isn't stupid, he must realise that."

"Yes. At first, he wanted to wait with the telephone call until the plane had taken off and was in the air. Sven managed to convince him that even if he waited until the plane was in the air, the authorities could easily order the plane to turn around and land in Frankfurt again. Should the authorities agree to wait until the plane was halfway across the Atlantic, then they would insist that the escort accompany him all the way to Buenos Aires.

So, even if they waited for the call until the plane landed in Buenos Aires, the escort could prevent him from leaving the plane. There is no private jet that can fly from Germany to Argentina non-stop. It would need a stopover either in America or maybe Spain, but both countries would be delighted to return Esteban Vargas to Germany. A small risk would always remain for the Argentinian, but for the BND likewise. It was up to him to decide."

"Oh, so now we have to wait until tonight. When did you say? Twenty to ten?"

"Yes."

"I'll be on tenterhooks until then. I'm sorry for being

brusque earlier, it's just that so much has been happening that I never dreamt of when I agreed to take the map to a police station in Germany."

"Of course, don't worry, I understand. What about eating now?"

Ivanna looked at Dennis and contemplated whether she could ask another favour. She decided to risk it. "I would like to visit Toby in Traunstein and check to see if the MRT was clear. Maybe he can come home, and if nobody's told him yet, then I better let him know what's going on with his wife and kids and Olivia and Hannes and their children."

"I promised Matteo that I would return to Ramsau later, pick him up and visit Freya together with him. If it's all right with you, I'll drive to Ramsau now and then we can all go together to Traunstein."

"That's great, thank you."

Chapter Forty-Three

SATURDAY, LATE AFTERNOON, 1 OCTOBER

Dennis drove the car and Ivanna sat in the passenger seat. They chatted light-heartedly with one another. Ivanna was now hopeful that the events would take a happy turn and finally be over. Matteo sat in the back and was quiet. Dennis and Ivanna knew that he would be thinking about Freya and left him in peace. When they arrived at the hospital, Ivanna went to find Toby while Matteo and Dennis climbed the stairs to intensive care.

"I'm hoping that Freya might be out of intensive care now," Matteo told Dennis. "The doctor said that if all went well, she could be moved to a normal ward today. Maybe it will cheer her up not to be alone in a room."

It was not to be. As soon as the nurse saw Matteo, she called to him. "Mr. Stocker, how nice to see you. Dr. Marzoll asked me to let him know when you arrived because he would like to speak with you. If you just hang on a second, I'll ring him to let him know you're here." The nurse rang a number, informed the doctor of Matteo's arrival, listened for a moment and then answered, "Will do."

"Dr. Marzoll asked me to show you to his room," she told Matteo. He felt it was like a déjà vu and worried about what the doctor had to say.

After shaking hands, a short greeting and sitting, Dr. Marzoll came straight to the point. "Mr. Stocker, Freya woke up in the night screaming. She had had a nightmare and remembered everything that had happened to her during her abduction. The nurse tried to calm her, but she was frantic, covered in a cold sweat and ranting. The nurse called me, and I saw no alternative than to give Freya a sedative. This morning when I visited her, she was calmer and sitting up in bed. She told me that she remembered being raped and – she was crying – said she thought it was by more than one man. She wanted to know if that was the reason why she had miscarried. She became hysterical and I had to give her another sedative. Under the circumstances, we have decided to keep her in intensive care until her condition stabilizes. This afternoon a psychiatrist visited but Freya refused to speak with her. In another week, Freya will be physically sufficiently recovered to return home. However, you may like to consider sending her to a psychiatric rehabilitation centre for some time. There she would receive professional psychiatric sessions, both privately and group therapy. There would also be occupational therapy, physiotherapy, swimming, hikes in the fresh air. I can give you some brochures of several suitable centres."

"No, no, thank you. Freya needs her family and me. I can take some time off work, and I can go on hikes with her myself. I'm sure she will feel more comfortable in her home surroundings."

"Well, you may be right, and I certainly hope so. Take the pamphlets anyway, in case at any time you feel overwhelmed. Umm, I suggest you wait six months before you try for another baby but after that there is no reason why Freya shouldn't conceive again. The psychiatrist here at the hospital wants to speak to you before Freya returns home, presumably at the end of next week."

On the one hand, feeling depressed and tremendously sad, but on the other, seeing a shimmer of hope on the horizon, Matteo went to the intensive care unit and knocked on Freya's door. No one answered but he entered anyway. Freya was lying in bed on her back, staring the ceiling. When she saw Matteo, she turned onto her side, away from him, and said, "Go away! I don't want to see you."

Matteo was pained. The hostility in her voice hurt him more than any weapons could. He walked slowly and quietly up to her bed and touched her shoulder lightly. "Freya," he begged, "please... I'm grieving, too."

Freya pressed the buzzer in her hand to call the nurse, and then she started screaming. Matteo backed off and turned around to leave the room. His eyes swam with tears that blurred his vision, and he nearly bumped into the nurse, who had rushed into the room.

*****

Ivanna found Toby in a room with two other patients. He was lying in bed resting. He had some narrow strips of plaster pressing the wound on his forehead together but otherwise he looked quite well. He was pleased to see her.

"Ivanna, how did you get here? I tried to ring Mel earlier but only got the voicemail. How is she? And the kids? Have you heard anything? I thought they would be safely back home by now."

"That's a lot of questions all at once," Ivanna said

laughing. "They're not home yet but everything is under control. Tell me about yourself first. Did the MRT go well?"

"Yes, all is clear. No fracture of the skull and no internal bleeding. I still feel a bit woozy, and my head is sore. The doctor wants me to stay in hospital overnight for observation. I agreed. To be honest, I thought a little peace couldn't harm me before I'm let free amongst my kids. They can be so noisy!" Toby answered, smiling. "Now tell me why they're not home yet."

Ivanna told Toby the whole story. Despite her assurances, he was very worried. "I've got to go now," Ivanna excused herself. "Dennis and Matteo will be waiting for me, but I promise I'll send a WhatsApp as soon as I hear anything new."

Ivanna went to find Dennis and Matteo. She was shocked to see the state that Matteo was in. She thought that Freya must be very ill but didn't want to pry and ask questions, and he didn't offer any information. She gave him a silent hug and then they all went to the car and drove back to Ramsau.

Chapter Forty-Four

SATURDAY, EARLY EVENING, 1 OCTOBER

When Ivanna, Matteo, and Dennis entered the operation centre, everyone stopped what they were doing, turned to look at them and started clapping. Ivanna suddenly realised that even Matteo and Dennis were clapping, and all eyes were resting on her. She was surprised and embarrassed. "What for?" she asked, genuinely clueless. Dennis put an arm round her shoulders "Do you really not know?" he asked.

"No, I haven't the foggiest."

Mr. Buchenmeyer came to stand next to her. "You found a cave full of millions of euros' worth of treasure, and thanks to you and your bravery, we've caught probably the most dangerous drug boss in the world."

"But no, that's not true! Toby found the cave and Matteo and David caught the Argentinian. All I did was find a map and show it to a police officer in Bonlanden."

"Matteo and David? I thought it was a capercaillie!" Dennis joked, attempting to lighten the atmosphere. It worked, everyone laughed. Several officers who had been standing with their backs to a table now moved away to reveal a huge cake and lots of champagne flutes. Robert walked to the fridge and returned with two bottles of ice cold Sekt. He was about to open one, but Ivanna stopped him. "No, wait! Please let us wait until Toby's and my relations are safe before we celebrate."

"She's right," Mr. Buchenmeyer said. "Let us wait. It'll only be another hour or two." He went to Matteo and touched him on the shoulder. "Can I have a word please?"

Matteo followed Mr. Buchenmeyer into a private office. The latter sat on an easy chair and beckoned Matteo to sit next to him. No desk between them? Matteo wondered what was coming. Mr. Buchenmeyer took time before beginning to speak. "Matteo, I spoke to Dr. Marzoll today. No, no," he added quickly as Matteo began to stand up angrily, "don't worry, he didn't reveal any medical information, nor did I ask him to, nor will I ask you. I merely asked how serious Freya's condition was. He told me that her physical injuries will recover entirely in time. However, she had been through a great deal and her mental condition was not good. He also told me that he had recommended some rehabilitation centres to you but you weren't keen. No, no, let me finish. It is your decision what you do, and you know Freya best. I just wanted to ensure you that the BND will cover all the costs for Freya's treatment, so please don't worry about the cost or the bother of applications."

"That's very kind of you, but rest assured, I would never have let money influence my decision. I still hope that by the end of next week Freya's condition has improved enough so that she can come home. I miss her terribly."

"Of course. Now, I've spoken to Mr. Ebner, and we've agreed to give you six months' paid leave as soon as Freya returns home. If you need any longer, just let me know.

There will be no paperwork or bothersome applications, a telephone call will be sufficient." After saying this, Mr. Buchenmeyer gave Matteo his card with a personal telephone number.

Matteo looked at the card. He was moved. "I don't know what to say, thank you, I'm very grateful."

"Well, I'm afraid you're not off work yet," Mr. Buchenmeyer smiled. "While Freya is still in hospital, we would like you to write up full reports for every day this past week. You can take your time, though. Visit Freya as often and for as long as you wish. If you prefer, you can work from home or in the hospital. The press may want to speak to you, but we will try to keep your role anonymous and you out of the affair as much as possible. Now then, what about you? Do you have any questions?"

Matteo hesitated. He knew Freya wouldn't want anyone to know she'd been raped. But there was the matter of the DNA that Dr. Marzoll had secured, and justice. He decided. Freya didn't know Mr. Buchenmeyer and there would be no need to tell her anything. He had a lump in his throat and gulped. "Freya was raped," he gushed, and then paused before continuing. "Dr. Marzoll found semen from three different men. He has secured their DNA. Freya was pregnant with our baby and miscarried." So, Matteo thought, now it's out, I've said it. He felt strangely lighter, as if a weight had been lifted from his chest. He looked at Mr. Buchenmeyer, who had gone very pale and didn't speak.

Matteo continued. "I would like to request, when you retrieve Rollo's body from the cave, if it hasn't happened already, that you send his DNA to Dr. Marzoll. Benni and Danny and the three Bulgarians were already in Straubing when Freya was kidnapped. Theoretically, the Turkish couple, that is the man, may have been involved, but I don't think so, they were busy elsewhere. That leaves the three bodyguards who were together with the Argentinian and Rollo in Hotel Kempinski. I don't know what's happened to them, whether they fought alongside Dragovic and the mercenaries or whether they left the country beforehand. Nor do I know whether they are alive or dead. Could you please send the DNA of all the prisoners and those who died during the battle to Dr. Marzoll? If it can be proven who was responsible, then I want them tried for rape, murder, and grievous bodily harm."

"Consider it done." Mr. Buchenmeyer had found his voice again. "I know that the three men you shot in the hand before the fighting began were arrested. It will need looking into, their photographs compared to the photographs in the passports that the hotel manager sent to us, but it could be that they were the bodyguards."

"If so, then it is a pity I didn't know beforehand. I wouldn't have shot their hands but aimed for their crotches. There is something else. I don't know if the BND offers a reward for information leading to the arrest of Esteban Vargas, but if you do, I would like to suggest that you consider Friedrich Horn. If he hadn't rung me and then followed Vargas, David and I wouldn't have had a chance to catch him. Freddie has a meagre pension that he tries to improve with odd jobs but he's already over eighty."

"Right, duly noted. Anything else?"

"Yes, sir. When you find out when Ludwig Fuch's funeral is, could you please let me know? I would like to attend."

"Yes, that goes without saying. Matteo, on no account did I realise that the Argentinian's men would be so brutal and violent. One hears of rape in war as a means of demoralising women, but I'm talking of war far away from here in the Middle East or former Yugoslavia. This wasn't a war, just the arrest of one evil man. If we had realised that something like this could happen, then we would never have asked for your help. I know this doesn't help you now, nor Freya, but if there is anything, anything at all, now or in the future that can be done to ease your pain, then please ring me. I need a few minutes, but could you then please send Ivanna to me."

Matteo left the office, looked for Ivanna and sent her to Mr. Buchenmeyer. Then he searched for Robert, Dennis, and David. Something had suddenly become clear to him. He wasn't going to be able to get through Freya's convalescence alone. He knew in his heart that she would hate anybody knowing about the rape, but he needed help, too, and his three best friends were entirely trustworthy and discreet. He saw them standing together and went over to them. "I need to tell you something," he said.

Chapter Forty-Five

SATURDAY EVENING, 1 DECEMBER

Ivanna knocked on the door and entered the office. Mr. Buchenmeyer stood up to greet her and shake hands. He commended her for the role she had played in finding the treasure and catching Esteban Vargas. "I've spoken to your superior and highly recommended you for promotion. However, Sven has also told me that you would be suitable as a BND agent. Does that appeal to you?"

"Quite frankly, sir, no. I don't think I would be suitable as a field agent, and if I worked in the office, I would have to move to Berlin. I was born in Stuttgart and have lived there all my life. My parents and my friends are there. After the excitement of the last week, I'm not sure that I could go back to work at Stuttgart Airport indefinitely either. Even with a promotion, the work is basically the same. I don't know what I want to do yet. All I know is that I want to be based in Baden-Württemberg or in Bavaria, near my friends and family."

"I appreciate your honesty. When you do decide what would like to do, then let me know." Mr. Buchenmeyer handed her his card. "I would like you to stay here for the next couple of weeks. We need you to write a report for each day of this past week. Also, we expect to be flooded with requests from reporters and TV presenters begging to interview you. I'm afraid we shall need to train you for this challenge. The media have a lot of tricks and like to twist your words into a different meaning. We need you to agree not to mention some details. It is a matter of life and death for the officers involved. So, we would like to give you some training concerning the handling of the media. On the plus side, the media will be willing to pay you large sums of money for your trouble. You may not only accept but also keep the fees. If you agree, we can employ a manager for you, for as long as necessary, to organise your appointments and negotiate your fees. You have been granted six weeks' leave with full pay."

"Oh, the media, I hadn't thought about them yet, but yes, I suppose you're right, and yes, I would appreciate some training and a manager. I hope the media circus doesn't last too long, because I'd really love a holiday. Somewhere warm where I can lie on the beach all day and get my head around things."

Mr. Buchenmeyer smiled. "I expect you'd get fed up after a couple of days, but do whatever you please! I know you're anxious about your relations, but we have at least an hour before we can expect any news, so if you have any questions now is the time to ask."

"I have three questions, actually. How did the Argentinian discover that I had the map? What role did Erik Benz play? And what will happen with the treasure and with the cave?"

"Right. Let me answer the last question first. As soon as forensics have finished their work, a team of experts will number the crates, and they will be transported to Berlin.

This may take a week or two, but until the last crate has been removed, the cave will be closely guarded day and night by the army. In Berlin, every item of every crate will be photographed, documented, and valued. The authorities will try to find the owners. This will be easier in the case of museums and castles than for private people. However, in time, documents will be made public, and citizens can make a claim. It is too early to say what will happen with the rest, but I expect that in a year or two, you and your cousin Toby will receive a reward."

"As I've already said, we shall decline any reward. What about the cave?"

"That is an interesting question that I cannot answer. Personally, I imagine it could be made into a small museum, but it won't be my decision. The clothing and tools you saw have already been removed and sent to Berlin. Now to your first two questions, they hang together and so I'll answer them together. When Erik Benz's body was found by the mountain rescue team, they also found his suitcase, lying just a couple of metres from his corpse.

"There was a ledger inside the case and several diaries with names, dates, and telephone numbers. He noted down everything and so we know that soon after joining the federal police in the motorway unit, he started his criminal career by letting drugs or banknotes disappear from the car boots of smugglers that had been caught. He wasn't greedy and only ever took a small amount.

"That was the secret of his success, nobody ever noticed anything. Zehra discovered a lot of information after scouring his bank accounts, and her colleague in Berlin continued her work and has written a documentation about Benz's criminal deeds. He copied the relevant passages from Erik's diaries, so we get an insight to his thoughts and feelings. Let me print a copy out for you, then you can read it in peace." Mr. Buchenmeyer pressed a few buttons on his computer and then handed Ivanna the printed document.

Ivanna thanked Mr. Buchenmeyer and left the room. She went to the main room, where the cake was still untouched on the table, and found an empty chair where she could sit in the corner and read.

Erik lived with his wife, Heidi, and two daughters, Alison and Sandra, in Plattenhardt, the neighbouring village to Bonlanden, where Jürgen Gross worked at the police station. He belonged to a bowling club that met every Thursday evening to play tenpin bowling. One of the other members, Detlef Riek, was known as Didi, an antiques dealer. Didi was a shady character involved in the handling of stolen goods. He was always on the lookout for any way to earn easy cash.

From Erik's diary:

May 1998. Last night at bowling, Didi took me aside and asked if I would be interested in cooperating with him. He knew that I worked for the Federal Police and suggested that I let him know when and where we were planning a raid, or when house owners were going on holiday or other such things. He said I would be rewarded, and I told him I was interested but needed to think about it. I'm going to agree to 'help' him, at least occasionally, it's not as if my pay is exactly brilliant.

July 2001. Apparently Didi spoke yesterday to Jürgen Gross, our new member, asking him to 'cooperate'. Jürgen asked me about it, but of course I denied working together with Didi. Jürgen said that he was going to refuse and wondered whether to report Didi.

I managed to persuade him not to make a report, after all, nothing had happened, it had only been an enquiry. I was relieved that he agreed because in the meantime my cooperation with Didi has provided me with a steady source of additional income. We've had some nice holidays, and I could afford to let Alison and Sandra start riding.

September 2022. I called in at the police station in Bonlanden on my way home tonight. Heidi needs our car this evening and I wanted to ask Jürgen if I could drive to bowling with him. He was talking to a young woman about a map she had found in her grandfather's loft, disclosing where stolen Nazi treasure had allegedly been hidden. I immediately thought of Didi. I can't wait to hear what he thinks about it. If it's true, then there must be a lot of money involved.

September 2022. Last night I told Didi about the map. He was totally fascinated just thinking of the enormity of the matter, if the map was real. He said that there are less than a hundred serious artefact collectors in the world. He added that it was a small secret world, and he didn't have the right contacts, but he knew somebody who knew another person who did have the right contacts. I can't wait to hear back from him whether 'this secret person' is interested.

September 2022. Didi contacted me yesterday. Apparently, the secret person, known as the Lizard, has been informed and is very interested. Didi was a bit cagey on the phone. I don't trust him to give me a fair share of the booty. He probably thinks I'm stupid but I'm fully aware of the importance of the map. I have googled missing treasure and discovered that a lot of the treasure that the Nazis stole still hasn't been found. I'm going to find out who the girl is and where she lives. Jürgen will tell me and if I ask carefully, he won't suspect anything. Once I know who she is, I'll observe her flat and try to get the map.

September 2022. *There are two men following the girl. She's called Ivanna, Jürgen told me. I'm going to follow the men and find out where they are staying overnight.*

September 2022. *Yesterday I followed the men in their car on the motorway. I stopped them, which I'm perfectly entitled to, it's my job after all. Ironic that! They said they were on their way to the airport. It could be true, Ivanna works there. So, I examined their passports and then said I needed to check their mobile phones. They really had no idea who I am or what the Federal Police are entitled to do. It was easy to secretly place a bug in each mobile, they didn't notice a thing. According to their passports their names are Borya Koljic and Farouk El Hassan. I'm interested to see what they are up to.*

September 2022. *It was good that I bugged Borya's and Farouk's mobiles. That way I found out that they intend to go on a training course for Federal Police in Berchtesgaden. I hacked into the police computer system and then wrote a letter to a participant telling him that the course had been cancelled. Afterwards I entered my own name as participant in his place. It was easy.*

25 September 2022. *Tonight, it was obvious that Borya and Farouk, now calling themselves Benni and Danny, were involved in Ivanna's disappearance. At the Kührointhaus I chose a single room, arguing that I snore loudly. Nobody seriously contested me – I was the oldest participant, after all. When we had all been dismissed to retire for the night, I inserted a spyglass inside my door lock, sat down behind the door and prepared myself for a long wait.*

I saw Danny go into Tina's, Nicole's, and Zehra's room and I saw him exit again. About half an hour later, I observed Tina hurrying along the corridor to Sven's and Mark's room. I nearly fell asleep sitting up, when I heard a creak in the floorboards and saw Benni and Danny creeping downstairs. I forced myself to wait and was rewarded when I saw Sven, Mark, and Tina following them downstairs. I waited a further ten minutes and then descended the stairs myself.

26 September 2022. In the early hours of the morning: *Nobody was in the common room, so I went outside and saw three black silhouettes beginning to hike down the road to the car park. It was Sven, Mark, and Tina who were following Benni and Danny. I followed them to the forest where Benni's and Danny's car, a black Golf, was hidden. At least I presume that the car belonged to Danny and Benni. They must have captured Ivanna as she was walking to the hostel yesterday afternoon. I saw Sven fighting Benni, and Mark fighting Danny.*

Tina helped her friends and eventually, Sven and Mark overcame Benni and Danny and tied them up.

Tina freed Ivanna from the boot of the car. Funny though, everyone is calling Ivanna 'Alina', so she's pretending to be someone else, too. Then I observed Sven and Mark injecting Benni and Danny with something and putting them in the car boot. I didn't think that Sven would drive far, because he had to be back at the hostel by 8 o'clock the latest. So, I decided to follow him. I soon lost the car, I was on foot after all, but about ten minutes later I saw Sven sprinting back in the direction of the Kührointhaus. I rang Didi and asked him what I should do. "Wait, where you are," he said. "I'll ring my contact and then ring you straight back."

I told him to hurry up because it was nearly daylight, and I needed to be back at the Kührointhaus before eight o'clock.

Didi rang back quickly, I'll give him that. He told me to find the Golf and then ring him back with the coordinates. He said that the Lizard had people in the area who would drive straight to me.

I continued walking along the road until I came to the next private track for foresters. I turned into it and found the Golf almost immediately. I rang Didi up and told him the coordinates. Didi told me to wait until a car came to pick Benni and Danny up. "But I have to get back the Kührointhaus," I protested. He told me not to worry and said that the man who was coming, Rollo, would drive me back to the hostel.

I told him that there was a barrier at the beginning of the road and that it was closed for normal traffic.

He told me not to panic and accused me that I'd be

wetting my pants next. Bloody cheek! It's not him here, is it? Risking his career. Anyway, he said a simple thing like a barrier wouldn't stop the guy and then he rang off. I went to the car and opened the boot. Benni and Danny we're still deep asleep from whatever Sven had injected them with. I shook their shoulders, but they didn't stir. They were much too heavy to lift out of the boot by myself, so I left them where they were and went to sit on a log and wait. I was feeling pleased with myself. I had prevented the worst, which was Benni and Danny being captured and taken away for questioning. The Lizard will be pleased with me and sure to give me a large bonus. I think I'll take my wife on a luxury cruise, maybe to the Caribbean.

Eventually, Rollo turned up. He told me to help him remove two corpses from his car boot onto the forest floor. Two corpses? That was a bit of a shock. I asked Rollo what for and where he had got them from, I mean, how could you get two corpses inside half an hour?

Rollo tapped the side of his nose. He told me the less I knew the better, then I wouldn't experience the same fate as the two bodies. He said he needed two bodies to replace those of Benni and Danny, otherwise the police would wonder what's happened to them. Then he said, after the fire, the bodies would be unrecognisable, and the police would presume they're those of Benni and Danny."

I asked him what fire he was talking about. I was getting quite anxious, so much was happening that I had no control over.

Rollo told me to shut up and stop asking questions and to help him get the bodies out of the car.

Once the two bodies were out of Rollo's car, I helped him lift Benni and Danny from the Golf into his car boot, then put the two dead bodies into the Golf. Rollo took a canister of petrol from his car, unscrewed the top and started emptying it inside and outside all over the Golf. He splashed petrol everywhere and took particular care to make sure that the two bodies were well saturated. He laid a long string under the Golf's petrol tank and started walking backwards, unrolling the string as he went. Judging that he was far enough away from the car, he lit the end of the string and then ran to his own car, ordering me to do the same.

Rollo said that the fire should eliminate any traces. He waited a minute until the burning string reached the Golf and the first flames began to lick up the sides of the panelling. Then he turned the motor of his own car on and began to drive away.

As we drove out of the private road, we heard a deafening explosion. Rollo accelerated and drove back to the Wimbach Bridge. It was still early, just after six, and the car park was empty. Rollo drove straight along the road to the barrier, pressed a remote, the barrier rose, and he drove through, up the hill and around the hairpin curves. I was amazed. I asked him where he had gotten the remote.

Rollo got angry and told me to shut up and stop asking questions. He said that I was too curious for my own good.

I shut up, feeling a bit scared. About a hundred metres before we arrived at the Kührointhaus, Rollo stopped his car and told me to get out.

I did as I was told, walked back the last few metres to the hostel and then entered as if I'd been for a walk and sat down to breakfast with the others.

As I was eating some bread rolls with butter and jam, I contemplated the events of the night. I didn't like the fact that Rollo had turned up so quickly with two dead bodies. I didn't like it at all; it had been a bit too convenient. Who were they? Did he just kill two thugs who had been talking? Rollo was a big man with a temper quick to flare up. Would I be the next to die?

I began to realise that I'd gotten involved with criminals that were way out of my league. The more I thought, the more scared I became. I decided that it would be best to leave Berchtesgaden as soon as possible, and as secretly as possible, so that nobody knew where I was. I'd return to Stuttgart and tell Heidi that I needed to disappear for a while. She doesn't know anything about my criminal dealings, but I will think of something to tell her afterwards, when the whole business has blown over. I hope I will be lucky and the Lizard and Rollo and any other thugs that the Lizard employs will be arrested. Nobody needs to find out about my role in the matter. But first, I need to disappear, as far as way as possible, maybe Spain. The criminals could easily find out my address in Stuttgart-Plattenhardt. I'm glad my children go to boarding school and I'll tell Heidi to visit her parents for a while.

26 September: On the hike to the Archenkanzel, I pretended to twist my ankle, and as soon as Matteo ran off to inform Robert that we would return to the Kührointhaus, I ran back to the Kührointhaus myself to get my luggage and then hide somewhere until I had the opportunity to disappear completely. I knew that I didn't have long before Matteo came looking for me, so I made haste, went to my room, and packed my personal belongings. It would have been better to leave immediately without my luggage, but there was far too much incriminating evidence in my bag. If it were found, and it would be found if I didn't remove it from my room, then I would go to jail for a very long time. I heard someone running up the stairs and opening all the bedroom doors. Damn someone was looking for me! I went into the bathroom and hid behind the door, leaving it open. Presumably the person had looked in my room but luckily not searched it. Soon I heard steps thumping back down the stairs.

After collecting my stuff, I crept stealthily down the stairs to make sure that nobody was in the common room. Hells bells! Matteo was sitting at a table already and about to make a telephone call. I had my Nordic walking sticks in my hand. Creeping up softly behind Matteo, I whacked him over the head with one of the sticks, dropped it and ran outside before anyone saw me. I went to the storage building, and using my Dietrich lock pick, I went inside and locked the door behind me. Now I was safe, at least for the moment.

*****

This was the last entry scribbled hurriedly in Erik's diary. Ivanna stopped reading the colleague's report. She knew the rest from Matteo and Robert. He had hidden behind the door and then slammed it in Robert's face and dashed outside to escape. She looked up and realised that Toby was on the telephone, and it sounded like he was speaking to his wife. She paid attention to him, but the conversation didn't last long. He turned around in his swivel chair, and seeing Ivanna said "They are all free. Unharmed and safe at home. Do you want to speak to Mel?"

"She will be exhausted, please give her my love and tell her that I will ring tomorrow."

Toby gave Mel Ivanna's message, then put the receiver down and turned towards the expectant faces looking at him. "Both families are safe and back in their homes. Nobody is injured, although they are still a bit shocked. It was good that Hannes was in the bathroom and the mercenaries either forgot him or didn't know about him. He rang up the police with the car number plate and they started a search immediately. They found it outside a farmhouse that was for sale. It should have been empty, but the lights were on indoors, so the police rang for backup, arrested the mercenaries and freed the hostages. The mercenaries are now on the way to Straubing and there was no need to release the Argentinian and bring him to the airport. Apparently, he was just told that the police had changed their minds. So ... how about opening that champagne now?"

The team in the operation centre, part civilians and part agents and officers that had become friends during past week, cheered and clapped and, as soon as Robert popped the cork on the champagne bottle, held their glasses out.

Matteo took a sip of champagne and was truly happy

that Toby's and Ivanna's families were safe. However, after five minutes, he put his glass down and quietly exited the room. How could he be happy when Freya was so miserable? He felt overwhelmed at the task ahead of him. He was heading towards his car to drive home, when he noticed Robert running after him. He stopped and waited. "Have I forgotten something?" he asked.

"No, but I don't feel like celebrating. I was hoping that you would drive me home and have a beer with me."

"At your place?"

"Yes, or we can go to yours if you prefer. But I'm not going to let you sleep on your own tonight." He gave Matteo a slap on his arm.

"Oh, all right then. Not that it's necessary, but let's go to yours then." Matteo said, secretly relieved and blessing the stars for having such good friends.

The End

Further Historical Details

Art Theft During World War II

Art theft and looting occurred on a massive scale during World War II. It all started with Adolf Hitler's unsuccessful career as an artist. He was twice denied admission to the Vienna Academy of Fine Arts, in 1907 and 1908. Nonetheless, he thought of himself as a connoisseur of the arts, and when he became Führer, he had a dream to create the European Art Museum in Linz, which would collect all the greatest masterpieces in the world. The hunt for masterpieces kept in conquered countries began.

Approximately twenty per cent of the art in Europe was looted by the Nazis, and there are well over a hundred thousand items that have not been returned to their rightful owners.

Many of these works were seized from collectors and artists who happened to be Jewish. Others, the Nazis confiscated and slated for oblivion because they did not conform to Hitler's narrow definition of what Aryan art should be – that is, representational and wholesome in their subject matter, as opposed to the often abstract, expressionistic compositions that characterised so many modernist works, which they labelled as 'degenerate.'

The Eagle's Nest

As a symbol of power of the National Socialist regime, decisions were made at the Eagle's Nest. It still stands for the insanity of the regime and the world on the Obersalzberg, where plans for war and mass murder were formed.

In defiance, the building stands perched over a sheer rock

wall. A road was cut into the mountain through previously impassable terrain. It is an architectural masterpiece. To reach it, there is a golden brass elevator buried in the heart of the mountain, through which one can reach the Eagle's Nest. All this was created with the sole purpose to impress and dazzle people.

The building became a legend in the post-war period, and apparently the use of the Eagle's Nest was seen as essential as a visual motif in popular U.S. war films and series.

The Eagle's Nest was originally designed by Martin Bormann. In fact, Hitler seldom visited the Eagle's Nest.

Today the Eagle's Nest remains in its original state. In 1960, the occasion of the 150th celebration of Berchtesgaden's incorporation into Bavaria, the Bavarian government relinquished its control over the building to a trust that ensures that the proceeds are used for charitable purposes.

The building's main reception room is dominated by a fireplace of red Italian marble presented by Italian dictator Benito Mussolini, which was damaged by Allied soldiers chipping off pieces to take home as souvenirs. The building also has heated floors, with heating required for at least two days before visitors arrived.

There are two ways to approach and enter the building, the road and the Eagle's Nest elevator. Hitler did not trust the elevator. He continually expressed his reservations at its safety and disliked using it. His biggest fear was that the elevator's winch mechanism on the roof would attract a lightning strike. Bormann took great pains to never mention the two serious lightning strikes that occurred during construction.

The Salzkammergut

The Salzkammergut (literally translated: Property of the Salt Chamber) is one of the most beautiful holiday regions in Austria, with its name coming from its history. As the premier spot for salt (*'Salz'*) mining. As salt was and is important, it was under direct control by the emperors in Vienna – that's where the name *'Kammer'* came from.

Sparkling clean lakes, green hills, wonderful mountains, and romantic towns and cities make up this magical region that is filled to the rim with scenic beauty and a rich local culture.

Nazis in South America After World War II

After 1945, the scale of the horror of the Holocaust came to light. Faced with unprecedented cruelty, much of the world responded with unprecedented vigour. The new term 'crimes against humanity' was coined in the subsequent Nuremberg trials, as Allied lawyers called senior Nazis to account.

Yet fewer than 300 Nazis faced judgement in the Nuremberg trials, while up to 9,000 Nazis, by some counts, were spirited away from Europe after World War II, helped by sympathetic agents and friends. Many found new lives in South America. By the late 1940s, much of South America, particularly Brazil, Chile, and Argentina, was a haven for thousands of Nazis eluding justice. German prosecutors in recent years have estimated that Brazil accepted between 1,500 and 2,000 Nazis. Chile took in between 500 and 1,000, and Argentina welcomed up to 5,000 Nazis to their country.

National Cooperation

The BND collaborates with national security authorities in many ways.

Their closest partners are not only the two other German intelligence services, the Federal Office for the Protection of the Constitution (BfV) and the Military Counterintelligence Service (MAD), but also include law enforcement authorities such as the Federal Criminal Police Office and the Federal Office for Information Security.

Every national authority contributes within the German security architecture. As a Foreign Intelligence Service, it is their task to deliver information and background knowledge that are of special importance to German, foreign, and security policy.

This information ranges from intelligence on foreign terrorist cells, to smugglers' activities, to details on the origin and course of hacker attacks from abroad.

Cooperation platforms for a smooth exchange of information

Cooperation platforms like the Joint Counterterrorism Centre (GTAZ) ensure a smooth exchange of information with domestic agencies. This is where forty national security authorities exchange information on terrorist suspects or the concrete threats of attacks.

An important special feature of the GTAZ is that intelligence services and law enforcement agencies can work together here in compliance with the separation rule and without losing time.

The Alpine Police Handle Body Recoveries

In coordination with the Bavarian State Ministry of the Interior, Alpine Task Groups (AEG) were established in mountainous regions for Alpine accident investigations and operations. The five AEG units are spread from the Allgäu region to Berchtesgaden, collectively forming an Alpine Operations Unit. In hilly regions and urban areas with climbing facilities, specialists are trained to handle climbing accidents.

Members of an Alpine Task Group must have above-average physical fitness and extensive Alpine experience. Suitable officers are trained as 'State-Certified Police Mountain and Ski Guides'.

Nazi Theft

Practically daily, high-ranking Nazi henchmen, officers, generals, but also politicians, who had managed to flee to the Salzkammergut to lie low, emerged with pockets and luggage heavy with jewels and gold that they intended to use for their life after the war.

Adolf Eichmann buried twenty-two boxes of gold during his escape from Bad Aussee. When an official search was later conducted, only a few empty boxes were found.

With 120 kilograms of raw morphine, left behind by a local medical unit, a profitable drug trade was carried out in the post-war years.

Drug trafficking

Drug trafficking in major Western European ports continues to be a huge problem.

Capercaillie

The story about how the capercaillie brings the Argentinian to fall, sounds unbelievable, however it is a true story, albeit with different characters. In exactly the same place as described in the book, a capercaillie became famous for frightening several hikers on different occasions. In fact, the bird was defending its stomping ground. But the tales became so frequent that eventually a report and photographs appeared in a newspaper, along with advice on how to pass the bird.

Unfortunately, a couple of youths read the article, and finding it amusing, went to the Bindalm with the sole purpose of finding the capercaillie and taking photographs of them annoying the bird. The youths were drunk and one of them had a crossbow with him. It ended how it had to end. Two arrows hit the capercaillie from behind. It was injured but didn't die. The bird became aggressive and eventually an official Forrester had to end its life. The youths were caught and charged with cruelty to animals. Their parents paid for expensive lawyers and because they were drunk and only seventeen, their punishment was very mild.

About the Author

THANK YOU for reading my book!

I began my writing career in the late 1990s with magazine articles in England and Germany, followed by non-fiction books for Frech Verlag. My love of storytelling soon led me to fiction, inspired by years of family tree research and a lifelong fascination with history. After completing a creative writing course in Cambridge and retiring from my career with Lufthansa, I published my first novel, The Missionary. Since then, I've written three more novels and several short stories.

My historical mystery The Matchstick Boy won the Coffee Pot Book Club Silver Award for the best historical mystery and the Reader's Choice 5 Stars Award in the USA.

Originally from Yorkshire, where I grew up surrounded by siblings and animals, I now live near Lake Constance. When I'm not writing, I enjoy walking in nature, travelling across Europe with my husband, and visiting our three children and six grandchildren.

Author's Note and Acknowledgements.

When our son moved to the Berchtesgaden region and settled there with his family, I cannot say that we were unhappy about it, in spite of the five-hour drive to visit. The region is in the south-eastern-most corner of Bavaria, Germany, bordering Austria. It is known for its stunning alpine scenery, the picturesque Lake Koenig, and a rich history that includes being the site of Hitler's Eagle's Nest. It is characterized by high mountains, deep valleys, glaciers, and wild rivers and home to the only alpine national park in Germany. In other words, a popular district for tourists, and we had every excuse to go there as often as we wished to visit our grandchildren.

Having an imaginative mind, seeing the scenery surrounding me, and knowing the area's history, I knew I would write a novel, set here, one day.

The idea for the plot came after reading a newspaper article about a sixteen-year-old girl who had found a bar of gold whilst swimming in Lake Koenig. She handed it in to the police, who investigated where it came from and who owned it. The bar's identity number had been defaced but officials managed to restore it. Reports said the find was not connected to the Nazi era but it revived rumours of Nazi gold supposedly sunk hurriedly in the lake as the Allies captured Salzburg and began to march towards Berchtesgaden. Police divers checked the lake for more gold, but found none.

There are many people I would like to thank for helping this book to end up in print.

My family for always being supportive and for putting up with me.

The book blogging community, I would love to name you all but am afraid I might leave someone out. Thank you for your help.

My fellow author friends, there are too many to list, but I want you to know how much you have helped me.

Alexandra Plenk, 4th generation Berchtesgadenerin, for her generosity in sharing with me her rich knowledge of the geography of the area and also her specific detailed historical knowledge of Adolf Hitler in Berchtesgaden.

Richard Sheenan for the professional complete editing and fact checking of the first edition.

Mary Anne Yard for her professional constructive critique.

Grace Augustine for the copyediting of the second edition.

Sarah Houldcroft for tons of advice, the layout and technical know-how.

Dee Dee for her wonderful cover design.

Finally, and most importantly, thank you dear reader for buying this book and being supportive of the publishing industry.

If you enjoyed this book, then please think about leaving a review on Amazon or Goodreads. Your feedback helps other readers discover the book and supports indie authors in a big way. Even just a word or two makes a huge difference!

Other Books by Rowena Kinread

UK Readers Choice 5 Star 2023 USA
Best Historical Mystery 2023

A dark chapter of Swiss history – moving, gripping, true.

This novel is based on a true story. It portrays the inhabitants of a remote village in the Swiss Alps and their dependence on the local matchstick factories in the mid-19th century.

After a series of disasters and bad harvests, the villagers are left close to death by starvation. People find work, and supposedly their salvation, in the matchstick factory – but the cost is high: illness, death, exploitation. Even the youngest children must toil 14 hours daily.

When little Josef dies in a mysterious rock avalanche, his brother Jakob suspects foul play. The village remains silent. Years later, Jakob's profoundly deaf daughter, Gretl, is assaulted by the factory director. Jakob dares to do what no one has ever dared before: he accuses the rich and the powerful.

A poignant novel about injustice, solidarity, and the power of truth – inspired by real events.

5 Star Review

While reading the story you will continue to ask yourself is this a true account because it is written so well and the telling is so good, you really believe you're reading True Crime history.

This book is totally in a category all its own, it is a truly great read, an awesome solid five star scrumptious delicious dessert of a book that I highly recommend.

Janalyn, the Blind Reviewer – 5 Stars

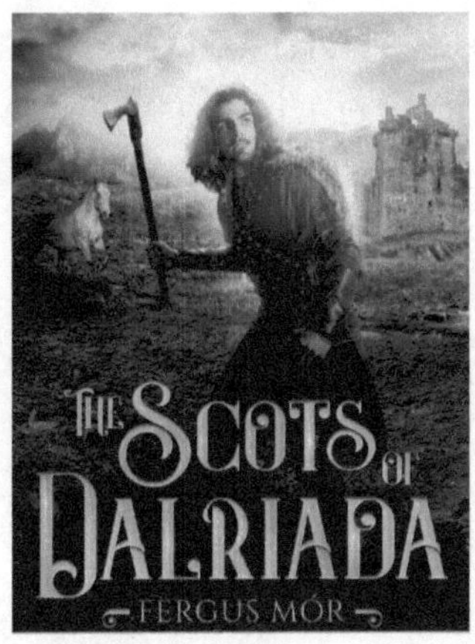

Three brothers Fergus, Loarn and Angus, Princes of the Dalriada, are forced into exile by their scheming half-brother and the druidess Birga One-tooth.

Fergus conceals himself as a stable lad on Aran and falls helplessly in love with a Scottish princess, already promised to someone else. Loarn crosses swords against the Picts. Angus designs longboats.

Together a mighty power and always on the run, the brothers must attempt to outride their adversaries by gaining power themselves. Together they achieve more than they could possibly dream of. Fergus Mór (The Great) is widely recognised as the first King of Scotland, giving Scotland its name and its language. Rulers of Scotland and England from Kenneth mac Alpín until the present time claim descent from Fergus Mór.

Full of unexpected twists and turns, this is a tale of heart-breaking love amidst treachery, deceit and murder.

Feedback from top Amazon and Goodreads' Reviewers

Both thrilling and intriguing, all the way to the end. The Scots of Dalriada is a definite recommendation by Amy's Bookshelf Reviews....

Amy's Bookshelf Reviews

... an entertaining and enlightening story of a period I had previously known nothing about....

Avonna Loves Genres

Was I ever tempted to push the book aside and stop reading it? No...

Barry Litherland

... I also loved the horse: it would be worth reading the book just for that story, though it creeps in gently and takes a while to work out.

Building in the Badlands

The best kind of historical fiction is the kind that feels real, makes you feel each tragedy, each bit of passion, each gut wrenching turn. The Scots of Dalriada certainly ticks all the boxes.

David's Book Blurb

Within the narration are some lovely descriptions: 'the leather bridles...polished until they shine like dogs' noses.'...

Marian L Thorpe

... good for people interested in Historical Fiction and especially an underappreciated figure from Scottish History.

Romances of the Cross

The story reads with immense authenticity, and leaves the reader caring about this distant time, distant country and distant people. An epic achievement.

Twila's Reviews

... a rousing book of historical fiction ... A relevant and entertaining read!

Zea Perez, Author